KNIGHT

ELLE SAMHAIN

The Shintori Chronicles: Book III

Other Novels by Elle Samhain

Aegis: The Shintori Chronicles Book I

Hemlock: The Shintori Chronicles Book II

To family.
By blood and by trials.

CONTENTS

CONTENT WARNINGS 9

CHAPTER ONE 11

CHAPTER TWO 41

CHAPTER THREE 70

CHAPTER FOUR 108

CHAPTER FIVE 150

CHAPTER SIX 200

CHAPTER SEVEN 228

CHAPTER EIGHT 262

CHAPTER NINE 294

CHAPTER TEN 322

CHAPTER ELEVEN 354

EPILOGUE 378

ACKNOWLEDGMENTS 384

ABOUT THE AUTHOR 385

COMING SOON 386

CONTENT WARNINGS

graphic violence

blood

gore

gun violence

monster horror

body horror

explicit sexual content

mentions of suicidal ideation

mentions of off-page domestic and sexual abuse

mentions of off-page parental neglect

death and murder

drowning

CHAPTER ONE

THE DEVIL

The world around Moz was blindingly bright. Each inch as far as his eyes could see was a cold, sterile white. Beneath his fingers he felt a cool stone surface and he used the sensation to determine that wherever he was, he was laying on his back. His hand had been limp on his ribcage until he spread his fingers and planted his palms on the floor to prop himself upright. Drunk dizziness overcame him and a blur of dark colors he did not notice before swirled in his vision.

Where am I?

He sat still for a long moment, becoming aware of the sweet whispers from somewhere around him. As he became steady his focus began to sharpen, the world came into view - but became somehow more confusing.

It was, in fact, a white marble floor that he was sitting on and the black shape was the darkness of his own clothes as his long legs were stretched out in front of him. An arcade of ivory columns formed a long hallway that he sat directly in the middle of. Beyond the arches were white stone walls and the frames of white doors could have easily been missed if Moz's assessment of his surroundings was any hastier.

He rose to his feet slowly and another wave of dizziness threatened to lay him back on the ground. Moz held out his hands before him to steady himself, straightening up only when he was sure that he was balanced in the knees.

"Hello?"

He was surprised by the cascading echo that rang around him and he looked up. Arcades upon arcades were stacked in countless floors above, the ceiling their columns held up was much too far from the ground for Moz to see even with strained eyes.

Where had he been before this place? Not even the Necropolis hosted such vast structures. Nervousness rattled his muscles and nearly convinced him to stay put. But he felt alone in the bizarre building and he was certain that nobody would be coming for him.

Moz looked ahead of him and noticed the small splash of azure at the end of the hall. Was that the way out? He stepped forward, carefully at first before his stride hurried. Whispers grew louder as he got closer to the blue, realizing it was an archway leading outside. A small blur of red moved through the field of sky. Was that a person?

After what felt like hours, he finally made it to the entry to a large balcony, opening to the most incandescent sky he could ever recall seeing.

"At last, he wakens!"

He whirled around to see the small figure standing just beyond the archway. She stood no taller than Moz's waist and she smiled at him with a knowing mouth. The corset and tiered skirts of her dress were wine red, the buckled belt around her waist matched the mahogany leather and brass boots that peeked out from under the asymmetrical hemline. Her golden hair was tied back in a braid that wound around itself many times, forming an odd sort of cone that bobbed on the back of her head and was anchored down only by the brass headdress she wore strapped around her chin. She looked up at Moz with dark eyes lidded in heavy red makeup.

"I did know that, however, didn't I?"

He didn't answer the question because it had only confirmed his recognition of the odd figure. Moz had seen her image in countless illuminated manuscripts and in the stained glass windows of temples across Shintori.

"Neri, the Goddess of Oracles. That's you, isn't it?"

She didn't answer him either. Her face lit up and she instead turned around, shuffling hurriedly towards a bell that was fixed to the wall of the porch.

"There is no time at all for that! I must let the others know!"

"Others?"

She stood up on her toes, grabbing a gold and burgundy braided rope to swing it side to side. A sweet ring reverberated off the rear wall of the porch, echoing off the lush white clouds that floated low. Not a moment longer than it took for Moz to blink, he was surrounded by strange and fantastic people.

His eyes gravitated towards the figure in the center, bathed in the same bright white that stretched tall in the vast hallway. The hood of her white cloak was gently draped over white tendrils of hair, the same shade on her lips and lashes. Her eyes, however, were the most brilliant shade of green and echoed the smile she regarded Moz with.

"*Moz, my bravest son,*" she spoke and he was convinced his heart had stopped. He sank to his knees, overcome with adoration and devotion when it dawned upon him what was happening.

His lips trembled, unable to even whisper the name of his goddess Ara. The Mother of All Things. *How am I here?*

Dark flashes of memory overcame him: the Knight, swarms of Morgana's Legion, the whir of an arrow, and Avery's crumpled body. His shoulders sank and the overwhelming devotion gave way to grief, tears welling in his eyes.

"Fear not, for she lives," the goddess next to Ara spoke. She was cloaked in a gown of leaves and her honey locks of hair were wild and untamed. The sharp cheekbones on her face were flecked with many freckles and she was warm with the sun. She looked down at Moz with such firmness, her steady demeanor reassuring. No doubt this was Yve; the reason for all the things Moz had ever seen on earth.

"Why… why am I here?" He croaked, his voice a cacophonous scratch in comparison to the sweet melody that was their voices. "Am I dead?"

"Never before have you felt such genuine fear," Ara spoke again and each hair on the back of Moz's neck stood straight up. "You are one and whole, relieved forever from your duties as a harbinger of death."

His eyes widened, his mouth dropped and went dry. He tried to speak, failing thrice before his croaking words finally were audible.

"I'm... Saved?"

Ara answered only with her smile, far more radiant than any sun Moz would ever see.

"Your tasks are far from over," a new voice spoke and he turned his head towards the source. Mona, goddess of the witches. She was holding a hand over her pregnant belly and her expression was far more grave than her counterparts. "The Knights are not done; not even the Knight of the Sea you still harbor. You must reach Yumi and take her to Eyon. Complete the ritual so we can void Beldam's plans."

"I'll do anything… but you need to tell me she'll live. Please let her live."

As he begged for Avery's life, the tears made their way down his cheeks.

"Go home. Protect her life with your own hands and she will live. Protect yours too, from those who wish to twist our intent."

The world around him began to dissolve, fragments of Mona's face fading into nothingness piece by piece. He desperately turned to Ara, wanting to hold on to the holy image of her face for as long as he could.

"But what if I can't? Even as a Knight I failed!"

The voices warped into senseless mumbling as he plunged underwater and his surroundings melted into white nothingness once again. Terror gripped him by the spine, yanking him forward at the speed of sound.

Moz flew upright in the bed, gasping heavily for air as he looked around the room. Blankets clung to his sweaty skin and he kicked them off in a desperate effort. He took deep breaths with his head bent down; his heartbeat raced wildly and he feared he would die in his fright.

Fear. What a strange thing fear was. It was so tangible now in the shaking of his hands, the racing pulse in his wrists, the slick coldness of his skin. He looked down at his right hand and noticed a new field of color etched into his skin. A deep red rose of the Goddess lived in his flesh, a word inked black into the knuckles of his calloused fingers. *Safe.* He was safe.

But there was the safety of another who was of higher importance to him.

Moz carefully climbed out of the bed and stood on the foreign floorboards that creaked and groaned under his weight. With a quick glance around the overcast grey walls, he pulled his black shirt off the chair in the corner. It wasn't until he flexed his trapezius muscles as he put the shirt on that he realized he was so terribly sore. He stepped carefully out the bedroom door and into a narrow hallway illuminated by daylight falling through a single window above the staircase.

The wood stairs sighed under his feet and the voices he heard floating from downstairs quieted.

"Moz, is that you?"

It was not a goddess nor a spirit that called out his name, but Maria's familiar voice. He entered a cramped living room and was met by the faces of his friends, their rigid postures slackening in relief.

Maria jumped up from her sagging leather chair and threw her arms outward like she might have hugged him before stopping short when she realized it might hurt his injuries.

"Where is she?"

She pursed her lips seriously before speaking. "A Brightloch physician took you in. In the room to the left, just down the hall. Lily has been tending to her, but she's been in and out for two days now."

He didn't answer her and instead followed her directions, his limp hurried in comparison to the crawl he had taken down the stairs. The faint whisper of Shank's voice floated on the air behind him, but he didn't care to listen. Moz approached the door, open too slightly to even peer through. He pressed his palm flat against the wood as he stepped through cautiously.

Lily was sitting in the corner of the room with an open book flat in her lap as she looked up at him. She held up a single finger to her lips, hushing him without making a sound.

In the center of the room was a bed with meticulously folded blankets; the person inside them seemed so small. Avery's bare arms were outside the blanket at her sides, the white fabric pulled up to her armpits. Her eyes were closed as Moz approached the bedside and he saw her lips were parted just enough to let air pass. The slight rise and fall of her chest was so small, but he could not recall ever seeing a sight so comforting. A large sheet of white gauze was taped around the front of her left shoulder and a faint stain of rust-red burned through the top layers. Moz turned and looked back at Lily, hoping she could inform him of Avery's condition.

"The arrowhead was removed," she whispered with a nod of her head and it told him enough. Avery would indeed live.

He had not realized his body was tense with fear until he loosened with relief. Moz sank down, crouching on the balls of his feet with his face in his hands. *The gods would let her live.*

There was a quiet scraping of wood and he felt a warm hand on his shoulder.

"I think you should sit," Lily murmured gently.

Moz looked over his shoulder at where she stood, his expression must have been a look of confusion that prompted her to explain.

"Because you're very important to someone who is very important to me," she said.

He smiled weakly and stood up halfway before falling back into the bedside chair, emotionally exhausted. Lily cast him one last smile before leaving the room, shutting the door behind her.

Moz sat in silence watching the rise and fall of his witch's chest. It was such an unsettling sight when he had lost so much time and one of the last things he could recall was her wicked smile before she carved a pathway to his freedom with Hemlock. The mercy in her touch when she had helped him out of his shackles starkly contrasted the violence she had unleashed on his captors, but neither could compare to seeing her so small and standing at the door of death. The goddesses had promised she would not be stepping through it this time, but her mortality still had shaken him.

"I would go to Od for you every time," he murmured, lonely in the heavy silence of the room.

He half expected her to stir, but she laid as still as carved marble with every curl and hard line of her jaw whittled into the shape of haunting beauty. Avery wasn't a Berserker Witch, a title bestowed upon her by fearful tongues and eyes that only saw her bloodshed. She was the Saint of Death, his loving and merciful Lady of the Veil.

Moz thought of the inky black miasma that had crept over her features when she was Ransom's hostage and the evil twist to her mouth when she had watched him with animal eyes. He wondered if Avery had heard his words when he spoke them to her possessed body:

I trust you. With my heart and with my life.

His newly found fear flexed when he remembered the first time he had seen her face and the worst thing he had done to her was act rather rude in a convenience store. He thought of the smell of cedar and coffee on her hair that he could still catch in the moments he had been able to hold her, of how her face had been a map of beauty even when it had been frowning at him. The changes in her were his fault and he considered that maybe it would have been better if he had never interfered at all.

His regret turned and shifted into the terrible shape of greed. Sure, he would have done things a little differently - but he was *Saved* because of her. Moz felt the hot lick of hunger to create where he had once destroyed, to repair what he had broken the best way he knew how. To pay the ransom ten-fold as just the start for what he owed Avery.

For his Saint of Death, he would learn gentleness.

The push of a needle into an arm speckled with body glitter and bruises. Her flesh was flooded with warmth and then Avery felt nothing; void of fear, free from sadness, drained of pain. That was what would keep her safe here.

How else was she to stay safe, with no family to look after her? What was it she had been told?

"A lure, but not made for you. You'll be safe here always, just as long as you follow my lead."

A woman's voice so soft and sweet, but struck a sour note of bitterness deep in Avery's ribs. Lights danced in the dark, casting her skin in teals and magentas. Her feet rolled under her not in a dream, but in the fog of a memory - she had been the prettiest thing on eight wheels. Or so the men told her.

Her pours were heavy-handed; all the better to steep the discontent of patrons who were unlucky enough to walk through the door into a bitter blackness. One that tasted delicious between the gnashing teeth she would rarely see. Sometimes she did witness the snapping of bones and monstrous limbs unfurling, the club erupting in roars that drowned out the staggered beats of grimy music before Riko would turn them loose onto the unsuspecting streets of Ardua.

Still Avery felt nothing. She rolled, she poured, she danced.

"You are the best and the finest of them all, Baby. I won't leave you like they did."

For the praise of a beautiful woman with bronze eyes and a smirk so devious, she would have gladly sat in her numbness. Why else was she doing this, playing the role of both sheep and shepherd? She hearkened the word of the hungry wolf.

But now she was the one with a taste for blood.

Exhaustion sat heavy in the creases of Avery's eyelids as she crept back towards consciousness. Around the furthest edges of her mind, she felt an unexplained longing for her parents that she had not suffered the bite of for years. She blinked it away with resentment, unsure at first of what the field of gray above her head was. As her vision focused she realized it was a wood ceiling painted a rather dreary shade. A quiet and low murmur came from somewhere beside her and she strained to make out the words.

"-the birds soared upon the southward winds, their song everlasting as Azura searched for her maiden Goddess. No returning melody echoed the call from the lips of sweet Iris."

Avery let her head roll toward her right shoulder and the source of the voice. She was looking at the top of a head, dark tendrils of hair astray in every direction. The voice was suddenly recognizable as she pieced her environment together: *Moz*. He didn't seem to take notice of her awakening and carried on reading.

"With the return of the sun come Lume, the flock traveled back, leaving no wind unsearched until one day they-"

"Moz," her voice felt so loud when she said his name compared to the soft and warm murmurs of his reading.

He looked up from the book and froze in astonishment. His shoulders sank as he exhaled deeply, forcibly pushing out the tension he had no doubt been holding.

"Avery," he whispered when the initial shock faded from his face. "How do you feel?"

She took a mental assessment: the shoulder where she was shot ached as the numbing agents were beginning to wear off. The blankets felt much too heavy on her tired body and she longed to move. But there she was: looking into a room with eyes that still saw and ears that heard Moz's comforting voice.

"I'm well. I'm alive."

He closed the book and suddenly sat up from his chair, leaning over the bed and cupping Avery's cheeks gently with both hands. Though his hands were roughened, the gesture was soft and she felt the tension in her muscles ease just a little when she was met with the familiar scent of clove and tobacco on his skin. Avery was certain he could feel her racing heart through where their foreheads touched and she looked up at where she could see moisture collecting between the dark lashes of his closed eyes. His voice shook as he spoke.

"Avery… I was afraid. That never happened before. I couldn't… the Knight couldn't even protect you."

She couldn't think of anything to say and instead covered his hand with hers. He blinked his eyes open and the tears spilled when he let out a single laugh that sounded more out of sadness than amusement.

"And I can't pretend that protecting you from how I feel is protecting you from the Knight."

The air between them quieted as the words sank in and she knew for certain that he could feel her heart racing even faster with the pulse point of her wrist against his.

"You can't kiss me and leave again," she finally whispered.

"I won't leave. Not unless you want me to."

"I don't."

Her own words shocked her and felt like a shout as they hung in the silence. *Am I just delirious?*

She stared into his eyes, her vision completely overwhelmed by mossy green irises with Moz's face only a breath's reach from hers. With a tilt and a dip of his head she felt his kiss that she had only experienced once before but remembered so fondly, no matter how much she had tried to convince herself that it had meant nothing. Where it was a kiss grasping for affection before, it had changed into a cautious touch. His thumb gently brushed her cheek, the way his lips melted with hers was organic and sincere. He planted a smaller kiss before leaning away, still cradling her face in his hands.

Moz was still there with his forehead to hers and the rush she felt was replaced by a warming sense of calm. *Still there.*

"I believe you, I trust you," she said quietly.

Her words triggered a memory for Moz and his eyes widened just enough for her to see the flicker of light flash across the forest in his eyes. The longer she looked, the less embarrassed she felt to stare at him so closely; she wanted to be seen.

"You *did* hear me, didn't you?"

Avery nodded, the movement small with their foreheads still pressed together. His laugh was sweet but laced on the edges with rough exhaustion.

"Of course you did," he joked before adding with a more sincere, "thank you for coming back for me."

Did he expect her not to? Avery recalled thundering through the forest, angry and desperate as she searched for the Legion horses that carried Moz to the prison in exchange for her exorcism. She knew now that she should have felt lost following them blindly, but it had been quite the opposite - she had a sharpened feeling of purpose. It was a fearful flavor of rage that she never wanted to taste again, but she would gladly wield it as a weapon for him.

"I'd come back for you every time," she whispered.

Moz leaned his head back just far enough to study her features with a flitting and discerning gaze, as though to cut open her words to find a deeper meaning in the shapes of their skeletons. She had given her feelings the bones but they were still only vague revenants. Avery realized this was the first time she had really spoken to him since they had emerged from Od. She had been possessed and then he was gone.

His stare felt intimate and the gravity of what each of them had done for the other suddenly weighed on her. Following one into the realm of the dead; sticking a head into the mouth of the ravenous lion to save the other. Neither of those seemed like things they would do for someone they just tolerated and maybe kissed every now and then.

"That wasn't an open invitation to make a habit of this, by the way," she added jokingly. "I was incredibly pissed the entire time."

He laughed, stroking her cheek with his thumb tenderly when he answered, "Duly noted."

As he pulled a hand away from her face, a field of red across the back of Moz's hand caught her eye and a brief blink of panic washed over her until she realized that it was not blood, but rather ink.

"Moz, what is that?"

He straightened up, reaching behind him to pull his chair up to the bedside and the serious gesture alarmed her. When he sat down, however, he was smiling. Beaming proudly, even.

"Avery, I'm Saved."

Saved? Her instinct was to jump out of bed and pull him into a hug, but she winced just trying to prop herself up on her elbow.

"My gods, Moz! What are you… how?"

"I meant to say that, the fear. Avery, I'm free. I'm going to live and finally grow old and… well, wait, after the Knight is gone. That's the only thing standing in my way now."

The excitement in his face morphed into a stern fix of his mouth as though he was just remembering. Avery felt the disappointment too. She shifted as best she could towards the edge of the bed, holding her right hand out to him.

"We're going to free you, I promise."

Moz looked at her with soft eyes and a smile to match. He gently wrapped his hand around the back of hers, lifting it just high enough to meet him as he planted a kiss on the inside of her palm. His thumb rubbed the spot with firm reassurance before he slid his fingers between hers.

"I believe you, I trust you," he echoed back her words, adding "I love you."

Avery froze, stunned by the display of emotion. He *what?*

"*Shit*, I did not mean to say that. I just, well, with what happened I couldn't go another day of…" his stammering trailed off when his hand slipped away, looking clearly embarrassed. "Do you need water?"

"I do," she answered, both meaning it sincerely and wanting to grant him a reason to leave; he looked like he needed to kick himself in privacy.

He stood up, the chair nearly tipping over behind him with the abrupt movement. Moz opened his mouth as though he was going to say something, and then closed it; she couldn't think of any time she had seen him so clumsy with words and motion and she tried her best not to laugh. He slipped out of the room, closing the door behind him.

Love was an awfully big word and not one that could simply be taken back. Especially when so many awful and world-changing things had been happening to them. She felt its presence hanging in the air where Moz had been sitting and tried to recall if she had ever used it in this way before. Avery didn't want to use the word until she was sure that she would have loved him even if they were lucky enough to have been ordinary people.

She shook her head, still laying on the pillows when she thought of the silent bell on a red cord around her neck that he had gifted her before he held her. "Still bizarre."

"Moz?"

The small voice sounded different when it wasn't coming from within his own head.

Moz stopped in his tracks, turning around slowly after Avery's door was closed. He looked upon the boy with white hair, his eyes a shimmering gold and very much human.

"Jack, what are you… how?"

"The Beldam gave me a choice. Live amongst a new Reaper as a demon and come back to Od as I please. Or live with you, my dying breath the same as yours."

Jack threw his arms around Moz, who hugged him in a tight grip with his fists locked together behind Jack's back. The boy was wearing Moz's spare parka from his pack, black with a fur-trimmed hood and far too long on his shorter frame.

"I chose to stay with you," Jack added after a long moment, stepping away from Moz and looking up at him with tears dribbling all the way down his smile. "After everything we had been through together, I couldn't go to another Reaper. You're my brother, Moz."

"Shit, don't cry, kid," Moz said and laughed, the corners of his vision becoming blurry with his own tears. "I'm gonna take care of all this as quickly as I can for you, alright?"

"Don't save the world on *my* behalf."

Moz chuckled. Now that Jack no longer served him as a familiar, the boy was free to be himself. He had taken himself far too seriously in his rat-form, the glimpses of his quippy and childish behavior surfacing only so often.

"I have some things to give you if you're going to be doing this with us," Moz said. "I'm not sure what you've maybe had your eyes on, but you can take anything but my sword."

Jack pouted when the consecrated sword was excluded.

"I reckon I've got a few things I could spare th' boy," Tristan offered, standing up from his chair.

Moz's smile faded. How did the exorcist feel about the ex-demon? He doubted that Tristan would grant Jack his immediate trust.

"Thank you, Tris. I was actually hoping that if I paid him enough, Kurosaki would… wait, where's Alice and Kurosaki?"

The room fell silent.

Maria slowly looked from Shank to Tristan, none of them offering an answer but their looks of sorrow made Moz's stomach drop and he knew that the answer would be grave.

"Moz," Jack said in a faint voice. "Alice is gone."

Moz turned, looking down at Jack with narrowed eyes. "What do you mean, *gone*?"

"Alice is buried in Credence Lot. It's about five blocks north from here," Maria spoke in a hushed voice. "Kuro-saki is there. He needs you."

"I'll go with you," Jack offered, a hand on Moz's shoulder. "Don't worry, they'll take care of Avery while we're gone."

"Let's go."

Maria walked to a rack overstuffed with coats and cloaks next to the front door; the wood post looked as though it may buckle under the weight at any moment. She handed him his black coat and grey cowl, gripping them tightly when he first tried to take them from her.

"Moz, treat him kindly," she warned before she let go.

Moz frowned. Did he really need to be reminded to be decent? He didn't answer as he put on his coat and stepped outside. Bounding down the front steps of the physician's home, the sound of Jack's boots pounded behind him as the boy chattered his teeth exaggeratedly.

"It's cold as fuck!"

Moz didn't bother to point out that the chill bite of the air was only a hint as to what would come after the Novara equinox; Jack only talked aimlessly when he didn't want uncomfortable silence.

"What happened to Alice," Moz asked in a low voice, his head ducked down when Jack's steps fell in rhythm to his own with striding effort. The shoulders of Brightloch locals brushed against his own as they walked along the outside of the cobblestone road. On a normal day, Moz might have clocked the nose of the man who nudged him harder than most, but he was far too weary as they trudged north to the graveyard on the hill.

Jack matched Moz's sad and quiet tone, "I saw the whole thing, Shank had me. Alice and Avery were trying to get to the Reaper kids. Alice was amazing, she broke their front line like she wasn't even afraid. Nobody saw the guy come at her with the sword until it was too late. One of the children was killed too- the young lad named Vinny."

Jack fell silent, ducking down to look up at Moz's face. Moz didn't bother trying to hide his watery eyes but dug his fingernails into his palm to keep the tears from breaking.

"I know what you're thinking Moz," Jack said when he straightened back up. "But those kids weren't your fault. In fact, there was divine intervention that you completely missed."

Moz stopped walking, looking at Jack's back until the boy turned around.

"Divine intervention? What are you talking about?"

Jack shoved his fists into the pockets of his oversized parka. "Well, we ran into Malo on our way to the prison. He laid his hands upon us for a blessing. Well, some of us anyway."

"Malo? The forest god blessed them?"

Jack nodded. "The people who died were the ones who refused a blessing. You already knew this, but I noticed everything as a rat. Overlooked, but always looking."

"Don't point that out to Kurosaki, okay?"

"Yeesh, I'm not an asshole. I haven't told anyone else but I just thought I'd mention it to you. But Moz, I think we were *all* supposed to die on that field."

The words chilled his blood and they continued in silence, Moz's thoughts trailing off to the glittering depictions of the forest god set into the windows of the Brightloch temple. He hadn't visited the temple in years but he began to think that a 'thank you' was in order. Or perhaps to rave to the sky about why the god didn't just give the blessing to Alice and the child anyway. *Only the ego of a god.*

At the top of the hill stood the wrought-iron fence around Credence Lot. Jack paused as Moz pulled open the creaking gate.

"Shouldn't we leave an offering like Avery d-" Jack began.

"No."

"Well, have it your way, Master," Jack's tone quickly turned to sharp sarcasm, as though he preferred Avery's method of leaving three copper coins at the foot of each gate they passed through. While it was strange, even Moz had to admit her habit was endearing.

"Please stop calling me that now."

"It's only weird if you make it weird!"

Moz walked up the cobblestone path that wound up the hillside, looking at the headstones that ranged from elaborate sculptures of angels to simple slabs beginning to disappear under the overgrown grass. They found the solemn figure alone in front of a plot still fresh, the grass on top of the patch of turned dirt had yet to be replaced. Moz stopped, holding out a closed fist to stop Jack from coming any closer.

"Give us a minute."

Moz approached alone, his feet treading heavily not because he feared creeping up on the assassin by surprise in this moment of vulnerability, but to give him the chance to demand Moz leave. He heard no such protest.

"Izaya," Moz called out Kurosaki's seldom used first name.

Kurosaki didn't answer as he sat on his folded knees, looking down at the soil. Moz slowly sank down next to him, looking at the bouquet of lilies that were already wilting where they lay on the patch of bare earth. They sat in silence for a long moment as Moz was unsure how to approach the tragedy before him.

"Izaya, I'm going to pick up some work and we're going to get her a proper marker. I'll do anything I can, anything you need for me to be there for you," Moz said gently.

When Kurosaki said nothing, Moz looked from the unmarked grave to his face. He was staring blankly at the wilting flowers with his brown eyes red and cried to raw dryness.

"Her brother doesn't know," Kurosaki murmured. "Todd trusted me to bring her back and I killed her."

Moz didn't know how to respond. He knew that if anyone was to share the blame with the Legion swordsman, it was him. Alice wouldn't have even been there if he found another way to fight off Ransom's possession of Avery. Would it then have been Avery's grave that they stood over?

He pushed away the dark thought abruptly. Movement amongst the tombstones and far crypts caught his eye. Moz looked up to see a bobbing black orb floating behind a marble mausoleum, two more swirling around gravestones. His eyes narrowed; Kurosaki's grief was attracting the fledgling demons. He turned his attention back to Kurosaki, not wanting to alarm him further with the presence of the Leeches and their lack of weapons.

"You didn't kill her, Kurosaki. We all let her down, but never you. She loved you more than anything."

"That's even worse. You've always been a shit pick-me-up," Kurosaki answered in a flat voice.

"I know, but I'm trying. You know how it goes."

Moz didn't know why he had expected him to give at least a half-hearted and knowing chuckle; some semblance of what they used to be. Kurosaki looked up from the plot of dirt, his expression stony when he saw the bobbing orbs.

"Look at these fuckers," Kurosaki said, his voice low and gravelly. "Feeding off humanity at its most vulnerable points. I can't even grieve without needing to be weary for my own life. Joke's on them."

Moz looked from the orbs to Kurosaki and his concern bloomed when he realized what his friend was implying:

Kurosaki would purposefully neglect to protect himself. He expected Kurosaki to have already drawn his gun for any full-fledged Leeches that could be lurking nearby, but the withering man continued to sit in sorrowful stillness.

"Izaya, why don't you come back with us? I think you can have some tea and think a little more sharply. We'll talk from there about how we'll end this. For her."

Kurosaki sat in silence, his hands gripped tightly together with his arms wrapped around his knees. After a long moment had passed, during which Moz cautiously watched the Leeches, Kurosaki sighed and stood up.

"For Alice."

CHAPTER TWO

THE TOWER

Maria stared blankly at the wall. The physician's home was much quieter now that both Moz and Jack had left for the cemetery. Behind the couch where she sat, she heard the soft murmur of Tristan's voice as he spoke encouraging words to Lily, assuring her that her adopted sister was going to be a bit bruised but ultimately alright. To her left sat Shank, an open book held in their hands but their head bobbed as sleep threatened to overcome them. Each one of them was so… very… tired. But Maria would not sleep. Instead, her mind played on a loop of what had happened two days ago when they carried the bodies in.

They had all been covered in blood, so much more than Maria had realized until after she dunked her tunic into bleach. The physician had asked no questions when he opened his door. He had introduced himself as Dr. Halesworth and then hurried to show them his spare room.

"You didn't remove the arrow," the doctor noted as they carefully laid Avery down on the bed. "My guess is that you've done this before."

"There's no time for stories," Lily snapped as she rolled her sleeves up. "Snap the shaft as best you can so we can see how deep the head went in. Where in the Goddess' name is your disinfectant? We need to stop the bleeding NOW!"

Dr. Halesworth looked at her skeptically with a raised, bushy grey eyebrow. "And who made *you* the doctor?"

"Padmont University. Or they were about to. Now just do it!"

Whatever words came next blurred in Maria's memory, she had just stood against the far wall watching. The color had drained from Avery's cheeks and her freckles vanished against the dark veins that snaked around her face. Her lips turned a ghostly shade of pale blue.

Her gaze shifted with widened horror to the figure standing in the far corner, watching Maria with sinister eyes. The girl was soaked to the bone, her blonde hair sticking to the face that was bloated and blue. Her brick red blouse was smeared with swampy mud and blood from the gaping wound that slashed across her forehead. Someone once an ordinary comfort to Maria had become the revenant of her waking nightmares.

"F… Firefly?"

The phantom opened her mouth and the screaming of cicadas filled the room. Maria clamped her hands over her ears, but neither Lily nor the doctor noticed the sound as they snapped the wood shaft of the arrowhead with a blade.

"Cheat death, cheat death, Baby Cruz cheat death," Firefly sang, her voice splitting with the voices of many people she wasn't in life. Maria had rebuilt the body for her, but her friend never came back.

"Bel-dam, Bel-dam, Baby Cruz cheat death," the reanimated corpse began to move, stepping from the corner with squishing soaked shoes.

"It's just a ghost, it's just a ghost, goddamnit, she's not even real," Maria had squeezed her eyes shut, talking to herself to drown out the revenant's mocking chant.

"We're gonna lose her!"

Maria's eyes opened and she looked at Lily.

She was standing over Avery, her braids pulled back with a tie and her beautiful face was twisted tight with frustrated grief. The doctor had the wound clamped open as he dug carefully for the arrowhead in Avery's shoulder.

He pulled out the narrow tong-like tool and frowned. "There's no retrieving it, it's lodged too deep in muscle and we risk further traumatizing blood vessels. We stop the bleeding as best we can and pray to gods she can live with it inside her."

"That's not good enough."

They both turned to Maria when she spoke. Her voice had been so calm when she pulled up a chair, forcing the doctor out of her way. Firefly watched her with a sinister sneer from over Lily's shoulder and Maria blocked her out. She had to stay calm. She couldn't afford to fall into her personal Od if this was going to work.

Maria pulled out a knife from one of her pockets and slashed open her palm, wincing and slow. With her uncut hand, she pulled Avery's blanket down below her breasts and put her cut palm against the flat of Avery's sternum.

Maria's chin-length waves of hair floated upward as if she were suspended in water and the whole of her eyes glazed over inky black as she sank back into the corner of witchcraft she swore she would never return to.

To save, never to resurrect.

The whole time she had been trying to remind herself that this time was different. She wasn't stitching back together limbs, reassembling crushed ribs, or restarting Firefly's dead heart. Avery still had a fighting chance and she had to try.

The room around her had disappeared and her field of vision filled with Avery's tissue and muscle sinews. She heard the blood pumping so clearly in her ears just under the faint thumping of Avery's frightfully slow heartbeat.

Maria held her hands up in front of her to level with her own chest, her fingers dug and searched empty air as she peered into the wound. Her movements dug her vision deeper and deeper inside her friend. Maria couldn't believe how much blood there still was.

Finally, she saw the stone arrowhead anchored deep into a muscle by one of its toothy hooks. Maria paused, thinking fast on her feet about the options they had. She could snap the arrowhead into pieces and pull them out one by one until she could pull every last bit out. That risked leaving one lodged if she missed. *Or…*

She gently closed her fingertips to touch the pad of her thumb, as though she were taking the pectoralis major into her left hand. Then she pulled slowly, feeling the resistance of muscle fibers. Her right hand worked with her mind to gently shift the arrowhead out from under the sternocostal head of the pectoral, slowly and deliberately. Wriggle by wriggle she inched the stone weapon out as she worked around blood vessels with held breath.

And then it was out - Maria flinched with excitement! The gory arrowhead had clattered to the floor, but her work was not yet done.

"Lily, use the butterfly seals and get that wound as tight together as you can," Maria said, unable to see her past the vision of Avery's insides.

As Lily brought together both sides of the wound with butterfly strips, Maria began working under the skin. Her fingers closed around broken fibers, reconnecting them with the muscles in Avery's shoulder and clavicle. The white hot heat of her magic soldered veins and arteries shut - even she was unable to undo the damage done to the vessels, but she could at least lessen the severity.

When she was satisfied with her work, she leaned back in her chair with her eyes still glazed over and her vision was focused on the superficial wound. She welded the skin back together and the stink of burning flesh overcame the room until the wound was sealed shut.

Maria's feet found the floor again when she shifted forward and her vision returned.

Lily leaned over Avery's body and examined the marred, pink skin under the butterfly bandages. She then turned her incredulous gaze from Dr. Halesworth to Maria.

"Her ability will be limited in that arm," Maria had said softly when she rose from the chair. Before she left the room, she added, "Always trust a witch to get shit done."

She couldn't get Lily's bewildered expression out of her mind as she stared now at the grey wall of the entry room. Just when she had nearly untangled the maddening feelings of needing to kiss Lily and why the attraction felt different than anything she had experienced before, she jumped back into the realm of dark magic.

She felt the looming sensation in the back of her skull, knowing Avery was asleep on the other side of the door behind her. Not long ago, Maria had worried that Avery had sunk too deep into Mona's magic given to her. That she was less Avery and more Berserker Witch; and that was to be feared. It wasn't Avery's gift she had been afraid of - it was her own.

But Maria had sunk her teeth into the rubies of Mona's pomegranate again. The dripping crimson was running down her chin from a single bite and *good gods* - she was hungry for more.

More, more, more, more.

What could possibly compare to reanimating the dead?

— ❧ —

Old wood creaked and Avery opened her eyes, the depth of her nap was shallow enough for her to hear the heavy feet walking into her room. A spectacled man with unruly curls of grey hair turned his head down to her.

"I'm glad you're awake," he greeted her, his low voice naturally soothing to Avery's ears. "If you'd allow me to, I'd like to examine your wound."

Avery nodded and slowly propped herself up onto her elbows. Aegis had been curled up at her feet and he perked his head upright to observe. She was wearing a taupe buttoned tunic and she fumbled to undo the top three buttons to give the physician access to her wound.

With gloved hands, the physician peeled back the gauze bandage on Avery's shoulder. She winced as the fibers parted away from a thick scab.

"You have healed enough that the stage of infection risk has passed," he stated. "Your body will heal just fine on its own from here on out."

The physician turned around towards the bedside table where he had placed a tray of antiseptics and bandaging gauze. He cut a strip of gauze from the roll and then again to split it in half. With one half, he covered the open mouth of the antiseptic and bobbed the bottle upside down once to wet the gauze.

He turned around and gently pressed the square against the wound. His careful stare flicked up and looked at her face expectantly and then his back straightened up.

"Good that it didn't burn. Hold tight and let me change the gauze."

With the other square, he folded it thrice and taped the fabric over the large, angry scab. The physician took the tray on the bedside table away, pausing in the doorway to look back at Avery.

"Very well, then. I took an oath to heal all those who come my way." The man's tone then grew cold despite his speaking of a respectable ethic and gentle behavior only moments before. "But I refuse to harbor criminals and witches. You have healed, now be on your way."

Avery blinked, stunned into silence by the physician's sudden change in attitude. When she didn't move from the bedside, his face ignited in fury as he stood in the open door frame.

"You have thirty seconds to leave before I turn you in!"

"Avery, this coward means business. Get your things and leave!"

Avery dove towards the chair in the corner where her cloak was folded neatly underneath her boots. In the next room, she heard Moz and the physician shouting at each other, their anger equally matched. With the cloak latched crookedly around her, she hopped as she struggled to put on her boots as quickly as possible and follow Aegis out. She winced at the glowing pain still lingering in her left shoulder and her uncareful movements were harsh on the wound that had not quite finished healing.

"Out, out, OUT!"

Boots shuffled across the floorboards on the other side of her wall; even Tristan swore colorfully in disbelief at what was happening. With her clothes and boots back on, Avery reached for her rucksack and Hemlock where they waited under a rack of hats and scarves. Out of spite, she stuffed a wide-brimmed black hat into her backpack.

"As a little 'fuck you'," she mumbled angrily as she rushed out the bedroom, Aegis darting ahead of her to flee the house of the angry physician. They were shooed out of the brownstone house, the door slamming on Avery's heels as she was the last to leave.

Avery looked upon Brightloch with wide eyes as she put the stolen hat on, drinking in every sight of the strange world. From where she stood on the stoop of the physician's home, she looked across a crowded avenue lined with brickstone shops and quaint half-timber homes. Paper streamers of gold and fiery red were tied to the iron street lamps, crisscrossing high above her head. The chatter of people and the racket of carriages on cobblestone roads were white noise under the angry words of her friends as they conspired their next course of action.

"I was hoping we could get the Knight out of Brightloch before the Novara harvest festival," Shank said, noticing her look of wonder at the strange decorations, "but with the time it took to care for you and Moz, it's tomorrow."

"Moz! Ave! You're gonna wanna see this!"

Jack's voice called out from somewhere in the street and Avery weaved through the crowd toward the head of pale hair she spotted standing in front of a bulletin posted to the outer wall of a bakery. Avery looked for Moz, confused as to what the demon was doing in human form. Moz reached the boy first and was already pinching the bridge of his nose in frustration when she stopped next to them.

"What's the matter?"

Avery looked at the notice before either of them could answer and jumped in surprise when she saw her own face staring back at her. Beneath a hasty ink rendering of her own face read the headline: *Berserker Witch! Wanted: For Murder, Treason, and Necromancy.*

"This is insane!" Avery cried out. "How did I commit treason?"

"Avery?"

She turned to Moz when he mumbled her name.

"Is my nose really that big?"

"Moz, are you fuckin' kidding me right now? These posters are everywhere," she spun in a circle once to confirm that the same posters were nailed to several other shop fronts on the same avenue, "and you're worried about your *nose*?"

"Look, your poster at least looks like you! Sure, they forgot your *endearing* freckles but it's more or less you! They made my eyebrow way more jacked up than it really is and gave me a fucking snout! I was looking forward to the day these assholes finally made the effort to put out a wanted poster for me and look what they've-"

Moz stopped when he looked down at Avery, her annoyance no doubt showing on her face. He grinned, laughing quietly before ducking his head to kiss Avery's forehead with warmth.

"Don't worry, we'll figure it out," he assured. Jack looked on with a dropped jaw and an exaggerated bewilderment on his pale face.

"Uh, *hello*?!"

Moz turned to snap something back at Jack, but her eyes fell to the poster below theirs on the board. It read simply in printed red letters:

KING'S BOUNTY.
REWARD FOR EVERY MONSTER DEAD.
INQUIRE WITH YOUR NEAREST
ROYAL GUARDSMAN.

Monster? So that's what they were calling the demons here. It wasn't wrong, but it didn't feel entirely right either. Those were people once. She frowned and looked away.

"We need to keep our heads low until we figure out how we're going to get Princess Yumi to Eyon. First priority is to get to her," Avery said, her voice hushed as she worried about who might have been listening. Moz pulled the cowl up around his mouth and nose as he backed away from the notice board. Avery followed his lead, pulling her long waves of hair forward to aid the hat in concealing her face.

"It's going to be hard to break the perimeter of the castle," Jack said as they rejoined the rest of their group.

Avery looked up at the towers that loomed over Brightloch with glittering roofs and iron spires. She looked back down at the street corner where uniformed guards stood, watching over the single road that led uphill to the castle grounds.

"Maybe we're overthinking this," Avery mumbled.

"Avery, what are you going to do now?"

"Watch, I'm going to get into the castle," Avery answered Aegis as she pulled her rucksack and Hemlock's scabbard off her back, handing them over to Lily. "Hold this."

"Avery, what are you..."

Lily trailed off when Avery turned her back, stomping toward the royal guards head on. She knocked the hat she stole from the physician backwards off her head with the strap gently tugging at her neck as the hat fell against her shoulders.

"Hey! Pigs!" Avery shouted.

"What the hell, Avery? Don't be an idiot!"

Avery ignored Lily as she strode towards the guards who looked at her with confusion. One guard muttered something to the other, his head turning towards a wall plastered with posters. When he turned back in her direction, his face was alert with recognition. As he reached for the baton holstered on his belt, Avery lunged upward fast with a swinging fist that connected with his unprotected face. Her knuckles cracked as the man reeled backwards and a dull pain radiated in her opposite shoulder with the thrust of her arm.

"Witch's curse on your face!"

Horrified gasps echoed in the street around her as she ducked out of reach of the baton. The guard who she had not punched reached his hands out, holding a binding rope ready to take her captive. Avery grinned, she already got what she had wanted - a fast track to the castle - but now she was having fun.

She yanked the hand that reached out for her, biting down hard on the flesh above his pinky. The man howled in pain, tugging his bleeding hand away from her gnashing teeth.

"Okay, Avery, I think that's-" Moz was approaching from behind and the guard looked up with wide eyes of surprise.

"William Mosley! You are being placed under-"

"Yeah, yeah, I fucking get it."

The guard she had not bitten grabbed both of Moz's arms, throwing him down hard onto the cobblestone. He wasn't putting up a fight at all and Avery knew that Moz was simply letting himself be captured so he could keep a watchful eye on her. The guard with the bleeding hand yanked both of Avery's hands together and began to bind them. With their faces pressed flat against the stone, Moz looked at Avery with a scowl.

"You're full of bad ideas," Moz said.

Avery grinned.

Lily had her hands thrown up in the air - utterly dumbfounded - when she watched the guards throw her best friend into a fireman's carry and cart her up to the castle.

"You DUMBASS, AVERY," Lily shouted when she finally dropped her arms. She could have sworn she heard Avery's snicker in response from somewhere up the hill.

"Un-fucking-believable."

She turned her annoyed gaze from Shank to Tristan, her hands on her hips and growing warm with worry-flecked anger. "Has she been pulling this kind of shit the whole time?"

Tristan shrugged, hoisting Moz's sword onto his shoulder that he handed off when he decided he needed to run headfirst into trouble as well. "More 'er less."

Shank flinched when Lily let out a loud groan of frustration and turned back to look at the looming castle behind them.

"Gods, she is so... so... DUMB sometimes, how has she not gotten herself killed yet?"

Jack was staring down at Aegis with wide eyes when he said, "what I wouldn't give to still be able to hear Aegis' side of this conversation."

Lily held her hand up to cover her eyes, shielding her embarrassment for her friend away from the eyes of the gods. She sighed and dropped both her arms, shrugging the strap of Hemlock's sheath onto the small space of shoulder she still had left from her own weapons.

"Okay, I'm done yelling," she said and took a slow exhale. "Where was the meetup point for getting the kids?"

"The east gate. They're letting Brightloch people out but no one in because they think Moz and Ave are terrorists," Shank answered, nodding their head subtly toward the end of the avenue they had just come from. "Would help if we still had those body bags they came in, the pity of the guards would have come in handy again. Aegis is to climb through the gate and let the kids know when we're in position."

"Do you think they were able to gather more Reapers from their outpost?" Maria asked, looking up at Shank's face inquisitively.

"I reckon it woulda been hard to get there an' back that quickly," Tristan was the one who answered. "An' it looked like they only had the gator an' bear to use. Did anyone see a familiar fer' Rowan?"

Kurosaki, Jack, and Maria all shook their heads.

"Doesn't matter, we left Ina with them, remember?" Shank said. "Or did you not notice that we were missing a giant dog?"

Tristan looked down, swiveling around. "Don't get mad at me, the ground's too far down fer' me to see!"

Shank tried to hide their laugh by looking down at the ground, arms folded and shoulders bouncing slightly. When they looked up, they had regained composure. "Anyway, Ina will have gotten out any message they needed to send if they couldn't make it to the outpost alone. Let's not worry about them - or whatever nonsense Avery has gotten herself into - too terribly much."

Lily sighed, "Easy for you to say. Let's go. I cannot *wait* to tell Byron what shit his sister has pulled now."

As Shank followed her lead down the boulevard towards the looming wall in the distance, they said "I am *so* glad someone with some initiative and good sense has finally joined before we could get ourselves all killed."

"Day's not over yet."

— ❦ —

"Your Highness, we have the wanted Centralian criminals under arrest," the officer addressed the King before stepping aside to reveal the bodies his peers had dragged inside by the arms.

One face was shrouded in a black mist, an ethereal mask Yumi had only seen once before in her life; one of these criminals was a Reaper as well. Her heartbeat pounded in her throat and she jumped up from her seat only to stand frozen in place. The sudden appearance of golden hair in her periphery startled her and she flinched, not caring at all for the suspicious eyes that fell upon her from the court. Never would she grow used to the simple fact that nobody else had ears and eyes open to the dead.

"As I promised," she recognized the spirit Owen's voice without turning to look; he spoke much clearer than her father right beside her "we've come to rescue you before those who wish to use you for harm find you. Do not be frightened."

For a moment, she could have sworn she felt the lines inked into the flesh of her torso slither and writhe. The Knight in her stirred within the walls of her skull to assess the new presence. Unseen eyes peered through her own and the Knight laughed.

"*Scum of the pond here to bend us to her call and beckon? We would not be the first. Let us crush her bones, little Knight.*"

Yumi ignored the demon lurking within her and she focused back on the captives, bent over on their knees with their hands bound behind their backs. As the inky mist faded, the woman's face came into view as she looked upon the King and his court, daring them for bloodshed.

Her dark hair hung in long, thick waves that narrowed her angled face as her fierce gaze scanned the hall. Yumi was compelled forward as she looked upon the so-called criminals bound and buckled like animals for slaughter.

The young woman's steel eyes fell on Yumi and she froze, burning hot under the woman's gaze. A smile flickered on her freckled face and it was then that Yumi noticed the smears of blood on her lips and the red crevices between her teeth.

"She sunk teeth into the flesh of the guard! I watched her do it! 'Twas the very thing that brought her here!"

The faceless spirit spoke over the dull murmur of the dead and Yumi caught sight of the droplets of crimson staining the marble, dripping from under the sleeve of the officer nearest the woman. Why did she bite the guard when she had a sword? She had seen the sword of the damned strapped to her back in the visions Owen had lent to her. Yumi realized then that the sword was missing. They truly had been dragged in with no intent to kill.

"The Berserker Witch," she murmured, if only to confirm herself that this was exactly the day she had been waiting for. Yumi then feared nothing.

"Princess, be careful," Mara warned her.

Still she clutched the pale rabbit in her arms a little tighter as she approached, ignoring the hum of the spirits that grew thicker in the air around the Berserker Witch. She was watching Yumi with eyes that had perhaps seen too much, their intense gaze of steel tracking Yumi when she crouched down low to meet it.

The witch's face was one that had spent recent days under a blistering sun with a faintly pink nose and cheeks, the short white scars on her cheek painted scattered constellations through her freckles. Up close, Yumi smelled the cedar in her thick hair and the lingering coffee on her skin. Her heart beat in a fury and Yumi knew that what had fallen into her lap was far better than any of the suitors that had come through the castle gates, hoping to take her for themselves and become King.

"You are the very essence of wilderness," Yumi whispered.

"The Knight, Yumi!"

She turned her head to assess the man bound and knelt to her right. He watched right back, his vicious eyes narrowing upon contact. She recognized him easily from the posters the Royal Guardsmen had pasted all over Brightloch: William Mosley.

"You can hide nothing from me."

His flat voice occupied the same space her Knight and Mara did. Yumi said nothing in response, though her silence prompted him to become rather talkative.

"You have to make them free us, we can't keep you safe from prison. Don't let the posters fool you - the person who put the bounty on us only wants to see us dead, Avery too. They're coming for you, but we can stop it if you help us. We'll take you to Eyon."

Yumi held his intense gaze for as long as she could tolerate before standing up, turning to face the throne upon which her father sat.

"Father, you must let them go free," she called out in a steady voice, finding strength in clutching her rabbit to her chest.

King Harthmoor leaned backward in the seat of his throne, looking back at her incredulously through his sneered nose. Her father's attitude disgusted her quite often.

"Yumi, what would inspire you to suggest such nonsense?"

She held her breath for a fleeting moment, knowing that what she was about to say would go against the wishes her father had held for years. He had decided she would be quiet and docile before she had even been born as a Reaper; and then she worsened matters by becoming a horrifying Knight of Od.

"There are people who wish to capture me, Father, and use the Knight of Od for evil. You must let them protect me," she said and the room fell silent, the face of the king growing cold and hard before igniting in anger.

"Yumi, you must not speak of these things! You have gone against our agreement and-"

"We have no choice now but to face these things and speak of them, Father," Yumi's volume scaled back, trying to calm the situation as best as she could. The secret her family and the Oracles of Neri shared was now out in the open, leaving the court with gaping mouths and a hum of whispers rising from the tense silence.

Her father stood. "My daughter, you know I cannot let them go. They pose a danger that I cannot allow to roam Shintori unchecked. Not when we have been warned by Ardua and Centralia of the terror they leave in their wake. We will turn them over to the Sentry task force who-"

"All of those terrible things happened to Ardua and Centralia when they chose to stand in the way of the Knight. I would hate to see it again here. For gods sake, the supposed Berserker Witch is not even armed!"

King Harthmoor pursed his lips as he looked down at her from his throne platform, his hands balled into fists as he began to register her words as a threat. Several chairs scraped as members of the court hurried from the hall, unwilling to become a participant in the scene unfolding before them - or afraid of the revealed Knight. Those who stayed looked on in sour skepticism.

"You will give them proper hospitality so that we may do what must be done," Yumi commanded.

"And what is it that must be done, my reckless daughter?"

"It's certainly not staying isolated in the castle and wishing to foolishly wait out the storm. We'll go to Eyon. There is still time to undo what the Oracles have foretold."

King Harthmoor looked down on her with intense eyes, his thick and greying brows furrowed. His gaze shifted towards the guards and he nodded his head once. The guards paused, unsure at first if they should follow the command. They began reluctantly unbinding the witch and the other Knight; Yumi smirked, pleased with her fear-inspiring leverage.

"Be warned, Witch," King Harthmoor boomed as Avery stood up, wiping the blood off her lips with the back of her hand and Yumi couldn't stop staring. "The next time you injure a fellow of mine, you will be imprisoned. If my daughter, if a single hair on my dearest daughter is harmed, you will die."

"Well, the whole idea is to not die," Avery quipped.

Yumi couldn't help but grin upon hearing Avery's voice for the first time outside of Owen's visions. It was a robin's song, a sharp melody to Yumi's ears.

The witch then looked over her right shoulder, her expression nervous. Yumi followed her gaze, swearing she caught a flicker of movement from the open doors of the Grand Hall's entry. Had the witch seen it too?

"Your Highness, I wouldn't wish to burden you further," William spoke with solemn respect that starkly contrasted his companion's bite of sour sarcasm, "but there are more of us. I regret having to ask this of you but-"

"We will welcome them all as well," Yumi cut him off as her attention returned from the doorway to the conversation, wanting to leave the hall as quickly as possible as her father's face continued to grow a deeper shade of furious red. As angry as he might have been, the King did not recant his agreement.

Yumi turned towards the guard hovering behind Avery, seeming to pretend for the sake of his dignity that his hand wasn't still leaking blood. "Leave us, you are no longer needed here. I expect no trouble from the Guardsmen towards our guests. Give them free passage to and from the castle grounds as they please."

When she heard no argument from her father behind her, she smiled. What delicious control the Knight gave her when she needed it most.

Doesn't it feel good? To command attention instead of evading it? It should be you who they call Queen of the Dead, Little Knight.

William frowned, making no effort to hide that he had overheard her Knight of Spirit. He turned, looking down at Avery.

"Let's go get the others. We can't leave Brightloch until we can fund a voyage and I'd like to get help from Shank in figuring this out."

Avery nodded, looking up from her bloody hands to the hallway with a frown. As they turned to leave, Yumi ran to block their path and held up her free hand to stop them.

"You can't leave without me," she said, trying hard not to sound like she was begging. "I need you to tell me more about what's happening."

William and Avery exchanged a look she couldn't place before he turned to look at Yumi.

"I'm gonna be straight with you," he spoke in a flat, unkind voice. "Based on what I can hear from your Knight, you seem pretty on the fence about where you stand. It's playing you for a fool."

Avery looked at Yumi, her blue eyes wide in alarm. The look gripped Yumi's lungs and she struggled to take in a breath before speaking.

"That, that's not true. I don't want what they do! I don't want the veil to break! I can't even imagine the state of the world if we fell to that level of chaos!"

"It would be easy for you to say that even if you did. That shit doesn't hold any weight with me."

Avery looked up at William. "What choice do we have but to trust her, Moz?"

Yumi looked at him in confusion. "Moz?"

He pinched the bridge of his nose between his fingers and sighed, walking past Yumi. "Yes, that is my name. We're leaving and will be back, you stay put."

Yumi's gaze slid to Avery, who shrugged. As the witch walked past, Yumi found that Avery was easily shorter than she was. She found herself wanting to laugh; the terrible necromancer witch was small.

"We don't ask about the name," Avery joked warmly as she followed Moz towards the entry wing. Yumi hurried to follow, nearly tripping over her navy skirts.

"I apologize," Yumi said, "for back there. I don't have the best relationship with my father."

"Don't worry, I completely get it."

"Did you see-" Yumi started.

"Avery, let's go!"

Avery turned, looking at Yumi apologetically.

"We'll be back!" Avery called out as she bounded down the castle steps after Moz. Yumi watched them leave, waving from the top step and she wondered if this would instead be the last time she saw the odd pair.

CHAPTER THREE

WANDS

Pebbles clattered to the ground one after another, followed by a groan of frustration.

Maria turned around, watching Lily as she hid her face in her hands. The young woman sucked in a deep breath and stared at the small rocks with a focused intensity. The pebbles floated upward into the air, rotating like stars in the changing sky. Maria grinned and thought about offering encouragement or telling Lily she was getting much more precise in her movements; she decided not to risk breaking her concentration. Instead, she looked forward, towards the focus of their stake-out and her expression sank into a frown.

"They've been gone for quite a while," Maria murmured, wringing her hands as she looked from the gate towards the thick wall of trees. It had been hours since Avery and Moz allowed themselves to be captured. What a foolhardy plan; they must have been meant to be.

The pebbles clattered again behind her and a gentle hand touched her back as Lily spoke. "Don't worry. They'll take good care of each other."

Maria turned to look at Lily, smiling weakly. For the long hours they had waited for Avery and Moz to recover from their ailments, Lily had been nothing but comforting towards Maria. The woman seemed to know that all Maria needed to keep a sunny outlook was a gentle touch and kind words. Maria looked back to the iron gate just as Tristan spoke.

"I reckon no word from Ina yet?"

Shank was crouched on the other side of Maria, pinching the bridge of their nose, and looking a lot like their ever-frustrated friend. "Don't you think I would have said something if there was?"

Shank grew concerned whenever they found themself away from the wolf familiar for long; their worries always translated to impatience and a short temper.

"Ina will be fine," Maria offered gently, trying to ease their fears.

"You said that about Croxi," Shank snapped back.

Maria tried not to let herself be hurt by their words, knowing that they would take it back as soon as Ina returned. She knew she didn't have the same optimism when Tristan had to kill the vessel of her familiar.

"What's that going to do?"

Lily was pointing at the glass vial of glowing green fluid Tristan held gripped in his hand, ready to pounce into action at any moment.

"Th'guards over there," he nodded towards the sentries that paced with calculated movements in front of the gate. "I reckon there's no reason to hurt 'em, but there's no way they'd let Ina and the Reaper kids pass through. 'Specially not Oonlok or Grim. So I reckon the best thing in this case was a fast-actin' hallucinogenic. Won't hurt 'em, but enough to render 'em useless. Added bonus is they won't question seein' a grizzly bear when the world around 'em is spinnin' an spittin' rainbows."

"Holy shit! How do you administer that?"

"Simple. Ya' just pop off the cork an-"

"Hush," Shank quieted the group, holding up their open hand. After a drawn-out pause, they whispered "they're here."

Maria saw the blur of movement on the other side of the gate, a shifting of shadows just low enough to be a prowling cat. Behind Aegis, Ina's larger form emerged from the forest, her thick coat blending with the darkness of the forest underbelly. The black wolf watched them from behind the gate.

"She says they're ready," Shank relayed the signal from their familiar.

Tristan popped the cork from the vial with a satisfying *thwunk* as he stood up from behind the bushes. Standing close against the trunk of a tree, he pulled a white tablet from a small pouch around his waist and dropped it into the vial. The green liquid began to fizz and foam; Tristan reeled back his arm and threw it with mighty force towards the posted guards.

Plumes of neon smoke began to bloom from the grass where the vial had landed and Tristan pulled his red cowl over his mouth and nose. The guards began to cough, holding their gloved hands over their mouths and falling out of formation with desperation to find clean air. Their steps became staggered and their cries of confusion were slurred, none so much as warned Tristan to stay back as the exorcist jumped into the green fog.

Maria heard the clanking of metal and she knew Tristan had easily located a key to open the gate. Muffled voices came from somewhere within the opaque cloud - the Reaper children. The large form of Oonlok emerged from the hallucinogenic smoke, leading Theirrin, Cassie, and Rowan to clear air. Cloths that had been worn around their mouths dropped one by one as they inhaled the clean air outside the plume.

Cassie opened her hand, a ball of fire sparking just above her palm and she held it up to act as a lantern in the dark cover of the woods. The warm embrace of light bounced on her pastel pink hair and across her green goggles.

"Take us to the Knight!" the young pyro-witch squealed with glee.

"Our trail's back here," Shank called out, their lantern bobbing just visible between the trees. The rest of the group met them, watching as they picked up the fragment of red ribbon they had dropped to mark their path.

As they followed Shank and Ina through the forest, a feeling of unease fell upon Maria. She looked upward towards the trees and expected to see the peeping eyes of spirits watching them from the thick canopies, but felt worse when she found nothing.

"You okay, Maria?" Lily asked from behind her.

"Yeah, it just feels creepy out here. Like someone's watching."

Maria could visualize the shrug even though she wasn't facing Lily. "If you can't see it, it's not there."

Maria sighed; while she knew Lily was trying to be comforting, the mortal woman couldn't even see the countless black orbs of Leeches that floated amongst the thick limbs of the trees around them. Even so, nearly everything that had ever gone wrong in her lifetime had always snuck in from somewhere just beyond her line of sight.

— ❦ —

Avery saw the top of Tristan's head first, his ale-blonde hair sticking out in a sea of dark hats. Through a break in the crowd, Avery caught a glimpse of Lily's face staring back at her. Her friend pushed through people, rude and uncaring that she was shoving villagers out of her path to Avery.

"You're stupid and reckless!" Lily shouted, giving her a hard shove before pulling her back and throwing her arms around Avery's neck. Lily's hug tugged the strap of Avery's hat against her neck, sending her into a choking cough that transformed into a laugh.

"I'm.. happy… to see you too," Avery answered between fading coughs as she put the wide-brimmed hat back onto her head to keep herself from choking again.

Lily let go and stepped back, the joy on her face quickly melting into sharpened focus. "So what's happening? What did they say? They just let you go?"

As Lily spoke, she took Hemlock and Avery's rucksack off to hand it to her. Aegis circled around Avery's feet, brushing up against her boots more than usual.

"Glad to have you back, girl."

"They offered us all shelter in the castle," Moz said "on the grounds that we escort Yumi safely to Eyon. We're still screwed for money though, a voyage won't come cheap."

"They wouldn't just give it to us?"

Theirrin's voice came from the back of the group and Avery stood on her toes to look past Shank to see her face. Her young and freckled face was even more hardened than it was when they had met; the death of her friend had clearly taken a toll. The young Reaper appeared lonely and small without her grizzly bear familiar, Oonlok, behind her. Avery guessed that Oonlok and Grim were left somewhere hidden; it would be hard to go about town trailed by an alligator.

"No," Moz answered. "Even just the shelter was given tentatively. There was no way they were going to give up naval resources for us, too. We can't leave until we get fast cash."

Avery turned to look up at Moz. "Sticky fingers?"

He shook his head. "Not us. Our faces draw attention everywhere we go as long as these posters stay up. Speaking of, shouldn't they be taking them down?"

"But you're saying you'd turn a blind eye to the rest of us doing it?" Jack's face lit up with glee.

"I'm saying that if you get caught, I'll kick your ass," Moz warned. "For now, we should head to the castle and replenish before we worry about funds."

Jack excitedly raised his arms in the air and whooped, "That's not a 'no'!"

"Lead the way, Moz," Maria said before looking over her shoulder nervously.

The Reapers followed him back up the cobblestone avenue leading to the castle grounds. Avery found that the hill was much steeper than it was when she was being lifted up the hill by armed guardsmen.

"Carry me, heathen!"

Avery shot Aegis a sour look as he circled in front of her as though to prevent her from going any further without picking him up.

"You're the worst cat ever," she mumbled as she took an exaggerated step over him.

Aegis fell behind her, trotting to keep up. She wondered if every demon was this annoying or if this one in particular just loved to push her buttons.

"You're slowly killing me, Avery!"

"Man, I miss talking to Aegis," Jack said from behind her, hearing only her side of the conversation with her familiar.

"Take him, you can have him."

"And here I was thinking we were having a fun time. What are you - hey!" Aegis protested when Jack obliged, scooping Aegis up into his arms and cradled the cat onto its back.

"Who's the baby?!"

Aegis wriggled himself out of Jack's arms, landing nimbly on his feet and running ahead so he couldn't be caught again. Avery snickered before they stopped at the large iron gates of the castle grounds. Through the metal rendering of the Harthmoor crest - an eight pointed star and a flaming sun - Avery saw Yumi in the gardens of ornamental topiaries run towards them. Had she waited there the entire time?

"Let them in!"

Metal clanked loudly on the other side of the gate as gears and chains grinded to force open the castle gate. As she stepped through the opening gate, she caught the scowl of the guard turning the crank. Avery stopped and stared at the mustached man as she tried to figure out what she could have done to warrant such a sour look. To him personally, at least; it wasn't *his* hand that she had bitten. As far as she could tell, anyway - they did all look the same to her in their navy tweed uniforms.

Yumi approached them as they entered the gardens and the cobblestone became the crunch of white landscaping pebbles under Avery's beaten boots. The Princess stopped an awkward distance away from Avery with widened topaz eyes fixed onto Hemlock. Even with her expression twisted into concern, Yumi Harthmoor was undeniably beautiful. Her long, silken black hair was cut with thick bangs just above her eyebrows and the precise cut of her jawline was fixed into seriousness as she studied the weapon in Avery's hand.

"That's the sword?"

Avery nodded, lifting the sword from her side. Yumi reached out a hand as though she was going to touch the leathery eyelids on Hemlock, stopping short in the air around it.

"Yeah," Avery answered. "It doesn't really come to life until I give it blood."

Yumi reeled her hand back in a combination of fright and perhaps disgust; Avery had to admit it was a natural reaction.

"Um, well, let me show you inside," Yumi changed the subject with audible discomfort and turned to lead them back into the castle.

Avery and the others followed Yumi through the towering wood entry doors and down the long hall of marble floors and gilded coffer ceilings. Never before had she felt so terribly out of place in her stolen tunic and dirt-caked boots.

From the corner of her eyes, Avery saw a shadow flutter across her periphery. She stopped, looking into a drawing room with wide open doors. No one sat on the brocade upholstered sofa nor in the chair at the writing desk, but the shadow was certainly human-like. Was it a Leech? She had never seen one vanish out of thin air.

She looked at her friends who had walked ahead of her. No one else seemed to notice.

"Did you guys see that?"

As Maria shook her head, Lily answered "No. What's up?"

Avery looked back into the empty drawing room.

"Probably nothing," she dismissed the shadow and hurried to catch up to her friends.

Yumi led them to a set of tall doors, pausing for a second while the guards posted at each side stepped in synchronized movements to open them. As they followed the Princess inside the hall, Avery realized it was the same grand hall that she and Moz had been taken to when they were bound and captive.

"Just to make everyone familiar with our guests," Yumi called out, capturing the attention of the King and the stout man he was speaking to in a hushed voice. Both looked up, confused by the rag-tag band of Reapers.

"I was unaware there were so many of... *them*," the King spoke the last word as though it were a profanity and Avery didn't bother to hide her scowl.

"You've already agreed," Yumi said firmly. "Proper hospitality and nothing less."

King Harthmoor's mouth tightened into a firm line and he was silent as he looked for a loophole in his past promise.

"I did agree."

The Princess turned back to face Avery and the Reapers with a smug grin on her face; the expression brought on a strange warmth along the back of Avery's neck.

"Well then, let me show you to your-"

Yumi's eyes suddenly rolled back in her head and her body froze.

"Yumi? … Yumi!" Avery panicked, not sure what she should do when the princess still stood upright with her face lifted towards the vaulted ceiling. How was she even supposed to help?

As Yumi lowered her face back down, her posture entirely changed. She shifted her weight onto her left leg, her hip jutted out in the smallest way that Avery wouldn't have noticed if Yumi didn't appear to have such strict posture under normal circumstances. Yumi looked towards Kurosaki, a strange grin spread across her face.

"*Kuro.*"

Her voice was warped, as though she was trying to speak in a tone that was higher than her natural voice. It wasn't familiar until Avery saw Kurosaki's eyes widen and the color drain from his face.

"I..I don't know how you knew about Alice, but that's a really fucked up thing to do," Kurosaki warned with a shaking voice as he turned on his heel to leave.

"45 Union Street. Apartment E7."

Kurosaki froze. He spun around, his mouth slightly agape. "Wha… what the *fuck* did you just say to me?"

"45 Union Street, apartment E7," Yumi repeated, now an uncanny echo of Alice's voice. "That's where I was living when you came to my doorstep, asking me to go with you and Mozzy."

"H… how?"

"Well first I tried Avery, but she didn't seem to see or hear me. Fuck if I know why! But then it dawned on me: the Knight of Spirit. I don't know why but she couldn't seem to hear me either at first. But then you got here and I saw you and I wanted so badly to talk to you again and whoops, I'm a princess now."

Tears streamed down Kurosaki's face as he grinned at Yumi - Alice's vessel.

"Fuck, it *is* you."

Alice smiled, Yumi's lips turning up the exact way Alice's had in life with a crooked curve to the left.

"And don't think I don't know about your plan," the sternness in her voice didn't match the smile. "I don't care if the Knights die, you aren't killing yourself when this is over. You're Saved, so you have to live out the rest of your natural life for the both of us."

"Alice, but you weren't-" Kurosaki started in a small voice.

Alice shrugged, the gesture didn't look right on Yumi's slender shoulders. "I guess the gods got some sort of rule for people who die trying to save children. Lucky me, right?"

"You're Saved?"

"*Too* Saved, if you ask me."

"Al... I miss you so much."

Alice smiled warmly. "Kuro, I've been with you this whole time. I've loved you so much, this entire time."

Kurosaki stood still, tears rolling down his cheeks as he spat sobs that he tried so hard to keep down.

"Al, I fucked up. I fucked up so bad and now you're gone. You loved me and you were my best friend and I should have let you go, I should have never come to your door that day... you'd still be home with your brother."

Alice reached out, delicately holding Kurosaki's cheeks in Yumi's gentle fingers.

"You don't owe me a damn thing, Izaya. I was scared a lot of the time, but these past months have been the wildest adventure of my entire life. I'm glad I got to spend them with you. You kill the Knights, and you kill 'em good. And if you decide you've had enough and want to go home, I'll be with you there all the same."

Alice leaned forward, softly kissing Kurosaki's cheek. As Avery watched the intimate gesture, she didn't under-stand why she suddenly felt her stomach drop. Kurosaki lifted off his rucksack, gently lowering it onto the ground before taking the rifle off his back.

"I guess now is the only time I'll get to ask what you want me to do with all of your guns."

Alice shrugged. "Keep what you want, give everyone else what you don't. Show 'em how to use 'em. Not like I have much use for them now, right?"

Kurosaki didn't answer her and his eyes filled again to the brim with tears before spilling down his angular cheeks.

"Hey, don't you cry, alright Kuro? Not to be a dick, but twenty-five isn't as young as you'd think. You're getting older now and life is short. Don't waste it missing me."

Alice held up her hand posed into a finger gun.

"Bang, bang, baby" she said softly with a small smile.

Kurosaki returned the gesture in her direction, his middle finger folding twice as though to pull a trigger. "Bang, bang."

Alice's head went limp, rolling forward until her chin touched her chest while her hand remained still held in front of her in a gun imitation. None of the Reapers moved or spoke, afraid of what would happen if they did.

Yumi slowly lifted her head, long strands of her dark hair hanging too close to her face as she looked at her posed hand in confusion. Her face twisted in horror as she pieced together what had just happened and she dropped her hand quickly.

"That was freaky as fuck," Jack broke the tense silence, his voice bubbling with excitement.

Yumi sprinted forward, pushing through their group, and fled the room in a flash of navy. Avery found herself both impressed by Yumi's speed in heavy skirts and sympathetic to her embarrassment. She pushed open the hall doors to follow Yumi, catching sight of her just before she disappeared around a corner.

"Yumi!"

Avery ran with pounding boots on the marble floor. Guards flinched as she passed them as they were unsure if they should stop The Berserker Witch from chasing the princess. She skid around another corner and caught sight of Yumi sprinting towards a door at the end of the hall. Behind Yumi, her lop-eared rabbit familiar darted in white zig-zags around Yumi's skirts.

"Yumi, wait!"

Yumi did not even slow when Avery called out again and she threw open the door, disappearing inside the room with her rabbit. Avery considered, for only a moment, that perhaps she shouldn't be chasing her down. She grabbed the iron ring handle of the door anyway and yanked the heavy door open. Inside she found not a room, but a stone stairwell dimly lit by lamps in wall sconces.

There was no way she could have chosen the wrong door when she had watched Yumi enter with her own eyes, but Avery's skepticism grew as she began to climb the spiral stairs.

"Yumi?"

Her call was left unanswered. Avery continued to climb and she could see only a few feet in front of her with the tight spiral she was walking.

A wailing gust of air whooshed down the stairs and a mass of white charged her head on. The misty form unhinged a jaw and shrieked into Avery's face, nearly sending her backwards onto her tailbone and tumbling down the stairs. She fumbled for the wooden rail beside her and crouched down to center her gravity and keep herself from falling. Avery whipped her head to watch the mist disappear into the darkness behind her.

A ghost? She was gasping for air, frightened by the jumpscare and she held a hand over her heart to ease the pounding thrum of fear. Finally Avery rose to her feet, brushing the dust and dirt off her taupe tunic. She continued up the stairs at a more careful pace in case she should encounter any more specters.

After she had been walking for several minutes, she realized that she must have been inside one of the cardinal towers of the castle. At the top of the stairs Avery came upon another door. She picked up the iron ring door handle and rapped it against the door.

"Yumi? Are you okay?"

The door flew open and Yumi met her look with wide eyes and bleeding nostrils. Avery's thoughts immediately recalled seeing Moz's nosebleed in the graveyard with Balthazar, days before the Knight surfaced.

"Shit, shit, shit, we need to get you help," Avery swore, uncaring about the status of her company before she pushed past Yumi and hurried into the room to find a kerchief. "We need to clean you up and then we need to get you help."

"What do you mean?" Her voice was unsteady and frightened as she closed the door and followed Avery into her room.

Avery didn't answer as she assessed the room. It was small, taken up mostly by the canopied bed with wine red bedding and an altar table covered in copper bells and incense. She whirled around and looked at the contents of a bookshelf that held more odds and ends than it did books.

"Do you have, like, an old rag? I don't want you to have to ruin your clothes or use your hand. Maybe if you have an old scarf or, hey, I loved that book!"

"Rambler and the Rook?"

"Yeah, I read that in school. It was one of my favorites. I thought that Griffin was a great- but wait, rag. I don't see anything. Just a second."

Avery ripped a section of fabric from the hem of her tunic and folded it neatly, looking up to hand it to Yumi. The Princess looked at her in horror but didn't argue as she took it to press against her dribbling nose.

"We need to tell Moz right now," Avery advised, "because if my guess is right, this could be a sign of the Knight coming. We need to delay that as much as we can."

"As of now, I'm not terribly fond of that man," Yumi spoke with her head tilted back and her voice nasally through her plugged nostrils.

"He has that effect on most people at first," Avery admitted, "myself included. But he warms up to you. I think his concern gets the best of him and he's worried about the Knight of Spirit."

"I'm not sure if he can help me," Yumi whispered.

"Of course he can!" Avery took Yumi's free hand, without thinking, to lead her to the door. She quickly dropped it; why was she acting this way?

"Sorry," Avery apologized in a quick stammer as she turned on her heel, diving back into the stairwell so she could turn her flushed cheeks away from Yumi.

They bounded down the spiral staircase. Yumi said nothing and neither did Avery as she mentally kicked her own ass for her behavior. But there was no time to play therapist and examine the things she was feeling and doing around the Princess. She winced and blinked her eyes hard as they opened the door from the dim tower into the brighter hallway.

Aegis quickly sat up from where he had laid lazily beside the door; he hadn't bothered to follow Avery up the hundreds of steps. She looked down at him as he slunk around her boots.

"Do you know where Moz is?"

"Last I heard from Bone Brain, he was planning to head down to the docks to try to find a ship to Eyon," Aegis purred back. *"He might not have left yet. Ina's still in earshot, try the hall again."*

"This way then," Yumi said, stepping past Avery to lead. Avery sighed in relief, thankful that Yumi could hear Aegis as well. There was no way in the world she could have remembered the path she had run through in the labyrinth of a castle to catch up with the princess.

As Avery followed, she caught Aegis glancing over his haunches at her several times. She frowned.

"What?"

"Later."

Avery frowned but hurried to follow Yumi. If she fell behind and lost the Princess, she was skeptical she would ever be found again.

Yumi had the bloody scrap held to her nose in one hand and used her foot to kick open the heavy door to the hall. Avery shot out a hand to keep the door from slamming shut on her and Aegis. She had to admit: the Princess had style.

Moz and Ina were standing in the hall, he was talking in a hushed tone while holding the strap of a full rucksack. He looked up from Avery to Yumi. When he saw the bloodied nose, he dropped the rucksack.

"No, tell me you didn't."

Avery shook her head. "Nothing's happened yet, but it's going to if we don't stop it."

Moz rushed to them, placing his hands firmly on both of Yumi's shoulders. His quick movement startled her and she tried shrugging away from the touch but Moz held a firm grip.

"Yumi, you have to do everything in your power - and maybe even more - to prevent your Knight from ever surfacing," Moz said, his tone grave. "You, of all of us."

"Why? Why me especially?"

"Because you're the last, the one she's been waiting for. The minute you let the Knight of Spirit walk this earth freely is the minute the Beldam can break the veil between the living and dead. Demons will slip through and feed on everyone here. The Reapers? They'll die. And us? There will be no coming back from this. You're the beacon for the end of the world."

Avery's eyes widened. "Reapers will die? This is fuckin' news to me!"

"I was trying to operate a 'no pressure' policy," Moz answered without breaking his intense gaze fixed on Yumi, "but the pressure's on now."

"Why will they die?" Yumi was the one who asked; Avery was afraid of the answer.

"The Beldam will simply have no use for us anymore. Why do you need demi-gods of death when there's no distinction between the mortal world and Od?"

Avery felt even the grand room grow smaller around her. "But… do the others know?"

Moz looked at her and shook his head, finally letting go of the princess as though he were already defeated. "If you don't count Tristan, no. Not unless they guessed on their own."

He turned his serious stare back to Yumi. "We're all counting on you."

Yumi was silent as if this was something she needed to consider or agree with thoughtfully. She looked back at Avery with uncertainty in her eyes and her stained philtrum was the only sign left of the blood that had been oozing. It hit Avery like a speeding car that with the bloody nose and evident stubbornness, Princess Yumi and Moz were hilariously similar.

Turning back to Moz, the princess asked, "what do I have to do?"

"I'm glad you asked," Moz beamed, turning on his heel and walking away from Yumi. Avery couldn't help but roll her eyes; clearly Moz would enjoy taking on a mentorship role.

He turned back to face them, several yards away from where Yumi was standing.

"Do you have any weapons?"

Yumi nodded. She reached down and tugged the velveteen sash around the waist of her dress to reveal the mahogany leather belt hidden underneath. On each hip, pouches were sewn horizontally into the material. Yumi unbuttoned the flap of one of them, pulling out a slender knife of gold.

"Great, come stab me."

Yumi's eyes widened in bewilderment at Moz's request. He had asked as if it were as simple as asking to pass the salt.

"What? No!"

"No, just trust me on this one! I'm not gonna get hurt, you'll see, you just need to see how your Knight reacts when… where are you going?"

Yumi had slid her knife back into her belt and burst out of the hall through the tall doors. Moz looked at Avery sheepishly.

"You think maybe I came on too strong?"

"You think?"

The doors swung again, this time with someone entering rather than leaving. Jack was still looking over his shoulder in the direction Yumi had left, laughing through his nose.

"What happened to her?"

"Didn't want to let me teach her," Moz answered.

Jack stopped as he frowned and folded his arms. "You know I'll always support you Ma- Moz, but I don't think this is a thing you should just let her go on. You can't just skip teaching her how to control her urges from the Knight, you have to be the one to bend. Both of you are bull-headed and this is the last thing you need to be tangling horns about. Figure out how she needs you to get through to her and do it."

Both Moz and Avery stared at him, dumbfounded by the eloquent criticism from the teenaged ex-demon.

Jack frowned. "What's the matter with you both?"

"That didn't sound like you, are you sure you don't wanna throw a dick joke in there somewhere?"

Jack snickered at Moz's skepticism, his cheeks puffing up as he tried to stifle back the laugh but spat air as he burst out, "Yeah, I do!"

Avery couldn't help but smile at the boy. She looked then to Moz and said "You go sort that out. Jack, make sure Moz keeps his head on straight. I need to go find Kurosaki and talk to him to make sure he's okay."

"Twin went to the grave," Jack informed her.

"Twin?"

Jack pointed to his own mess of light hair. "Though mine is natural, I'm the spitting image of Kuro! He should be flattered."

"There's nothing natural about you at all. Are you okay heading there by yourself, Avery?"

She nodded back to Moz. "I'm not worried. The people here have been huge assholes to us so far, but I think they're more scared than anything. I'll be left alone."

Moz frowned and didn't appear to believe this in the slightest. Which was fair, considering the last time the Berserker Witch wandered alone she was almost left for dead at the mouth of a haunted forest. "Be careful, don't let anyone give you shit."

Avery smiled sweetly but said, "It's me who hands out the shit."

Moz's mouth turned in a small and crooked smile just as Jack joked, "So when will you be posting the wedding registry?"

She rolled her eyes but hid her smile when she turned to leave the hall, passing Aegis where he had been waiting at the door. He trailed behind her diligently without saying a word. Avery found it odd but decided she would rather not risk the feline complaining if she brought it up.

They were granted their leave through the castle gate with nothing more than a sour look from some of the guards. Not that she expected them to eagerly wait on her hand and foot because Princess Yumi said so, but she would have appreciated it if they at least *tried* to hide their resentment.

When she got to the bottom of the hill before the cobblestone split into left and right to form one of the main boulevards, Avery stopped and looked down at Aegis.

"You wouldn't happen to already know where the graveyard is, do you? I was just going to guess."

"This way, come along now."

Avery followed Aegis as he trotted ahead, weaving around the feet of Brightloch citizens who would give a wide berth to the Berserker Witch but not her black cat.

She looked around, doing her best to memorize the route in case she had to travel it on her own again later.

Before she even saw the street names on ornamental plates hanging from the iron gas lamps, she noticed an eerie absence of Leeches and bobbing black orbs. Ardua had been absolutely littered with them and it was strange to be in a city where they were simply missing. As she lifted her head to look at the topaz and ruby banners draped above them between the second story window ledges of brownstone homes, she saw a lone orb bobbing lazily. It seemed incredibly uninterested in what was going on beneath it; it didn't even buzz with a *"bloodbloodbloodbloodblood"* like the ones she was used to back home.

The golden tones of the banners matched the changing of the trees planted on each block in even spaces. The leaves here turned much earlier in the year than they did in Ardua with the change in latitude and Avery wondered if their colors would later stretch up the mountainside that towered beyond the castle when hours of sunlight were rarer.

She took a deep breath when they passed a bakery wedged between a bookstore and a tailor. Through the large glass windows of the white facade, she saw a woman in a tidy beige uniform set a pan of fresh bread on a counter and the warm scent of comfort curled around Avery's nostrils. Though her stomach rumbled, she found herself wanting to investigate the bookstore before even considering food. She had the time for neither but made a mental note to retrace her footsteps when she found her first minute of freedom.

It was a shame the people of Brightloch didn't care for her presence; Avery could really see herself staying in a place like this.

"Hurry along, now," Aegis urged her when he noticed she had become distracted by the new sights and smells. She followed as he darted around a corner, and then another one.

Finally they came to a cobblestone avenue that ended at an iron gate. On instinct, Avery looked for each end of the ornate fence to find the edges of the cemetery. She'd never been able to look at graveyards the same since her dream about Balthazar's otherworldly graves. They approached the doors of wrought iron and Avery looked up, struggling to read the words that sat atop them like a crown.

"Credence Lot," she read aloud when she finally deciphered the shapes the metal bent into.

Avery fished through her pockets, annoyed that she was only finding lint until she felt the cold copper of coins. Her shoulders relaxed when she pulled out three - *perfect*. She knelt and arranged them into a tight triangle at the stone column anchoring one of the iron gate doors, just enough out of the way that they wouldn't be nabbed by the next person who walked by.

She stepped back and looked up at the gate.

"May we enter?"

Her voice was just below the volume she wanted to use as she worried about being overheard by passersby. Was this a normal thing to do in Brightloch? Or anywhere, for that matter? She wasn't even sure she would receive any kind of answer; maybe signs were as rare as Leeches in this city.

As Avery waited, she watched for movement inside the graveyard between the wrought iron bars. She could see grave markers winding up a hill alongside a cobblestone path, trees communing at the bottom of the hill and becoming sparser as the incline grew higher. It felt peaceful here, but there was still an edge of caution.

She flinched when she heard the sharp first note of a bird singing in the tree above her head. Avery looked up and saw the robin perched in a low branch that jutted over the fence from where the tree was planted within the gates. The bird's post was just above the line that divided the city of the living from the city of the dead, so Avery decided that this was the sign she had been waiting for.

"Thank you," she said politely to the bird and reached for the handle of the gate before her.

The metal gave with an awful screech as she pushed her way into the graveyard and she was careful to close the gate behind her once Aegis was at her feet again.

"Okay, let's find Kurosaki," she said to him, but Aegis didn't move.

"*Something's not right here*," he warned. "*Look over there*."

Aegis trotted forward to direct her gaze and Avery followed him. Around the trunk of a great oak, several black orbs bobbed with lazy and fluid motion. She watched them for a moment and tried to understand why they were there when she had hardly encountered any on her walk. Avery realized they were making slow progress towards the hill. She realized then that it wasn't because the demons were sparse, they were all drawn to a concentrated point.

"I think I figured out where he might be," she murmured and started towards the hill, where the fledgling demons were gravitating towards an immense source of despair.

Aegis followed until he circled in front of Avery and cut her off abruptly.

"*I believe I have put together why we saw so few of them before now,*" he said. "*There's no infant demons because they're all able to latch on so easily to souls. You saw the notice about the monster problem.*"

"I really hope you're wrong."

"*Me too, girl. Me too.*"

They climbed the path up the hill and the cemetery unfurled around them like a corpse flower as the trees thinned amongst the crowding of headstones. She spotted the head of bleached hair easily between tombstones for there was none directly in front of him yet.

Avery approached Kurosaki quietly, sitting beside him with her legs folded under her. She looked down at the freshly turned plot of dirt and sat in the silence with him.

"You two are so close," she finally said. "The way you made each other smile was so infectious, even when we were getting ready to storm. She was incredible, still is really. If anyone was going to be able to defy the final silence, it would be her. Alice will keep chattering in your ear until the day you die. Then some more."

There was a pause after she had spoken and Avery had expected Kurosaki to retort back with something wounded. When she turned to look at him, he was watching the new grave with a faint smile and evaporating tears on his cheeks.

"I wish I was lucky enough to know her as well as you did," Avery added softly as she took one of his hands in hers to give it a gentle squeeze.

"I was always learning," he answered back, his voice rough and jagged but quieted to match hers.

They sat for a long time together where Alice rested, sitting in silence because what could they possibly have said? Kurosaki held onto her hand and she let him. The bones in his silver-ringed fingers felt tired, the fatigue of grief seeped from his body to hers and Avery's heart broke for him. Alice, too. She would gladly and dutifully hold onto the grief for her friends.

He watched the wind stirring the grass around the patch of grave dirt and she watched the Leeches amongst the tombstones with wary eyes. As she scouted to make sure he would stay safe from the fledgling demons, her thumb absently stroked the back of his hand. When he unthreaded his fingers from her, he shrugged his black parka to open wider and he began to unbutton his shirt.

Avery frowned, curious as to what he was doing and she watched him silently. Under his dark shirt was a wide black strap crossing his chest from his left shoulder and looping beneath the right half of his ribcage. As he reached down, Avery saw the faint ghost of a long scar running laterally underneath his pectoral that stopped at his sternum. She quickly looked away, unsure if she saw something she was not meant to.

"I want you to have this," Kurosaki said, fishing out a pistol and holding it out to Avery by the barrel.

Avery's eyes widened with bafflement at the gesture. "Me? But why? I don't even know how to use it!"

"You were with her," Kurosaki said gently. "You backed her up until the very end and did everything you could. And even though you didn't know her long enough for her to start showing it right, she admired and respected you. Alice wants you to have this. I'll show you how to use it."

Avery looked from the gun to Kurosaki's face. He watched her with watery eyes, nodding once to encourage her. She cautiously took the grip of the gun into her hands, balancing the heavy weight of it when Kurosaki let go of the other end.

She had watched Alice and Kurosaki storm on firing rampages but the reality of what they had been doing had never fully settled in for her. That small labyrinth of metal and gunpowder was instant death for others. Or herself.

"Kurosaki, I know this means a lot to you and it means a lot to me to hear you say that," she said. Halfway through her refusal, she watched his eyes light up just the smallest spark and she knew then that she couldn't turn the gift down. He was already buttoning his shirt up, confident that he would not need to put the gun back in its holster.

"Thank you, I'll take good care of it for her."

Avery swore silently to herself that she would never fire it.

When he said nothing in response, she offered "We should probably head back to the castle, we were all so worried about you. How does that sound?"

"Yeah, I suppose we could," he agreed, standing up. He looked down the hill with a frown fixed on his mouth and Avery followed his gaze to the black orbs floating up towards them.

"It's okay, I'm fine," he then assured her as if he could feel the concern rolling off Avery's shoulders in crashing waves. "They're not going to be a problem."

She nodded. Avery began to walk down the hill back to the gates and Kurosaki followed. Aegis darted past them in bounds, looked around and waited for them to catch up before doing the same pattern again. By the time they reached the cobblestone avenue, none of them had spoken a word until Kurosaki broke the silence.

"Avery, are we friends?"

She was startled by the question that came so suddenly when they began passing the brownstones and shops.

"Of course we are, Kurosaki. What's on your mind?"

He was quiet for a long moment before the sound of their footfalls were swallowed up by the ambient sounds of the people around them. When he finally spoke again, his voice was low.

"I guess I'm just not really sure where I fit anymore. It's like I'm lost or something. Like I was held together by her gravity and now that she's gone, I'm just spinning out."

Avery stopped, but he kept trudging forward until she called out to him "Hey, stop for a second."

Kurosaki turned to watch her with downturned eyes and his fists shoved deep into his trouser pockets. She stared at him and hoped the heartache wasn't visible on her face. He didn't need her pity right now.

"Nothing any of us can say will ever take away what you're feeling right now," she said truthfully, "but we'll be here regardless. I'm your friend, Moz is your friend, Jack idolizes the ever-loving shit out of you. We're all your friends and you're never going to have to face any of this alone. Never. Okay?"

He considered her words before agreeing, "Okay."

Avery outstretched her open hand and waited expectantly for him to grab it. Kurosaki sighed before he obliged, interlocking his fingers in hers before they continued walking. She felt pleased with herself, like she had won some unspoken contest to get Kurosaki to show even an inkling of platonic affection not once, but twice. But when she glanced up at his face as they walked beside each other, she saw the water welling in his eyes.

Kurosaki squeezed her hand tight and she let him, saying nothing - she was just there.

CHAPTER FOUR

THE STAR

oz followed the voice of Yumi's enraged Knight until he found her behind the ajar doors of a library. She sat at a table littered with loose sheets of parchment and seemed so small surrounded by towers of stacked tomes. The heavy smell of old paper and polished leather hung in the air and Moz's gaze fell from the dust falling in the sunbeam from the single stained lancet window, down to Yumi's scowling face as she noticed him walk in. He felt a bite of familiarity but as soon as he recognized it, he locked the memory away to stash it somewhere it would not be found so easily again.

"What do you want," Yumi demanded.

Instead of answering her, Moz pulled out the wooden chair across the table from her. The old wood creaked under his weight as he leaned back. The Princess folded her arms across her chest and leaned back in her winged-back chair of royal blue velvet, matching his casual stance as though he had dared her to see who could care the least about their predicament.

He pinched the bridge of his nose, shaking off the attitude he must have given off and leaned forward to level with her.

"Yumi, I'm sorry. I'm sure you understand, we're under an *immense* amount of pressure right now. No games, no tricks. Just let me tell you what you need to know."

Yumi frowned. "Why didn't you just start there? Jackass."

Moz closed his eyes, inhaling through his nose, and pictured the insult rolling right off his back. She could have at least made this easier on him. When he opened his eyes again, he saw the annoyed arch in her brow.

"Let's start with rule number one: don't let the Knight out."

"Wonderful. Ingenious. You've said that already, next."

His expression fell through the emotional floor of disappointment and crashed into the cellar of irritation.

"Okay… rule number two: you can be healed from almost all wounds when you're in your own body. You are your most vulnerable when you transform into the Knight's true form. In that form, there is nothing to heal you from within and you will die."

That grim fact quieted Yumi easily and Moz tried not to let himself look pleased.

"That is why stalemates have been so common amongst our one-on-ones," he added. "No one wants to be the first to get in that state where we can be murdered. So use caution. Ideally, you'll never even have to be in that state at all. But if it ever gets to that point, make sure I am too. I'll cover you."

"You said *almost* all wounds. What is excluded?"

"Well, I've never seen it done so this is just a hypothesis. But I'm willing to bet money on how hard it would be to come back if your head was to be severed from the rest of your body."

"Fair enough," she conceded. "Then what happened to your face?"

"Croxi found blessed waters so now Tristan uses baby-proof bottles. Rule number three: for as long as the Knight lives inside us, we will not age or die of natural causes. We're more or less immortal as long as there's basically a piece of a god inside us. Much like being a normal Reaper."

"Okay, and isn't that a good thing?"

Moz huffed. "Maybe at first for you, but I'm getting real fuckin' tired of it. Do you know how long I've been around?"

"A long time?"

"A *long* fuckin' time. I'd really like to retire one day."

"Take a nap like the rest of us and quit complaining," she snarled at him with a scowl. The anvil that was falling through the house of his emotions had dropped out of the basement of irritation and was now on the cobblestone streets of Od. Moz pinched the bridge of his nose tighter than he had before, resisting the urge to slam his palms on the desk before storming out. It was tempting but not conducive to his "be a better person" mission.

"Yumi. You are not making this easy. We're on the same team here, what are you doing?"

She then did the unexpected: she relaxed her arms and the frown fixed on her face eased. Yumi leaned back in her chair.

"Alright, I think we're even now. Carry on."

"What are you talking about?"

"Avery said you were quite stubborn and unruly upon first meeting people. I believed her immediately just based on our first interaction. I am tossing that grenade right back to you. If you truly are sorry, all is well. Just know that no matter how bull-headed you think you are, I can be five times worse. Would you care to avoid that?"

Moz couldn't decide if he admired or hated her, so he chose to ignore the play altogether. He let go of his nose, undoubtedly red from the tight pressure, and folded his hands neatly in front of him.

"Moving on…"

"*You trying to pull a fast one over Bone Brain?*"

"What the fuck are you talking about?" Avery snapped back at Aegis just as her irritating familiar caught up with her as she strode down the hallway.

"*Have you looked in a mirror recently? You should see the look on your face when you're very clearly adoring the Princess.*"

She felt her cheeks flush hot. "It's none of your business what I think!"

"*You made it my business when you decided to inter-fere with demons. No matter how much Bone Brain wants to deny it, he's one of us. So, are you trying to pull a fast one over him? I would much rather you politely move on."*

Avery fell quiet as she thought, even her hurried strides stopped suddenly. She hadn't thought she was deceiving anyone, but intention and impact were two very different things.

"No, I'm not. The way I feel about Moz and the way I think Yumi is making me feel are good, and different... but somehow the same. I don't know how to explain it, I'm barely working it out myself... wait, why do I have to justify this to you?"

"Because you can hide nothing from me, girl."

"I'm not trying to hide any feelings. They're just in two places instead of one. I'm going to say something, but how? What do you even say to someone you haven't had a chance to explain that's how love works for you? Life has just been *happening*."

"I will never be able to understand you, though I will support you. But if you deceive one of my siblings, I may have to gut you."

"I'd like to see you try, kitty cat."

Just as she said it, she watched a door further down the hall and Moz emerged with the ever-telling pinching of his nose bridge. He caught sight of her just as he was shutting the door behind him.

"How did it go?" She asked but was not optimistic with his body language.

Moz sighed. "I almost ripped all my own teeth out. And my hair. But I did it, she's up to speed now. Where were you headed?"

"Just investigating the lay of the land. There's too many fucking doors down here and I'm tired of being lost."

He laughed warmly. "Me too. Mind if I come?"

"Not at all. So far all I've found back that way was a kitchen, a study, and a chapel."

Aegis sauntered off without his usual jab at Moz and with what Avery knew about the demon, it was because he knew he wouldn't have been able to keep his mouth shut about their previous conversation. Who knew a demon could be a bastion of self-control?

They walked together in a comfortable quiet, peeking into each room that had an unlocked door. A bathroom painted a dark navy to match the overly intricate porcelain sink. Another study spilling over with full shelves. A solarium with perfectly manicured pothos and monstera. A pantry. After the third study, they both grew terribly bored and trudged back to the main entry hall to see if another wing was more interesting.

As Avery was about to lead him down the western wing, she caught sight of the doors opposite of the throne hall. They were cracked open and it struck her as strange when everything else around them was trimmed and locked into perfection.

"What do you think is going on in there," she whispered, unsure if they would be walking in on a tense diplomatic meeting if they snuck inside. Moz carefully peeked through the gilded doors, opening them just wide enough for him to look inside.

"What's in there?" Avery asked, standing on her toes to look over Moz's shoulder.

"Tables? Instruments? It looks like-"

"The Novara Ball."

Moz and Avery both jumped at Yumi's voice from behind them.

"Fu- You again? Don't sneak up on us!" Moz narrowly avoided swearing at the princess and pinched the bridge of his nose. He was getting dangerously close to the red marks becoming permanent.

Yumi looked from Moz to Avery, one of her dark eyebrows lifted and momentarily disappeared under her straight-cut bangs. "You know you're allowed to go in there, right?"

Avery wasted no time slipping into the space Moz left when he had backed away from the door and she threw open a door to burst into the hall with excitement.

Her footsteps fell with satisfying thuds on a marble floor and Avery stopped, looking up in wonder at a grand coffered ceiling painted with the deep hues of a night sky between gilded beams. The tall lancet windows flooded the room with orange hues of the falling sun even with the unlit crystal chandeliers above their heads.

Avery's dazzled gaze skimmed over the unset tables on the far end of the hall and fell on a platform housing a grand piano. Beside it stood several chairs with black cases on top of them; Avery knew immediately that they were the instruments waiting to be played. Next to one chair, a larger case was propped and Avery's eyes went wide as she hurried to the platform.

Her boots clomped ungracefully as she stepped up to the black leather case and reached towards the brass buckle. Avery froze, turning back towards where Moz and Yumi watched her.

"May I?"

"If you wish," Yumi answered simply.

Avery hastily unbuckled the case, pausing when she looked in wonder at the polished wood of the cello. With delicate care she pulled it out, examining the surface of the maple wood. The instrument was meant to be played by a musician taller than she was and so she bent down, adjusting the endpin so it stood at a more appropriate height for her. She pulled the bow from a compartment in the case before sitting down.

The neck of the cello rested against her shoulder and chills ran up her spine, thrilled with the familiar feeling. Looking down, she ran the bow across the bridge to test the sound. She froze, both startled and delighted by the full-bodied sound that had not fallen on her ears since before she was even a Reaper.

Her fingers moved into positions on the neck that were programmed in her memory long before she was the true Avery Porter and she began to play somber notes she thought she had left behind wherever she had lost her humanity. The notes fluttered and took the shape of a song, the name of which she had long forgotten.

Avery flinched when she struck a sour note and felt embarrassed by how out of practice she was with Yumi watching. She corrected herself quickly and her song carried on in rich and deep notes. Moz walked onto the platform and opened the sliding fallboard of the grand piano before sitting down at the bench.

He played notes in the octaves above and below hers, clearly not knowing the song but kept pace with her in impressive improvisation. His higher notes skittered above hers, looping under her low rhythms and back above again. Her heart swelled at the sound - it fit so perfectly with hers.

Avery made music in sweeping gestures with her whole body, the world beyond the maple frame melting away. Her sound grew faster, rising up to the heavens and fluttered back down just before breaking. She stopped playing, wiping her teary face with the back of her hand that still clutched the bow.

"Avery, what's the matter?" Yumi stepped forward, ducking to look at Avery with worry.

Avery laughed, wiping the other side of her face before answering her, "No, no, it's okay! I just haven't played in a while and it made me really happy."

She looked back at Moz on the piano bench and he looked over his shoulder to meet her gaze. At her questioning look, he shrugged as the melody he played faded to silence and he stilled his hands.

"What? You live nearly forever, you tend to pick up a hobby here and there."

Yumi was stepping up the platform to approach the piano, her wondrous stare was fixed on Moz's hands as they rested on the keys. He looked up, confused at first by her behavior until he looked down at his own hands.

"Oh!"

Moz wagged his tattooed hand in the air before he rolled up his sleeve as far as it would go, revealing the black depths of the ocean and bottom of the ship just below his elbow. He stood up, showing Yumi.

"You can't really see the Knight, it's at the top," he explained. "Do you have one?"

Yumi hesitated before her finger reached for the collar of her dress, undoing the top button around the base of her throat. Avery whipped around to avert her gaze, nearly knocking the cello over as her face flushed hot.

"WHAT ARE YOU DOING?!"

"It's fine, Ave," Moz said. "It makes sense that the last Knight links the others together. Peter's got it on his arm opposite mine, Morgana and Sera have a leg covered. So naturally the Knight of Spirit would be marked on the torso to connect them all."

Avery gently set the instrument back into its case before turning back to Moz and Yumi. Yumi held open her dress, unbuttoned down to just below her collarbone. At the base of her throat sat a black sun, with swirling lines dancing around it. While it was only a faint glimpse of the tattoo, Avery instantly recognized it. The dark ink easily matched Moz's arm where he had a Knight in a stormy ocean sky above a ship.

"This is how they knew it was time," Yumi explained. "The attendants were helping me dress one morning, and there it was. Suszanna shrieked the loudest I'd ever heard, demanding to know what unholy thing I had done to my body. I was still so disoriented… the voice I heard before I was me said nothing about such markings. And though it isn't hard to be modest enough to hide them, it is troubling to know that they were put there not by my own doing."

The princess quietly buttoned the neck of her dress back up. The golden light of the falling sun danced across her skin, streaming in brilliant colors of the stained glass lancet windows. Her soft face was a beautiful shade of solemn and she floated past Avery to glide towards the hall doors.

"Here, come with me," Yumi's voice was warm even in her instruction.

Moz and Avery obliged, following the Princess into the main hall that split off into smaller wings. She approached the stairs, looking over her shoulder to make sure they had kept up with her before they had a chance to get lost in the labyrinth of hallways.

"Let me show you to your rooms," Yumi offered, her skirts drifting about her long legs as she turned around the banister of the stairs to lead them up to the next story. Moz and Avery followed up the stone steps and Avery looked up in wonder at the paintings that adorned the walls around them. Landscapes of the rumbling sea and the mountainside during the full blooms of Lume. Royal portraits of people Avery had never seen before followed her with their unblinking and serious eyes.

Yumi led them up to the next story and down a wing, following a long strip of ornate rugs woven with sweeping flourishes of umber and gold. She stopped at one door, gently opening the wood and iron entry with care. Behind the door, the overwhelming color of bright juniper flooded Avery's field of vision.

"Moz, this will be your room," Yumi stated.

Without pausing to let Moz quip a joke about the loud hue of the room, Yumi turned and kept walking before she stopped two doors down.

"And this will be your room, Avery," Yumi said as she pushed open the door.

Inside was a room of rich navy in the bedspread and wallpaper. A window of stained glass flooded the room in blue speckled with golden stars. Avery's wide eyes scanned the room; the royal family certainly used their celestial star and sun crest in any way they could. Beneath her feet, a thick rug of a deep charcoal and blue florals padded her aching arches from the stone floor.

A mirror stood in a corner and Avery avoided looking in it for longer than a glance-over, embarrassed to see what she may have looked like standing next to Yumi. Beside the mirror was an archway leading into a washroom painted the same dark navy and tiled with mosaics of golden stars on the floor.

"You send Owen if you need me for anything, okay?"

Avery turned and looked at Yumi.

"I can't begin to thank you enough for letting us stay here. It's been a long road and the shelter means a lot to us."

"It's really no imposition," Yumi said and smiled. "I appreciate what you are doing… for me. And it's the least I can do. Now rest up, tomorrow's a big day."

"What's tomorrow?"

"The Novara festival and ball. We'll use that as an opportunity to find a ship captain to take us to Eyon."

"Clever," Avery murmured as she looked up at the night sky painted on the ceiling of her temporary home. She looked back down to see Yumi was smiling at her.

"Good night, Avery," the Princess spoke with sleepy softness before she left, closing the door behind her. The gentle words sent nerves running up Avery's spine and she stood frozen in place for a long moment to sit in the feeling.

Finding she wasn't tired enough to sleep, she gently laid Hemlock down across the navy duvet before she stepped back out into the hall. She peeked left and then peeked right - Yumi had already vanished and there was no sign of anyone. Hurriedly, Avery rushed down the hall with swinging arms.

"Psssst… It's me," she hissed through the door two down from hers.

"Yes, I know," Moz's voice called through the closed door.

Avery gently pushed open the door to Moz's chamber, taken aback again by the gaudy green velvets and gilded furniture. Her horror at the awful decorating turned into laughter as she closed the door behind her. Moz seemed terribly out of place sitting on the floral bed sheets in his long black coat and as he peeled off his taped boots, looking around the ridiculously curated room. He shifted his gaze from the emerald canopy above his bed to Avery, dropping the second boot to the floor with a thud.

"I'm so tired that I don't even care," he said with a chuckle. Moz extended his tattooed arm out to her, his palm open. "Come here?"

Avery nodded, stepping towards him. He gently took her right, unscathed hand into his and pulled her into the space between his knees. With Moz sitting on the bed, they stood eye to eye and he propped his chin over her right shoulder as he hugged Avery close. In his arms she felt the same safety she found buried in Malo's tomb of branches. She was a fluttering moth flitting inside, inexplicably drawn to the glowing lantern of a heart that beat within his ribs.

He nestled his head in the crook of her neck and she felt the soft breath of his laugh on her hair before he said, "You smell good. Like pine trees and a cup of coffee."

"Oh thank goodness, I was beginning to wonder when climbing into the trees with my cowboy coffee was going to pay off," she joked, her knee-jerk reaction to feeling flustered by his proximity. The smell of clove and tobacco smelled just a little stronger on his skin and Avery wondered when he found the time to step out for a smoke.

"It's hard to believe," he murmured, the unexpected softness of his voice next to her ear sent more tingles running down her spine, "but this is the safest we've been for a long time. I've been moving for so many years and I would just like to rest. Really rest."

Avery had stood still until she realized her hand was cupped against the back of his head and she gently scratched her fingers at the crown where Moz's short hair became longer tendrils. She smiled even though he couldn't have seen.

"I'm glad you feel safe," Avery answered softly. "You deserve the rest. I'll let you-"

"If it's okay," he cut her off with a small hint of eagerness in his voice before he tamped it down. "If I could just be near you a while."

"Yeah, of course. I can stay until you want me to go."

"Please stay."

Avery nodded and stepped slowly out of his arms. She rounded the bed and carefully climbed onto the covers beside Moz, laying back against the tall stack of pillows with her hands folded neatly on her stomach and he began to laugh.

"What's so funny?"

"You look so rigid still. Take your boots off."

Avery looked down at her feet and frowned. It had become such a habit to fall asleep on the ground with everything still on. She sat up and unlaced her boots; the laces had become stiff with dried mud and she struggled until she was finally able to wriggle her feet free.

Avery laid back down onto her side, truly relaxing the second time as she felt every tension in her bones sink into the cushion of the mattress. She closed her eyes, sighing in satisfaction and opened them again as Moz was fumbling to get himself underneath the blanket.

"You sure are picky about your rest for someone so helplessly weary," she joked as she wriggled under the brocade cover for the sake of making it easier for Moz.

He flashed an unserious scowl down at her before laughing it off, settling finally into a stillness when he laid down on his back. Moz inhaled deeply with closed eyes, holding the breath for a short moment before exhaling with tangible relief. His head rolled over his shoulder to face her, his gaze looking directly into Avery's eyes. Neither of them spoke or moved, but Avery knew that the simple ability to be still was exactly what Moz had wanted.

She studied him in a way she never had found the time to before; the scrape on his cheek from Centralia had almost finished healing, his forehead and nose were faint pink with sunburn. His dark facial hair had been allowed to grow unchecked for too long to call stubble, but not long enough to call it a proper beard.

"You have quite a few more freckles than you did when I found you," he whispered and laughed before turning his head up towards the green canopy as though he was suddenly embarrassed under her stare. She grinned in admiration, knowing there was a time not too long ago that she couldn't even imagine what his laugh might have sounded like.

She didn't notice when exactly the rough edges of him had smoothed out, but now here it was. Moz was unguarded and she couldn't think of a single time before when he wasn't looking to find the next strike from within his own skin or the world she could observe plainly.

Avery then felt her smile disappear.

"I have to tell you something, Moz," Avery whispered quickly before she could take it back. Before she could shrink away like a coward.

He turned towards her. "Yeah?"

Avery froze when Moz's full attention was on her and she felt her neck flush hot.

"I have a lot of feelings for you, please don't get that wrong," she started and trailed off, not knowing where she had wanted to take her words.

His laughing smile vanished but he watched her without interrupting.

"But I think there's something you need to know about me," she murmured, her voice shaking. "There have been times I… where I was, fuck. Times where I had more than one partner. I mean, it was before I was me, I mean a Reaper. But I think it still applies and I wanted to tell you."

He raised a brow and even the small reaction sent her pulse racing with fearful anticipation of shouting or anger.

"Is *polyamorous* the word you're looking for," he simply suggested.

"What? Fuck, I don't know."

"You're telling me now because of Yumi, right?"

Avery froze. He began laughing again.

"My gods, Avery. The horrible, terrible thing you needed to tell me was that you have a crush on the Princess?"

Moz was laughing and Avery sat up abruptly, her face twisted in horrified confusion. "*That*'s your reaction?"

He sat up to meet her, his laughter fading. "Avery, that's not unheard of. Over the years I've known quite a bit of people with multiple relationships. Sometimes even family trees that look more like a family bramble. It's more common than you probably think. I'd bet you'd spot it even here in Brightloch if you started looking for it."

Avery was still frowning and her vision began to blur with water, not feeling that she was being comforted but that she wasn't being taken seriously. He was just *fine* with it? Moz scooped her into a tight hug before speaking.

"Hey. I don't want anything to make you feel as though you have to hide, not from anyone and definitely not from me," he leaned back, holding both her cheeks in his calloused hands. "Does the way you feel about her take away from whatever you feel about me?"

Tears broke from her eyes as she looked at him, suddenly feeling undeserving when Moz smiled at her kindly and she had been waiting for a fight. The feelings she held for either one of them were different: Moz felt like home, Yumi felt like a strange magic she was still learning. Neither feeling was any less enticing than the other.

She shook her head. "No, never."

Moz laughed once, his smile spreading wider like her answer had relieved a fear he kept unspoken before he pulled her into a tight hug.

"That's all I need, Avery. Please tell me if that changes."

Avery gripped him tight, holding handfuls of his black shirt as she stayed cradled on his lap. She wept despite her relief.

"If it's any consolation, her Knight makes it sound like you've got a pretty good chance. But no way am I courting her, too," he joked as he gently smoothed his hand over her hair.

As she wiped her face with the back of her hands, Avery couldn't help but laugh.

"Oh, is *that* what you've been doing with me?"

"I think considering our starting point involved you holding me at chef's knife-point in your apartment, I've been improving pretty well."

Moz gently tipped over with his arms still around her and they hit the pillows with gentle thuds. Her eyes immediately closed, the emotional upheaval had left her exhausted. The top of her head rested just under his chin and she felt the steady rise and fall of his breathing against her ribs. They really were safe.

She fumbled for one of his hands, threading her fingers through his to hold them against her cheek.

"Avery…," Moz murmured, sounding just between sleep and wakefulness.

"Yeah?"

"You.. are single-handedly… the most terrifying woman I have ever met. And somehow yet… the softest."

"That doesn't make any sense, Moz."

He didn't answer her. With the slower rise and fall of his chest, Avery guessed he had finally tipped over the threshold of sleep.

Moving slowly and carefully, she pulled her head back just far enough from his chest to have a clear view of his face. The peace on his face was a creeping, contagious thing and Avery felt her own breathing slow and level. In the full view of his marred eyebrow that was normally knit into a frown and the white scars of faded scrapes from years of fights, Avery finally let herself admit that he was handsome.

"Moz," she whispered, just audible enough for her to test his depth of slumber. No answer.

When she knew she was safe, she murmured, "I think I could love you too."

He didn't stir, never hearing the words. But this wasn't the right moment for them anyway, not when the world around them was burning and they had just found a pocket of air to breathe. So she tucked them away for later, keeping them close to her chest. Avery remained awake for as long as she could, relishing the warmth of Moz's fingers against her cheek.

When Avery awoke, sunlight streamed in through the stained glass window and made the bejeweled greens of the room far more horrendous. She blinked sleep away from her eyes, rubbing her cheek with her hand. Suddenly she was aware of the fact she was no longer holding Moz's fingers in hers and she looked about the room.

As if on a cue, she heard the faint halt of water pouring from a faucet on the other side of a closed door. Moz emerged from the adjoining bath and looked at her with a knowing grin. His presence felt like the warmest kind of ordinary until she realized the sound she heard was the draw of a bath and that he was wearing a robe.

"You fell asleep holding my hand," he teased.

"Yeah, well you fell asleep with your hand being held," she retorted back, her cheeks and ears flushing hot. "And mid-sentence, might I add."

She sat upright with her legs dangling over the side of the bed as he approached her. He bent down and leaned close, one hand planted firmly on either side of her. Avery felt the heat creep across her face and down her neck as her gaze rolled up from his bicep to the satisfied smirk on his face.

"Funny girl," he murmured as he studied her flushed features carefully.

Moz lifted one hand and pushed hair back from her face, tucking it tenderly behind her ear. With the movement, his face drew closer to hers and Avery found herself watching his mouth. She couldn't remember watching him this way before; unable to think of anything that wasn't the parting of his lips against hers. His hand that had brushed her hair away settled on the slope of her neck where it met her shoulder, his fingers touching the back of her neck with skin that felt so warm against hers. She watched his mossy stare flit across her face, as though he couldn't settle on which detail of her that he wanted to hone in on.

"Moz," she whispered.

"Hm?"

Before she could talk herself out of it, Avery reached her hand up and pulled his face to hers. They collided in a kiss so familiar and she instantly recognized the same glow of hunger she felt when Moz had kissed her unexpectedly for the first time. But without a sneak attack, without confessions on a physician's bed, this was on her terms.

The gentle touch she held on his cheek fluttered down his neck and her fingers settled firmly just below his collarbone. Fingers of his tattooed hand cradled her face and swam backwards into her dark hair. Moz matched the tempo of her kisses and their eagerness melded into a living, breathing thing. His hand that had remained planted at her side dipped underneath her thigh in a sure grip, drawing her closer to him.

Avery had only meant to kiss him but the hunger grew and roared the more he touched her. Crash after crash of lips and tongues and teeth and she could not will herself to stop. The peace and gentleness she felt the night before was devoured by the burning fear that if she wasn't here with Moz now, she never would be again. They could both easily be dead by sunset. His mouth trailed up her jaw and down her neck, the small scrapes of teeth sent each nerve ending in her body into a frenzy and her breath hitched.

"*Avery*," her own name against her skin was a low rumble, dark and heady as he pleaded with her. She knew the question and she could only nod eagerly.

Moz cradled her back gently as he found her lips again and she found the surface of the brocade duvet beneath her.

She couldn't decide if she felt weightless or ravenous, so she wrapped her arms around his neck to keep their bodies anchored together. Her hands dipped under the collar of his robe to touch his skin and she felt the flex of wiry muscles under her fingers. Nothing else in the world existed except for him above her so protectively and amorously, kissing her with a maddening fire that was both broken and stoked by the soft and involuntary sounds that fell from her lips.

She hadn't expected him to break the kiss and almost protested until the heat of his breath brushed past her cheek and to her ear so he could murmur:

"You are the sun in my sky and I would orbit these heavens in your gravity for all of time."

Avery's fingernails would have punctured holes in his shoulder blades had they not been cut to the quick and she allowed his skin the relief from her grip when she gently guided his face back to hers in both hands. Moz skimmed her face with kisses before he pressed his forehead to hers and in the seconds of stilled restraint, the devotion in his words felt real:

"And I would remain a monster for eternity with no hesitation if it meant I would belong to you."

Her heart dropped. There wasn't a single reason she could have ever asked that of him and it felt more raw than any "I love you" either of them could say. He was a gilded icon of justice, a golden waypoint star in her darkened sky. She would have ripped the world around them to shreds if it meant he would be free of his chains - and she had already started. Avery saw his eyes flicker to her left shoulder where she had taken an arrow during his rescue, the bandage exposed under the falling sleeve of her half-open tunic.

"You can't rough me around like I would normally request, but you certainly don't have to baby me," her words had been joking as she ran her hands down and smoothed the opening of his robe, but they sounded like spiced honey to even her own ears. She didn't want him to think for even a second longer that the Knight could own him forever.

Moz grinned, wicked and devilish with his mouth just out of her reach. His hand that had gripped her thigh to lower her down grazed across her hip to the hem of her shirt. The warmth of his fingers spread up the bare skin of her belly, tracing the lower curve of her breast as though he couldn't wait to finish unbuttoning her shirt before touching her. He helped her carefully shift her weight with her bad shoulder as she shrugged out of the sleeves, leaving her bare for his kisses to trail hot sparks from the center of her sternum to the base of her throat.

"Don't mistake my tenderness for someone who hasn't been burning at both ends for you."

The words spoken against her collarbone set her ablaze from the inside out. Avery was done with talking; she wanted to know exactly how much he had been wanting her. Her fingers shot forward and gripped the collar of his robe, wanting so desperately to pull it from him when Moz pried her fingers away and pinned them to the bed.

The thickening air of aggression around him thrilled her when Moz lifted his hands from her wrists to undo the button of her pants and strip her legs bare. Avery burned hot, naked under his stare that he let roam across her skin without the pretense of hiding his hungry gaze. He slipped his hands again under her thighs, stepping backwards with his feet back on the floor and dragging her with him until her knees hooked around the edge of the mattress.

"Okay, the safe words are the comprehensive instructions on driving an automatic transmission," Avery joked.

Moz sank to his knees, glowering down at her in a flash of displeasure at her remark. She was quickly forgiven by the time he was making a home of the space between her legs, kissing the tender flesh of her inner thigh with the selective reverence of a sinner.

"Avery, tell me the truth, baby," his voice was a low and dark rumble between her thighs when he looked up at her face. So close, but so far from where she needed him. The pet name felt like a finger jammed into an open wound, but she didn't know why. "Did you hate me?"

She kind of hated him right now for the tease. "Of course I did. It was so goddamn irritating the way you would - *fuck!*"

Avery's snap was cut off when she felt the wet heat of his tongue lap at her center. Her eyelids fluttered shut and her hand shot down, locking her fingers in his longer waves of hair to hold him right where she wanted to keep him. Moz's tongue was fast and precise - just as she expected it to be. A soft moan fell from her lips and her hips lifted to rut into him, until his tattooed hand pushed her back down into the bed. Avery's eyes flew open and she looked down at where he knelt at the bedside between her legs. *Just who does he think is in charge?*

Moz lifted his mouth just enough to say, with a dark gaze rolled up to her bewildered face, "then we wasted the opportunity for a classic hate-fucking because I'm far too smitten with you to do that now."

She glowered down at him. "It can easily be hate again if you don't hurry up and fuck me."

Avery saw the wicked grin again before his mouth dove back against her, lashing at her far too greedily to be precise any longer. She cried out, forgetting all the tender prose he murmured to her only minutes ago. This mouth was less poet, more animal.

"Try asking nicer, baby."

She would have been lucky to string a full sentence together at all, let alone lace the words with saccharine submission. That wasn't her style anyway.

The sensations wavered between agonizing and holy and Avery was sure she would be seeing stars painted on the back of her eyelids at any minute. Moz finally released her, kissing the inside of her knee. He stood upright and she followed, pulled by his gravity and the shadows in his eyes. This was not the Moz she had known; this was worse and she wanted it all.

She peeled the collar of the robe open again and he did not fight back. When it fell to the floor, Avery was horrified that anyone could be cut to such perfection. The plane of muscle across his chest, the lean surface of his stomach, the v-shaped cut below his waist that drew her eyes down to how clearly he wanted her. *Oh, fuck.*

She looked up at his face and locked her gaze into his stormy eyes, darkened with want as he watched her sink to her knees. It felt so heavenly to be desired by him and she hoped he felt the same when she put her lips around the head of him.

Avery's head bobbed with the steady stroking of her hand and she dragged a pleased groan from his mouth with the languid swirls of her tongue. His fingers slid into her hair and she looked through her lashes up at his face, eyes closed and head thrown back as he surrendered to every sensation she gave him. Moz had sunk into her so easily and the raw power she felt thrilled her.

"Fuck, Avery," he groaned before he looked back down at her. She was sure her eyes showed the pleased smirk that would have been on her mouth had it not been preoccupied with his dick.

His hand floated down to her shoulder and he gently pushed her mouth off him. For a moment, she felt the cold sting of rejection until he said:

"This needs to stop, I'm not done with you yet."

He gently guided Avery back onto her feet, his hands on her waist easing her back onto the bed with a carefulness that she knew held ulterior motives.

"Do you still want it?"

Moz was looking down on her with caution, laced around the edges with a dark lust. Avery's legs wrapped around his waist, pulling him greedily against her.

"I need it so bad, please, *please*," she begged him without shame, her short fingernails raking red tracks down the wiry muscles of his arms on either side of her.

Moz smiled that devilish smirk and reached a hand down to his straining length to line himself with her. The head of him prodded at her before slipping inside and he looked back up to her flushed face when she groaned.

"Fuck," he moaned, drawing out slowly before diving again. Moz's grip locked around her hips and Avery prayed to whatever goddess oversaw the affairs surrounding sex that it would bruise. "I've been dreaming of hearing you make that noise."

His movements quickened and his careful dips into her became deeper thrusts, pushing her knees towards her head to shift his angle. He held her hip steady in his tattooed hand, the other running up her belly to roll her breast in his hungry grip. She felt a hot flare of anger along the edges of where he buried himself deep inside her when she realized they could have been going at it much sooner than this.

Avery squeezed her muscles around his length and she watched the struggle to regain control flash across his face above hers when he warned her in a low voice, "*Not funny.*"

Despite the warning, he moved faster and Avery bit her bottom lip when she clenched around him again, daring him. She wanted to know what would happen as a consequence of ignoring him. Thankfully, she didn't have to wait long at all. It was entirely his fault that she had been conditioned to act up when he used that voice of low threats on her.

"Alright, that's enough," he growled, pulling out before flipping her over onto her front with enough roughness to stoke her fire. Moz pulled her up onto her hands and knees with such delicious strength - there was her monster of a man.

He brushed her long waves off her back, getting a clear view of her before he dove at her again. His hips pounded against her ass, driving even deeper and Avery could no longer stifle her whimpers. Her eyes rolled up and her fingers gripped the covers beneath her.

"You're doing so good, baby," he purred into her hair, his hands squeezing with a roughness that didn't match his honeyed words. *Oh gods, not the praise.* Avery could have melted right there in his carnal grip, but she wanted more.

His next words were a blur to her, but certainly involved more praise about how she was taking his dick so well.

"*Harder*," she demanded between pants.

Instead of arguing, his inked fingers closed around her good shoulder for leverage when he began pounding her from behind with the most basic drive of an animal. She cried out, ecstasy bubbling from her lips and Avery dropped down from her hands and knees. The force of Moz fucking her was too much for her jellied limbs and instead of pulling her back up, he dropped down with her. His primal grunts were getting louder and far more maddening now that they were closer to her ears.

Moz thrust into her with deeper sweeps against the bed and her head lifted with her growing moans. He tenderly took her neck into his hand, carefully guiding her just a little higher to look into his face above hers. Avery wanted his grip to tighten but she couldn't find the words. She felt absolutely *filthy* looking into his freckled eyes while he was inside her.

"I want you to look at me when you come."

"Then… get on … your back," she ordered him between hard breaths, feeling bold even in her compromised position.

He pulled out of her warmth again and obliged, laying down beside her. Moz's hands gently held Avery's hips when she straddled his waist and sank down onto him. She sighed when her head lifted up towards the canopy of the bed and she relished the feeling of every corner of her being sated by him. She began to ride him, rocking up and down to slide across his thick length.

His head rolled back when he breathed, "fuck, Avery… you feel *divine*."

She gripped his shoulders in a tight lock to steady her balance as she rolled her hips, pulling moans from his lips with her movement. When he looked back down at her rocking on him, his eyes blazed in burning forests. His grip on her hips tightened and he began thrusting again, fucking up into her. She cried out and she felt her nerve endings swell in a tide of pleasure, building in her so strong that she wasn't sure how much longer she could take it.

"I'm… I'm gonna come," she managed between moans.

His hold on her hips became his arms fully snaked around her body when he sat up to meet her, tugging her into him as hard as he could. He rained kisses on any surface of her skin that he could reach while still squeezing her rocking hips. Avery forgot she could ever hate him, or the boundary lines of where she ended and he began. They were a writhing tangle of sweat and limbs, moaning into the other's mouth between kisses when they soared off the edge.

Avery was gasping for breath when Moz smoothed her hair away from her sweaty face. His breathing was labored but the adoration on his face was effortless. She took her fingers from where they had burrowed in his shoulders for balance and she cupped his irritating and handsome face.

"We can't go back to not doing that," she said between the deep breaths that had turned into laughter. He grinned wide at her, the light reaching the forest floor in his eyes.

"Don't have to tell me twice, I'd do this all day if you'd let me."

The bath Moz had drawn for one became tender after-care for two. As they sat in the cool water with Avery's back to him, Moz washed the thick waves of her hair with an endearing care that she was afraid to joke about, lest he stop. The gentle touches were made with the same love as the ones that she hoped had bruised her. She didn't want to admit it out loud, but it felt nearly as heavenly as the sex had.

He listened to her softly recount their run-in with the forest god, asking thoughtful questions every now and then while his fingers combed through her sudsy locks. She listened to him talk about all the shrines for Malo he had seen in his lifetime, and she nodded, asking if he would take her to see them when this was all over. Avery felt it was good to be heard even when she was bare.

She sat with her knees pulled up to her chest, trying to afford him as much room as she could in the clawfoot tub for his long legs on either side of her. He didn't shift and Avery allowed herself to take up the space again. They sat in a comfortable silence, the last ghosts of their moans settled into the sighing floorboards as he absently traced the bumps of her spine with his thumb.

He stopped stroking her and said, "I love you, Avery."

The first time he uttered those words they tumbled out by accident. She hadn't blamed him for it - staving off death could heighten any emotion. But these ones were definitive, each word shaped with steady resolve, and she loved the way her own name sounded next to them. The way it sounded when he spoke it.

Avery looked over her shoulder at him. Moz's face wasn't watching her expectantly, trying to coax anything out of her. He just smiled, water dripping from the ends of his dark hair and the light from the single stained-glass window casting him in saintly emerald and gold.

Love was a big word with a shape her mouth did not yet know how to draw. She knew even less how he had learned it so quickly for her.

"Please stick around long enough for me to say it," she whispered.

"I'm so sorry that anyone ever made you feel that you weren't worth sticking around for," his voice matched the softness of hers but lacked the shakiness. "I'm not going anywhere. Not after everything and certainly not after you."

He reached out and touched her cheek precisely where a dimple would form if she had been smiling, like he had memorized its exact placement. Moz's words stung her in a place she hadn't expected; one that resembled less the empty arms of a lover and more the hollow cage of a home. Avery nodded and turned her cheek into his open palm, closing her eyes so she could focus only on the anchor of his touch.

"Thank you, Moz," she murmured softly. When she opened her eyes, he had been watching her with awe and he shut his parted lips as he gave pause to whatever it was he had been about to say. Instead, he kissed her forehead.

They climbed out of the bath with careful coordination to not fall into a dripping mess of bruises before they could wrap themselves in fluffy towels. Moz helped comb her long waves, his movements methodical and reverent. Avery pulled her dirty clothes back on, grateful her rucksack of spare items were just a couple rooms over. They parted with a kiss and a knowing, lingering look before Moz watched her leave. In a lovestruck fog, she wandered the two doors down to her room and found herself standing at the mirror in her own bath.

Her skin was flushed and her lips were swollen from prolonged kissing. The sensitive skin of her neck was washed with pink from the grazes of his short beard and ghosts of bruises were beginning to bloom in grey shadows. Avery turned on the faucet and splashed icy water on her face. When she thought she had grounded herself properly with the arctic shock, she shut it off and looked into the reflection of her dripping face.

And she began to practice:

"Moz, I think I might be in love with you."

She frowned at the flushed image of Mirror Avery. No, she would have to do better than that. He had used such tender prose when she had simply wanted to be devoured by him and the least she could do was put her own feelings to words.

"Moz, I think you're a pretty great guy and I, no."

She pressed her forehead against the cool porcelain sink and drew in a deep inhale of frustration.

"I'm going to be here a while, aren't I?"

CHAPTER FIVE

CUPS

When Avery walked into the entrance hall, her friends had already gathered in several pockets of discussion and plotting. Her eyes found Moz like metal on a magnet, his back to her as he spoke with Tristan and Shank. Immediately she recalled the feeling of his wiry muscles under her scraping fingernails and Avery fought to shoo the thoughts away. Shank's gaze traveled past Moz's shoulder towards her and they lifted their hand in a friendly wave. Naturally, Moz turned his head to see who had finally come down. When he met her gaze, he winked.

"Cheeky bastard," she muttered, shuffling her damp hair around to try to disguise the blush that crept across her face again. She tried not to think of what they had done barely an hour ago. It certainly would have been sinful to let herself remember his steady hands on her neck. Absolutely scandalous to think of the rumble of his low, dark laugh between her thighs. Outstandingly unladylike to even dream about how he put his-

"Avery!"

Avery flushed furiously when she realized she had been standing still and thinking of all those filthy things anyway. She looked to the other side of the congregation of Reapers and saw Lily waving her over. Her best friend was standing with Yumi, Theirrin, and Cassie. Each of them held serious looks on their faces when Avery made her way over.

"We're about halfway through a plan," Lily explained. "A small group of us needs to go with Yumi to the sailor's tavern. We're trying to find a captain for the voyage. We're still working out how we're going to fund it though."

"Didn't Jack mention robbery yesterday? I mean, it's a terrible idea but we're kind of crunched for time and resources," Avery offered.

Yumi looked back from Avery to Lily. "The tavern is also an inn, we may potentially be able to pilfer through the rooms."

Lily's face was aglow. "Genius! I knew I liked you!"

"Who's going to go with her?" Avery questioned.

"Well, seeing as none of the underage ones can and Shank and the boys are cooking up their own, ahem, half-baked plan over there, I figured you could go with her. You could bring Moz or Tristan too, depending on what they're cooking over there."

Avery mentally scolded herself to reinforce the work the cold bath had done. "Okay, yeah that works," she said instead nonchalantly.

Lily stood on her toes to call out, "Shank! Do we have a plan over there?"

"Absolutely not. Do you?"

"Point to the ladies."

Shank frowned but melded into their huddle, Tristan and the rest of the men followed. Avery felt the heat of Moz's presence directly behind her and when he shifted his weight on his feet he was close enough that only static could have passed between them. She felt her face flush furiously again and she looked down at her boots to hide it. He knew *exactly* what he was doing and that she was in no position to march him back upstairs and bring him to his knees at her altar of worship.

Avery made a tremendous effort to ignore the warm sensation of Moz's breath on the crown of her head and focused instead on Lily explaining the plan.

"-they'll be on the hunt at the docks for a ship captain who would be willing to ferry us to Eyon. If we could find someone who would be willing to accept payment after we've won this thing, that would be great. But if not, I am not saying Jack should not pick-pocket. If that happens, which I'm not saying it should, someone will need to spot Jack. I am not saying Kurosaki should do that."

"YES!" Jack threw his fist up into the air excitedly.

"And while that group is doing that, a much smaller group is going to break off and search the inn," Lily continued. "Yumi, Avery, and Moz: will that work for you?"

Avery nodded. "You got it."

"Perfect. We'll meet back here at high-noon. None of you get your asses caught."

Avery kept her head ducked and shielded by the wide brim of her hat when they entered the tavern. The townsfolk in Brightloch were just as skeptical of the Reapers' innocence as their King was; she could tell by the heavy sensation of eyes on her back as she followed Moz into the dim light of McAsher's.

None of the sunlight passed into the dark tavern unless someone opened the doors; there were no stained glass windows and the only illumination came from oil lamps on the counter and tables. Long tables of half-finished wood stretched down the length of the establishment and sailors the size of boulders sat in hunched forms on the benches.

Tailing behind Avery was the figure cloaked in black with a drawn hood. They fostered a sense of nervousness in the eyes that landed on them but Avery knew better; Yumi's hidden presence was a strange sensation of comfort that lingered in the back of her skull. She was safe.

The Princess whispered behind her with a mouth hidden by shadow, "The inn is upstairs along that staircase. If we're going to rob the rooms, we need a way in."

Avery's gaze scanned the humid room and then fell on the steep staircase that rose alongside the left wall to a balcony. On top of the balcony was a doorless entryway that appeared to lead down a hall that Avery couldn't quite make out the details of.

"Any plans, Berserker Witch?"

Avery smirked at the sound of her moniker through Yumi's lips. She stared up at the balcony before turning her gaze towards the bar, lest she attract any attention with her interest in the inn upstairs. The hidden Princess stepped forward to stand next to Avery and carefully they calculated their surroundings together.

"We need a way into those rooms. It's not a problem to scope out down here, but we really need to know what kind of people we've got boarding here," Avery answered.

Out of the corner of her vision, Avery saw Yumi's eyebrows raise in surprise. "I can get us into the rooms without a problem. You two just worry about finding a ship captain."

Both Moz and Avery at Yumi - the former down, the latter up - with looks of mirroring confusion.

"How are you going to do that?"

Yumi smirked with delight when she answered Moz, "I've got my own tricks."

The Princess closed her eyes and inhaled deeply through her nose. Yumi didn't release her breath for what felt like an eternity to Avery and so she reached for her wrist to make sure her heart was still beating. Avery flinched before she could grasp her hand when suddenly the hard exhale came and Yumi opened her eyes.

Puzzled, Avery looked around the room and then at Yumi again. Nothing appeared to have changed.

Very quietly, Avery began to murmur, "I'm sorry, Yumi, but I don't know-"

Yumi shook her head and cut her off very gently with her answer, "Look at the wall illuminated by the lantern. On the stairs. Be discreet."

Avery slowly turned her gaze to the western wall of the tavern, avoiding any quick moments that may attract attention to whatever Yumi had just done.

The warm glow of the sconce lantern enveloped the plastered wall from the staircase leading up to the hidden hallway and faded into darkness near the entrance of the tavern. The faint shadows of the patrons danced in faded shapes as they were cast from a light at the bar, she almost missed the one moving slowly up the staircase independent of any solid body. Yumi's detached shadow moved slowly up the wall along the staircase, careful not to attract any attention with sudden movement.

"You both find us a captain," she whispered. "I've got this under control."

She stepped backwards into the crowd, letting herself blend in amongst the tall mill workers and loggers. Yumi left Avery standing alone, the bodies of working class men who had recently ended the night shifts swaying her in a current of sweat and testosterone. She looked up and caught a flash of shadow disappearing into the dark hall-way of the inn.

"Okay, that's way cool," Avery murmured to herself.

She had not noticed Moz had vanished until he material-ized from the crowd, holding two glass mugs in his hand. Ale sloshed over the brim of the cups and dribbled onto his hand.

"Don't drink the whole thing of course, but we'll look awfully suspicious without them."

Avery took the mug out of his hand and grimaced when lukewarm ale sloshed over and dripped down the back of her hand. "Gross, it's warm!"

Moz leaned close to her ear so he could jab quietly, "yeah, this place isn't exactly the highlight of Brightloch, but that's exactly why we're here."

Avery scowled, turning to look at his face bent close to hers. He regarded her with a boyish grin and she saw all his faint freckles up close. *Oh gods* - she found herself think-ing again of his bite on her skin. Moz winked and hoisted his ale up in a sarcastic toast. "Bottoms up, my most favor-ite witch!"

Avery rolled her eyes but lifted her own mug to her lips, swallowing down room temperature beer as fast as she could. A wave of disgust rolled down her stomach and she shuddered.

"Fuck… okay, I'm gonna sit down," Avery walked away from a chuckling Moz, sitting down at one of the benches at the communal tables.

Moz sat down on the bench across from her and together they scanned the room around them while casually sipping their ales; Moz taking much bigger gulps than Avery's timid sips. *How can he possibly be enjoying this?*

As the patrons of the bar milled about, occasionally Avery caught a glimpse of Yumi's cloak that masked most of her face. She already could recognize the clever curves of her mouth, turned up just enough to give you the feeling that the Princess knew something that you didn't. The Knight of Spirit was blending into the shadows cast under the open staircase while her own shadow had gone missing.

As Avery sipped, she felt her skin flushing and growing warm. Against her better judgment, she shed her cloak and draped it gingerly on the empty spot of the bench next to her. She took her wide-brimmed hat off and tried to discreetly fan herself before setting it atop the cloak. Avery unbuttoned the top two buttons of her tunic to let air flow across her skin but felt no relief in the humid bar.

She must not have been as stealthy as she had assumed, as she caught a group of large men chuckling and talking in low voices amongst themselves while looking in her direction. Avery turned forward and prayed they hadn't noticed her watching them back.

They soon lumbered over in their direction and she felt nerves creep up her spine when they stopped behind her.

"We don't allow outsiders here. Especially the Berserker Witch and her homicidal lackey," the tallest man said in a gruff voice.

Moz snickered, blowing droplets of beer as he tried to sip through laughter. While he laughed, Avery felt anger flush her cheeks even warmer.

She never rose from her seat, never turned to face him. "Don't fucking try me right now. I have had to entertain this warm piss as a drink and I'm frankly a little upset about it. So could you just skidaddle on?"

Moz laughed again but didn't bother trying to hide it, "oh my gods Avery, *skidaddle?"*

The man looked down at Avery's frown, then past her at Moz. "Your ball and chain is bein' a bit of a hag, don't you think mate? Why don't you take your wife home before someone else shuts her up."

As the man spoke to Moz, his hands reached and grabbed her by the collar of her tunic, lifting her up out of her seat. Avery's eyes widened at the sudden escalation.

Moz slammed the empty stein down on the table. "What is with everyone thinking she's my wife? How DARE you accuse her of having terrible taste! Don't do Avery dirty like that."

Avery remained locked in place, the thick fingers of the burly man held her up by her collar. Moz didn't bother getting up from his spot at the long table; Avery had this one.

"Let go of me or you'll get my boot so far up your ass, you'll be tying shoelaces with your tongue," she threatened the man through gritted teeth.

Glass suddenly crashed as Avery was thrown across the table, sending mead bottles and plates splintering to the floor.

She came to a stop past where Moz was sitting and her dirty boots had scuffed streaks across the wood surface in her wake. Avery sat up and the scab on her cheek reopened as blood dripped down her chin. She held an open palm, the blood pooling fast.

Avery's gaze turned upwards to the men who looked on at her with smug sneers, and her face was twisted not with terror but with a sinister smile.

"You're fucked now, gentlemen," Moz tutted, reaching across the table to drink from Avery's beer.

Avery rose to her feet, standing tall on the table. With her hand cradling a pool of blood, she tilted her hand skyward and let it drip down her wrist. The blood offering dripped onto her bracelet made of leather cheated from the grip of Hemlock. Revenants seeped upwards through the floorboards, circling around the men hungrily when the golden eye of the sword blinked to life. Avery's eyes glazed over white as she sat in the veil between the living and the dead.

"*Go*," the witch ordered and the pub descended into chaos.

With her sword still under the bench, she leapt off the table and brought her elbows down hard on the shoulder of the man who had tossed her. He buckled under the blow, stepping back before shoving Avery hard back into the table.

Bar patrons who had nothing to do with the conflict were suddenly fighting each other, riled up by the action and taking advantage of the excuse to rumble. Avery leaned her weight onto her arms that planted firmly on the table behind her, kicking a boot hard into the gut of the man as he tried to follow through his throw. Before his friend could swoop in from her side, she grabbed the glass mug she had been drinking out of and swung it into the side of his head. Glass shattered, beer spilled, and blood bloomed out of the man's mangled ear.

"Damnit Avery, I wasn't done with that!" Moz shouted from somewhere behind her before she heard an impact of palms on wood.

"That was *my* beer, asshole!" She shouted back as she dodged a swinging fist from the first man she had kicked into the bar. From her lower position, she turned her body sideways and shoved her weight into the man's legs with her elbow jabbing his abdomen.

"You weren't even drinking it!"

The man picked her up by the back of her collar, spitting in her face. Avery wiped the spittle off, grimacing with extreme disgust.

"You don't know that I wasn't going to finish that!" She shouted back at Moz.

"Well, *were* you?"

She curled her fingers back and shoved the meat of her palm hard into the man's nose, sending him backwards and clutching his bloodied face as he howled.

"No!"

"Then I fail to see what the problem is! I finished mine, I wanted yours, you didn't! The math checks out, my love!"

While she hesitated to believe that this man could count beyond ten, Avery couldn't help but laugh a little through labored breaths. She knew he was only being childish to keep her entertained, but the booze was certainly helping. A sailor built like a brick wall bolstered himself with his elbow out before shoving himself into Avery, sending her falling to the floor.

"Oof!" The impact took her breath away for a mere moment before she saw his foot coming down fast at her face. She rolled under the table Moz was sitting at, stopping beneath the shelter above.

"Avery, what would Jack say if he could see you now," Moz chided from above the table.

"An innuendo, definitely," Avery said and laughed back, catching her breath.

The sailor that had knocked her off her feet was pushing the table, grinding wood against the floor with a harsh screech to get to Avery.

"Um, excuse me? Bestie, we're trying to have a conversation," drunk Moz complained to the man, getting pushed as he still sat on the moving bench. Avery couldn't see what was going on, but knew it wasn't good judging by the rain of broken glass that came pouring down Moz's side of the table.

Avery climbed out from under the table on Moz's side, swinging herself onto the tabletop with kicking legs. The tread of her boot connected with the sailor's cheek and Drunk Moz howled in laughter.

"GODS I am in love with that woman!"

The man stumbled backwards, but not far enough. His enormous hand closed around Avery's ankle quicker than she could recoil and he dragged her off the tabletop to toss her hard onto the ground. The wind fled Avery's lungs and she wheezed at the impact, gasping for air.

Finally, Moz sighed and stood up.

"I don't think she's having fun anymore," he said to himself, as if suddenly sobered.

Moz climbed up onto the table, shimmying his hips in a dance to music only he was hearing. He reached with his long arms to grab the sailor by both sides of the head.

"Where do you think you're going, cutie pie?"

Then he was the feral Drunk Moz again, bending forward at the waist and planting an aggressive kiss on the sweaty forehead of the sailor. The man looked up at him with a twisted and enraged confusion on his blood-flecked face as he tried to free himself from Moz's grip. With hard force, Moz pulled the man's head down and smashed it into the wood table at his feet. The sailor slumped down onto the bench, unmoving.

"K.O.!" Moz yelled with glee, throwing both fists into the air above his head.

"Moz! Did you fucking kill him?" Avery panicked as she stood up, looking wildly around the room for anyone else coming their way. No one did. Those who hadn't cleared out of the tavern were punching and rolling in their own squabbles.

"What? No! Weren't you listening? I said K.O. - knock out!"

"GET DOWN."

It wasn't Avery who yelled, but the cloaked figure on the opposite side of Moz. The Princess' hood was down and Avery had a full view of her face, clenched jaw and all.

Yumi's nostrils flared in anger. "Can you not go one single place without causing a fight? Either of you?"

Avery looked at the ground sheepishly. "They had it coming," she murmured to herself.

"I don't care if they had it coming," Yumi snapped back, pointedly letting Avery know that she had heard. "The plan was ruined and now we have to figure out another way to get money. Why must you always start fights? And *you*," she jabbed a finger in Moz's direction. "It is the middle of the day and you are already three sheets to the wind."

"Avery starts fights, I just finish them," Moz shrugged, his words becoming slurred around the edges. "And what do you even know about sail lines, I bet you've never sailed a day in your damn life. Miss Princess."

Yumi clenched her fists, anger welled out of her throat first in a low rumble, then a yell. "AAAAAAAAAAAAAGGGGGGGGGGGGGGHHHHHHHH."

Drunk Moz ducked his head down to meet her level and yelled right back "AAAAAHHH... SEE, I CAN DO THAT TOO! AAAAAAAHHHHHHHHH!"

"You are both embarrassing," Avery said and this time she was the one pinching the bridge of her nose in frustration.

Yumi held up her hand to form a barrier between her face and Moz's before she turned back to Avery, still holding the partition of fingers.

"There's no way we are going to find anyone here now. Not when these *men* are behaving like animals. Yes, William, present company is included."

"Moz," he corrected her with a huff and pushed her hand away from his face.

Avery would have hated to be him in that moment with the cold glare in his direction. Yumi's jaw flexed; she nearly said something in response but thought better of it. Instead she turned on her heel to walk towards the tavern door.

"Come," she called out to them. "We'll try another place after you have sobered."

— ❦ —

Both groups returned to the grand hall empty-handed.

"Not only did we not find anything, but Moz got day drunk."

"I'm completely fine now, and it was an accident," he quickly defended himself from Avery's announcement.

"Well, shit," Lily said, assuming the same position in the circle as the leader of failed plots.

"Jack and Kurosaki aren't back yet," Maria pointed out. "Maybe they're having some luck?"

Avery felt the stir of Moz behind her again as though he was shaking his head. "We need to go pull them out, they might have gotten into trouble. I trust that kid to keep a low profile about as much as I trust a guardsman."

"Feck, I reckon yer right," Tristan agreed and was already making his way to the door.

"Let's try this again" Shank said and heaved an exasperated exhale.

This time they strode through the castle gates as one large group rather than breaking off into parties. Halfway down the hill, Lily fell into stride with Avery.

"Pop your collar higher." Lily said in a low voice without moving her gaze from the road ahead.

"What?"

"Just pull up the collar of your cloak, your lover's bite is embarrassing. What are you, sixteen again?"

Avery felt her neck flush hot. "I didn't-"

"Yeah, yeah, save it. I'm not Mom. I'm just glad you finally slept together. If we all had to go another day of hearing 'calling it' from Jack, I might've actually killed someone."

"You can't just-"

"Not. Mom."

Avery didn't bother to argue with her any further, but pulled up the wool collar anyway and bunched it as high as she could. She followed quietly behind Tristan and Shank, keeping her head on a swivel to find a mop of blonde hair amongst the crowd of dark tweed and tulle - and anyone who may have been chasing them down to get their purse back. They peered down alleys, were shooed out of shops meant for paying customers only, and left wondering what could have possibly become of the Saved man and teen-aged ex-demon.

Just when they were ready to split up and try to extend their search perimeter, Avery heard the gleeful yell from behind her.

"Moz!"

They all turned to find Jack half a block south, waving his arms wildly as he hurried to catch up. Kurosaki was not far behind and looked less than pleased.

"Any luck?" Moz asked when they finally met with the rest of their group.

Jack shook his head disappointedly. "I don't know what it is, but this is a way tougher crowd. Nobody's got pockets I can get to easily and if they do, they're carrying a bunch of useless shit."

"Don't worry about it," Moz reassured him. "It was too risky anyway, let's quit while we're ahead."

He then turned, looking to Lily and Maria. "You got any other ideas?"

"I'm not sure," Maria started, "maybe we could…"

Maria suddenly trailed off while a woozy weight pressed down on Avery's skull. Avery pressed her palm to her own forehead, trying to steady herself as she focused on a crack between the cobblestones beneath her boots.

"Well," Shank said from behind her, "that should not have happened."

Confused, Avery looked up and caught sight of the hundreds of white orbs. They bobbed around the heads of dozens of townsfolk: women, children - the marks did not discriminate.

Avery froze in terror: Reaping targets. She had never seen more than one at the same time. She turned to her friends, who were looking on with the same horror painted on their own faces. If this many people were marked to die, something terrible was about to happen.

Her ears rang, the violent knell of the death chimes ringing one on top of another in a cacophonous clamor. The Reapers all threw their hands over their ears as though the sound were coming from somewhere on their mortal plane. Avery's skull buzzed, her fingernails clawed against her skin, her animal instinct begged to puncture her own eardrums to make the horrible noise stop.

"My Creations."

The voice was low, hoarse with the dust of a grave buried for millennia and cracked open again. Death bells fell to a fast silence. Even Moz was looking for the source of the voice - the orbs were invisible to his Saved eyes but he was not spared from the words.

"I have found the pests amongst my nightshade garden. But only fools believe they can hide from Death. You will lay waste to all as my demigods of destruction or suffer measures of unfathomable pain."

Yumi's nostrils began to gush blood and she held her open palms beneath her chin to collect the pooling crimson.

Moz clamped his hands hard on Yumi's shoulders, his movements staggered and drunk under the effect of whatever was sabotaging the Reapers.

"Yumi… Yumi, fucking listen to me! You have to fight it! Fuckin' fight it or a lot of people are going to die!"

Yumi looked up at him with her outstretched fingers and her eyes pleaded for him to help her as the fluid dribbled down her chin, following the slope of her neck.

"Kill them or I will lay waste to the insignificant things you hold dear. Your choice is slave or slaughtered pig."

As the last words echoed in Avery's eardrums, the heavy air of the grave that had hung heavy over their heads lightened and she was left to feel only the pounding beat of her anxious heart from her throat down to her ankles.

"No, no, no, no, FUCK!" She stammered with panicked frustration before she turned around to face Moz and Yumi. The blood had stopped gushing from the Princess' nose and she had her head thrown backwards up to the sky.

Avery rushed to her, pulling out a loose scrap of fabric she had remaining in the pocket of her trousers from the day before. Her fingers reached out gently to Yumi's cheek and she coaxed her to look down at Avery rather than the sky.

"We'll figure it out, there's always a way," Avery said as she began wiping the blood from Yumi's face. She wasn't sure if the words were meant to comfort the Knight or herself. "We'll figure it out, I swear to fucking gods."

Yumi frowned. "Don't swear or use their names in vain."

"Fine, I swear to fucking something else."

Yumi looked down at Avery with glittering topaz eyes, her mouth turned just the slightest in an amused smirk as Avery mopped up the last of the blood to the best of her ability. Yumi's skin was still stained with the glow of rust where the blood had settled into the pores of her skin. But at least now she didn't look like she had been sucker-punched in the nose.

"Oh gods. Avery look!"

Avery followed the direction Lily pointed in, confused when she found herself staring at a middle-aged couple crossing the avenue. Her eyes then widened with surprised recognition. She knocked the wide-brimmed hat back off her head to see clearer. No, it was not just a trick of the light.

"Mom? Dad?"

Avery looked upon the couple, who still had not stopped. She strode towards them, stumbling at first on the uneven ridges of the cobblestone.

"Katherine! Harrison Porter!" She yelled out, the fringes of her voice wavered with anger as she quickened her pace.

The man and woman stopped, looking about the crowded street to find whoever had called their names. Avery froze when she saw the little boy standing between them, both of her parents holding each of his small hands. The white orbs that bobbed around the three of them looked so much bigger next to the boy's small face.

"No, Avery, you don't have to-" Lily called out from behind her, trying to prevent Avery from approaching her parents.

The woman turned and her confused gaze stopped on Avery. Her mother looked at her with cold fear and the evidence of the years that had passed was clear on the face of Katherine Porter. The long waves of raven hair were turning grey around her small face and the worry lines around her blue eyes were permanently present. Katherine clutched the little boy to her, looking to the nearest bulletin board and back to Avery.

Her father was the one who dared to approach her; Avery's stomach turned in fear of his reaction to seeing her but she still could not pry herself away. Harrison's glasses reflected the lanterns, obscuring the warm brown of his eyes. He drew his coat around himself and stopped feet away from her, close enough for her to see the freckles she inherited but too far away to mistake the encounter for a joyous reunion. Avery knew better than that.

"It looks like you've gotten yourself into trouble, haven't you, Avery?"

His voice was as warm as a father's should be and her eyes watered.

"You didn't want me… because you thought I wasn't a real child. Because the Oracles told you I had no soul. You let terrible things happen to me when you should have been protecting me."

Avery didn't dance around what she really wanted to say. She had locked the feelings of abandonment in a box to keep them out of sight, out of mind, but still the words came tumbling out as if they had never left her thoughts at all. Harrison sucked in a breath, putting his hands on his hips under his coat and looked away before speaking. The death orbs floating around him scattered with the movement and then settled again, like blowing a thick sheet of dust off a table.

"Avery, please understand," Harrison looked back down at her, completely unaware of the death mark. "The Oracles told us you were a vessel and nothing more. A mere shell for something else to come. We didn't know what to make of that. What could we have made with that?"

"You could have made a family," Avery whispered; no effort she made could have hidden the cracking heartbreak in her voice.

She looked from Harrison to the little boy that Katherine held close, her arm wrapped across the front of his chest and held him secure against her legs as he watched.

"Avery, that's our son," Harrison said calmly, as though she would have been unable to gather as much on her own.

"One minute," she demanded, quiet and angry. "Give me one minute to speak to my little brother and you will never have to see me again."

Harrison turned, looking back at his wife as she shook her head furiously. He turned back to Avery.

"One minute. We reserve the right to revoke that at any point."

Avery shoved past Harrison and approached the boy cautiously, not wanting any sudden movements to frighten him as though he were a fawn. She knelt to level with the boy; he had their father's brown eyes and their mother's dark waves of hair.

"I'm sure with all these posters around, you've heard a lot of untrue things about me," Avery said sweetly, trying her best to undo all the fright that must have been instilled in the young boy from seeing his parents so alarmed by her. The neglect she had suffered had nothing to do with him. "I never got to meet you. What's your name?"

"Soren."

"Soren, wow! I think that is a really neat name. How old are you, Soren?"

"Six," he answered again with only a single word; shy, but giving the information that was asked of him.

Her eyes traveled up beyond the boy's head and to his mother, who looked down on them with fear. Avery scowled at her; of course it was six years. She would have just been left behind at age seventeen, burdening Lily's family while her parents conceived a shiny, new, mortal child on the other side of the continent. They went as far away from her as they could to try again.

Avery looked back down at her little brother, his small face absent of fear but knit with concern over the fright of his parents.

"Soren," Avery said gently, reaching for the little boy's free hand before Katherine swatted it away. She reeled back before continuing, still determined to get her message across. "Soren, when you're older and want to know what really happened, you come find me. Your mom and dad love you so much and I wish I was able to get to know you. I'm going to make sure this world is safe for you-"

"I think that's enough, Avery," Harrison grabbed her shoulder, forcefully pulling her up and away from the boy whose expression changed to fright. He had closed his hand around her arrow wound and Avery winced with seething pain, hissing through her gritted teeth.

"Don't grab her!"

Yumi yelled from behind them, running towards Harrison to push him away from Avery. At the sight of the Princes, Mr. Porter froze.

"Your Highness?"

"Don't bother with formalities," Yumi growled. "If what Avery says is true, and it appears to be, you are the absolute scum of Shintori!"

A hand reached from behind and laced fingers through Avery's. Moz turned her around, her back now to the Porters. He ducked down, looking at her directly in the eyes.

"Avery, you don't need them. I promise, you don't. You are wonderful and strong, and we all love you," Moz said, his efforts to uplift her were bordering on aggressive. He didn't let her answer before straightening up and pulling her into a tight hug.

"- and don't let me catch sight of you again," Avery heard Yumi call out as more arms enveloped her in a tangled hug. Tristan's thick and safe arms, Lily's gentle embrace; Avery found herself nearly suffocating in the comforting compression.

"For what it's worth, Ave," Maria's muffled voice came from somewhere behind her, "I think Soren will come find you. I know you will get the chance to be a great sister."

The image of the little boy's face was burned into her brain as Avery stood in the middle of the hug; all these people were fighting tooth and nail with the purpose of destroying the Knights and she had just looked upon the biggest reason of all why they needed to succeed. Her shoulders shook and she broke into tears, making no attempt to hide it.

One by one, the pairs of arms let go of her until she was left with only Moz. She continued to cry, her hands gripping hard on the back of his black coat. They stood for several long moments as her tears slowed and his embrace never weakened.

"I love you too, Moz," she croaked faintly.

Moz didn't respond but stepped backwards with a rigid posture, still gripping Avery in a hug until he spun her around to stand protectively.

"Archers, to the back."

"Moz, what are you-"

Her heart sank when she realized he hadn't heard her. Avery peered past Moz and down the cobblestone avenue. The crowd of people began to disperse as shrieks rang out, giving her a clear view of the black orbs accumulating around one person in particular. Demonic miasma, invisible to mortal eyes, covered them in a heavy cloud before they flailed onto the ground with ear-piercing wails. The skirts that splayed around the woman's legs ripped as dark limbs shot from her hips, the new extremities long and tipped with hooks. Bones snapped and the fledgling demon sank into the flesh of the woman, turning her flesh ghostly white.

Spider-like legs rose and the body of the woman hung like an ornament at the face of the beast. Avery flinched, her memories instantly taking her back to the possessed man who had nearly killed her just outside of Ardua's walls. She blocked out the screams around her, reaching over her shoulder for Hemlock. This time she was ready.

Beside Avery, Yumi stood firm with a throwing knife in each hand and a determined scowl as she watched the demon with calculating eyes. Avery wanted to advise her to stay at a safe distance but she knew that look anywhere. No one could tell Yumi how and when to fight.

Avery turned her attention back forward, the demon-spider now looming at its full height just beneath the roofs of the two-story townhomes. Her focus locked on the woman hanging from the thorax that reeked of rot.

"I'll disorient it with the revenants, wound it when I can," she said to Moz. "You take the kill-strike as soon as you can."

"You got it. But keep in mind though, I'm going to be fucking pissed if you die trying to impress a girl."

"Honor and ladies, Avery!" Jack yelled from the sidelines as he pulled out the dirk he inherited from Moz. "For honor and ladies!"

She did her best not to grin as she cut her palm on the edge of Hemlock; the pain had become almost unnoticeable with the countless times she had drawn blood sacrifice to the sword of Paion. The leathery flesh of the bronze eyelid shot open and the eye scanned their surroundings in fast flickers. Avery lifted her dripping hand up as the stirring revenants seeped up from the cobblestone beneath her feet.

"Go."

Their hesitation to Avery's command did not last as long as it had the last time they had confronted a demon. Shadowy hands lurched at the spider's legs, clawing and scratching. After their ghostly front line dove in, Moz charged at the demon with a gleaming sword as Avery carefully edged her way in.

A flying dagger whizzed through the air above Avery's head, missing the face of the possessed woman by mere inches and pierced the spider thorax. Black ooze seeped from the wound around the gilded knife.

The spider stomped its many feet, trying to pierce Moz with the lethal spikes on the tips of its legs. He followed the deadly dance of the demon, staying ahead easily as its legs lifted high for each strike. Whenever he found a window of time, he swung his blade at a leg in hopes of bringing the tall beast down to the ground. The skittering of legs was far too fast for him to cut and the stampede of knives only grew faster as the demon grew angrier.

A leg swung out, inches from clipping the top of Avery's head if she had not ducked. She stumbled out of the way, looking up at the spider's thorax high above her head. How was she supposed to reach it? Avery reeled her arm backwards before swinging Hemlock towards a tipped leg, missing contact by a mere second before the spider skittered again after Moz.

The spirits assaulted the demon in shadowy dives, targeting the legs out of Moz's reach. The demon wailed, backpedaling and crushing the street vendor stalls under its knifed feet. Avery dove away from the splintering wood, scrambling to change her position to get a better angle on the beast.

Loose boards of the stand clattered against the cobblestone ground, Avery looked around to see Lily's hands held upward. The loose projectiles launched off the ground, flying fast at the legs of the demon-beast. It hissed in pain as a board hit a slender limb, the leg buckling against the impact. The beast swayed, disoriented but not injured enough to fall.

Avery's eyes widened.

"Lily! Give me a boost!"

"The fuck? What do you mean?"

"The crate!"

Avery pointed towards a wooden box, revealed as the fruit cart beside it was reduced to shambles. She watched as the crate rattled before it was jerked up into the air. Avery yelped as the projectile came hurtling toward her. She leapt and fell on top of the box with a loud thud.

The box bobbed under her weight and Avery was sure it would crash to the ground and splinter beneath her. Instead it stopped, keeping her held still for a moment before Lily pushed the box toward the beast. Giving the beast a wide berth as it sparred with Moz, Lily guided the box slowly around its legs while raising Avery towards the central body.

Avery wanted to shout out encouragement to Lily, but bit her lip as she was afraid to draw the spider's attention towards her. In her peripheral vision, Avery saw the tops of the brownstone houses as she found herself level with the beast. Lily lifted the box just above the spider's back; Avery would have to jump.

"Avery, take it!"

Moz shouted from somewhere behind her; the kill was hers.

She swung herself onto the back of the beast, nearly losing her footing on the slick surface the miasma created on the spider's thorax. The woman's body at the head thrashed wildly, trying to throw Avery off as it wailed. Avery stumbled, falling before she scrambled to straddle the beast.

Avery wrought Hemlock down upon its neck. Black ooze spattered from the absent stump and the demon's body began to sink to the ground. The spider dropped to the ground, its legs collapsing like a tent.

Avery stood perched on the crumpled body of the beast, her boot planted firmly on the spider's back. Her gaze traveled up to see the little Soren Porter watching her, eyes wide not with fright but with delight. Katherine and Harrison were struggling to push through the crowd, swimming against the tide to their boy as the citizens fled.

Avery held the stare of her little brother even as Katherine fearfully gripped his arm and pulled him away from the demon's corpse.

"Mom-"

Soren's voice faded just as quickly as they did. Avery turned back towards her friends and jumped down from the demon's body. Lily was breathing heavily, her posture swaying as the energy her mind exerted drained her body's reserves. Avery rushed to catch her under the arm before she fell and Maria dove to catch her on the other side.

Cassie circled them to face Lily, her eyes bright with excitement.

"I have a proposal for you," the young girl said, her excitement cool as she grinned.

"Run it… by me later," Lily heaved out between breaths.

Yumi retrieved her golden knife from the thorax of the beast, wiping it with a black kerchief before placing it neatly back into her hidden belt. She looked down at the severed head of the demon before her serious gaze traveled up to Avery.

"Take the head to my father. He will reward you handsomely and certainly enough to sail a vessel to Eyon."

Avery approached the head slowly as if it would suddenly rattle back to life and bite her. The slain woman's hair was matted with black ooze and obscured most of her face. Avery wished it could have fallen enough to cover the haunting eyes: still black with possession, unblinking. A small pang of guilt gripped her heart. What happened to this woman?

Avery began to take off her cloak, intending to carry the head inside it to keep it out of sight. Yumi laid her hand on Avery's shoulder to stop her from removing her beloved garment of forest green.

"No, carry it unhidden. Let the people see what you have done for them," Yumi's words were coaxing; honey-thick and dark.

"Yumi, this is a-"

"It's what she wanted. You avenged her when you took its head. Now you must promise to stop it from happening again."

Avery paused. It sounded wrong, but maybe she hadn't known enough to be questioning the Knight of Spirit when it came to the wishes of the dead. "I promise I'll-"

"Not to me. To everyone." Yumi swooped closer to her, gathering Avery's hands in hers to hold them up. She continued to speak, kind and strange, "You promise to every-one by showing them the Berserker Witch had slain a Lost One. You show them that you are not their enemy, that something much worse than demon-beasts await them if they don't trust you. That Lost One was meant to kill all of those who had just been marked by death Herself, and you stopped it. Make them see that."

Avery trembled, the words were equally moving and terrifying. Yumi released her hands and stepped back, looking down at the head and back again at Avery expectantly.

Avery knelt, her hand shaking as she reached towards the head.

"I'm sorry, I'm so fucking sorry," she whispered to the woman who was long gone. "You didn't deserve this disgrace. I'm so sorry."

Her fingers gripped a thick section of black hair and she lifted the head, ooze squishing with the movement and Avery made an effort to keep herself from retching.

She stood up, looking away from the head as it dangled in her grip. The other Reapers looked at her with disgusted horror, Avery couldn't blame them.

"To the castle. And as quickly as we can, alright?"

Maria and Theirrin were the first to shuffle away into the direction of the towers and spires; the rest of the group followed them in silence. As Avery carried the dripping head, she began to notice the whispers floating around them as the people ducked their heads, speaking in hushed voices. They were none the wiser that they had been freed from the death halos.

What a damned fool Avery must have been for thinking she could parade a gory head through town in exchange for forgiveness. It was Yumi who was walking proudly with squared shoulders, beaming as though she knew her plan was working. The further they walked, the more people dared to stay within earshot of the pack of Reapers.

"Praise Onja!"

Avery stopped when the woman cried out. She looked at the woman, who grinned back at her with high, amber cheeks before she disappeared into the movement of towns-folk, the feather of her hat lingering in sight longer than she did. Avery looked down at the head in one hand and then at Hemlock in her other.

Was this Onja's doing? It seemed everything Avery had done was attributed to the goddess of victory and her survival credited to Malo, king of the woods. She felt anger bubble in the pit of her belly. If they had followed a predetermined plan made by the gods, the Beldam would have already won.

It wasn't Onja who had slain the elslith. It wasn't Malo who had stormed the Legion prison. That was by *her* hand, and by the hands of the Reapers she had grown to trust with her very life.

How strange it was to trust Death with life.

–––

The guards took the head, placing it inside the wood box and hastily nailing it shut. Avery raised a brow; did they expect the head to try to escape? They carted the box across the glimmering marble floor, through the tall oaken doors and back into the main hall.

"You claim the reward tonight at the Novara Ball," King Harthmoor commanded. "The people must feel an incentive to slay these demon-beasts, for they have grown complacent with the current state of terror."

"What's the reward?" Avery was skeptical, the posters they had seen around didn't name a specific number and left the King and his Royal Guardsmen free to make up any arbitrary number - or lowball any reward collectors they didn't particularly care for.

King Harthmoor looked from the ragged and bruised group of Reapers before him to the Guardsman nearest his throne.

"Officer, what was the height of this beast?"

"The Sentinel who witnessed the incident measured it to be of a height of thirteen feet, Your Highness."

The King looked from the Guardsman, back down to Avery through his nose with a smug smirk on his blonde-bearded face. "One hundred gold pieces for every meas-ured foot in height. For those of us who know math, that is one thousand and three hundred gold pieces."

"I know how the math works, you sack of-" Avery was abruptly cut off by an elbow to her ribs.

"She says 'thank you, Your Highness'," Theirrin spoke up, hoping to smooth out whatever insult she had been about to spit.

King Harthmoor frowned deeply. "You are excused. Be in the dining hall at sundown."

They shuffled out in shame, Yumi hung back and they heard the muffled sounds of her yelling when the doors closed behind them.

"Well, now what's the plan," Cassie asked, forcing the older Reapers into a huddle with her by corralling them with her lanky arms.

"We're going to have to break into parties again," Lily said to the youngest girl. "Some of us will need to already be down at the docks, looking for a captain who is willing to hang tight for the money. Some of us will need to be at the ball to both hand off the money and keep Yumi safe un-til we have the all-clear that we have a ship ready to go and that there are no Legion officers in the vicinity. A third and final group will need to be the one to give that all clear. There's what…"

Lily paused, faintly murmuring the headcount to herself. "Eleven of us? That puts us in groups of four when we include Yumi. How should we split this up?"

Tristan stepped in, "I reckon the heavy-hitters keep th' Princess safe. Moz, Ave, an Kurosaki. An' Yumi, of course. Those of us with range should scout, makes the most sense fer pickin' them off. Maria, Shank, Lily, Cassie - that's you. An' th' rest of ya should come with me to find a ship. Rowan, Jack, and Theirrin. Y'look more or less like kids and I reckon that should make 'em more willing to help. Hopefully."

"But we are kids," Rowan pointed out and Jack nodded his head with cartoonish agreement.

"Does this work for everyone?" Lily looked at each face as she took the poll and no one had any protests. Except for Jack.

"Why can't I go with Twin?"

"You literally just got a weapon yesterday," Moz answered with laughter bubbling under his words.

"This is clearly demon discrimination," Jack pouted, but the rest of the group had already moved on.

"Alright, well if everyone's already clear. Let's get to it. Ina and Aegis will be our message relays of course. I'll ask Yumi if Mara is willing to help as soon as she finishes… whatever is going on in there."

They paused and heard escalating yelling in the silence.

"Great chat, team," Lily quipped and stepped out of the huddle.

"Thanks, Coach," Shank joked, and Lily gave them a light smack on the bicep with the back of her hand.

Avery smiled. Lily had joined their cause days ago, but she still felt so glad when she saw instances of her meshing so seamlessly with the Reapers. Heavy wood slammed and she looked past her friends to see Yumi with her back against the shut door, clutching Mara to her chest and her cheeks flushed red with anger.

"Everything is fine," Yumi stated firmly before anyone could ask her.

"Solid reaction, no notes," Moz said. He then looked to Tristan. "You should all probably get a head-start in finding a captain. I think Ina is the obvious choice for the relay familiar between your group and the scouts. Aegis can hang back here."

As if on cue, the black cat slunk around Avery's feet. *"Who'd you kill to become King, Bone Brain?"*

Moz shot a sour look down at him. "You if you're not careful."

"Alright everyone, good luck," Lily said, and the group parted three ways.

Yumi knocked on the door, holding the forest green gown across her arms as best as she could without dropping it. The layers of tulle and satin were heavy not only with material, but with sentimental value. It had been gifted to Yumi from her late mother. She heard footsteps approach the door and she frowned at their heaviness that didn't quite match the Berserker Witch's small frame. When the door was opened, she wasn't looking into that sweet and wild face. Yumi sighed in annoyance.

"You're here for Avery, right?"

Yumi didn't answer, unsure of what she was to say to Moz. Her eyes scanned the room past his shoulder, thinking that perhaps Avery was somewhere that her gaze had missed; she was nowhere to be found.

"I'm gonna give you a tip. Just let Avery do what she needs to do. Your faith in her will carry you as far as you want to go. Though I can't see that being an issue, you certainly gave her a needed fluff of the ego today."

Yumi frowned as she pushed her way past him to lay the garment across the starry bedspread. "I don't need your help."

Moz's expression chilled over. "You could at least pretend for her sake that you tolerate me."

"But I don't even like you. You doubted me."

Moz looked down at his folded hands, pausing with thought before he turned his head back to face Yumi. Though his face was still serious, it had lightened just the faintest bit.

"You're right, I did doubt you," he confessed "and I'm sorry. I, of all people, should know. I should really fuckin' know better. Because the first time I let the Knight slip away from me, it was in front of all of the people I care about. It was in front of her. And I felt hideous shame and they believed deep down to their cores that I was going to kill them, that I was going to turn on them. But Tristan and Avery didn't doubt me. If I'm going to ever deserve that, even just a shred of that, I need to apologize. Yumi, I'm sorry."

Yumi locked stares with him with her arms folded, her gaze flickering back and forth between his eyes and the scar that marred his left eyebrow.

"She is going to steal our witch. Our witch is our witch alone."

The deep rumble was not from her Knight, but his. Yumi hesitated; *what did it mean*?

"I accept your apology," she started, her voice low, "but I'm not ready to forgive."

Moz grinned toothily and she was taken aback; he could smile?

"Maybe you'll forgive me if I tell you how to woo my girlfriend."

Yumi's cheeks flared a hot red. "You're going to *what*?"

"Though you're already ahead in the game in that she's already taken a liking to you," Moz continued, not listening to Yumi's stammering. "Is polyamory not as big a thing here? Or maybe you just don't get out on the town enough. That's not actually a problem. But like I was saying, you've already affirmed solid faith in her-"

"Stop. Just please stop talking."

Yumi held her hands up to her temples, walking to the door to leave as the room around her became overwhelmingly small.

"All I ask is that we keep proper boundaries. For me, that's being honest abou-"

Yumi slammed the door behind her, and he called out once more through the solid wood.

"Pigs and fishes, Princess!"

Yumi leaned back against the oak door, blowing her blunt bangs out of her face before she started down the hall again to find Avery.

"Jackass," she muttered to herself.

She stomped through the wings of the second story and came up empty-handed before she decided to search the main floor. Her ears were still hot with embarrassment and anger and she hoped that it would fade by the time she did find Avery.

Finally, she found the figure with long, dark waves standing in her mother's solarium with their back to Yumi. Avery was bent forward, examining the patterns of a striped pothos.

"Hello, Avery," Yumi greeted her.

Avery jumped as she turned around, startled by Yumi's voice and she felt a twinge of apology for approaching her so suddenly.

"Oh, sorry!" Avery apologized despite having done nothing wrong. "I just saw this plant and I thought it looked neat. Am I allowed to be here?"

Yumi nodded. "Yes, absolutely you are. That's called a golden pothos. It's one of the most adaptable species, so we have quite a few of them here. My mother didn't have the greenest of thumbs and when she was alive, she insisted that she would be the one to take care of all the solarium plants despite her inability to keep the finicky ones alive. This seemed like a good compromise."

Avery let out a laugh before smiling warmly. "I get that, I couldn't keep a house cactus alive in my old apartment. I'm glad she was able to care for these ones, though. The Queen sounds like she was a wonderful person to have known."

"She really was," Yumi felt the sadness creeping in around the edges of her words and she decided this was a great opportunity to change to a less melancholy subject. "Speaking of which, I found you a gown for the Novara Ball. It was hers, actually, before she passed it on to me. She was just a bit taller than you, but I believe we could make some temporary adjustments that would suit you quite well. I left it in your room if you wanted to try it on."

She felt confused when she watched the witch's expression fall.

"Yumi, that's very kind of you and I'm so grateful for the offer," Avery said in a quieter voice and Yumi was suddenly worried she had said something to offend her. "I don't think I could let myself wear such a meaningful dress to your family, I couldn't forgive myself if something ever happened to it. Would there be any way to go out and find something on my own that wouldn't be missed? Maybe a suit or…"

"A suit?" Yumi was confused. She had never seen any of the women in the palace wearing masculine clothing and she thought for a moment that there was some regional difference in language that she was missing.

Avery nodded. "Yeah. I've never felt myself in a dress. It kind of feels like I'm trying to wear someone else's body. Like it's me, but it's wrong."

Yumi wasn't sure what expression was painted on her own face as she tried to put together what Avery meant and felt immediate guilt when the witch spoke again quicker and louder, trying to backpedal on what she had already said.

"But I'm sure the dress is absolutely gorgeous! I would love to see it even if I'm not wearing it! I really just don't want anything to happen to it!"

Yumi felt awful that she had made Avery feel that she needed to take back what she was saying about herself.

Yumi smiled. "Do not worry, I understand now what you mean and I apologize for my confusion. I would be happy to introduce you to our tailor, I think now I can envision you so much clearer in a suit."

CHAPTER SIX

THE MOON

Avery looked at her reflection, briefly confused as a knee-jerk reaction when she didn't see the same person who had stared back at her from her old bedroom mirror. Her right cheek was speckled with the white spots of recently healed scabs. The sunburn across her nose and forehead was only just beginning to subside, leaving behind tanned skin and more freckles than she could recall ever having. With her hair pulled back into a ponytail, she had a full glimpse of her too-large ears and she frowned. Her exposed jawline appeared even squarer than it was, and she laughed, grateful that she didn't accept Yumi's ball gown. In the deep navy coat, she couldn't help but feel she was a rather handsome woman.

Her small shoulders were deceivingly broad in the brocade coat cut around her hips, making them disappear altogether. The two hairpins of golden stars Yumi loaned to her matched the adorning buttons closed all the way down from the base of her throat. The black of her trousers nearly matched the midnight navy of the fabric and she had resisted the urge to tuck the pants into her boots for the sake of keeping up a polished appearance.

"I must admit, you clean up well, girl," Aegis commented, slinking around the oak legs of the mirror frame.

"Thank you, Aegis."

"Though I have to ask, where do I fit in the schemes for tonight? You're not wearing a bag."

"You're right, I'm not. You are to stay outside and warn us in case we get any unwanted company or a demon outbreak," Avery instructed the cat.

"If you insist. But if we're making this decision based on poise and class, it should really be me in there," Aegis replied with a snide remark.

Avery scowled as she watched Aegis slink out of the room, his tail curling around the edge of the door before he disappeared.

— ❦ —

The "heavy hitters" met outside the dining hall doors and Avery let her shock show when she saw Jack stride through the gilded castle entry doors.

"What are you doing here?"

"Cassie decided she was more worried about Grim than she wanted to be a scout, so we swapped. Hi guys!" He grinned toothily and waved.

"And where is Moz? He should have been here already, we're about to walk inside."

"He's doing one last stroll around the perimeter with Aegis to determine where we should link the cat to wolf meetup point. He put me in charge of standing in his place until he gets here. It sounded like they were bickering a lot more than they usually do," Jack said and pouted. "I miss the cat bastard."

"For fuck's sake," Avery muttered to herself.

As she was ready to rearrange their entire plan, an attendant poked a head out between the hall doors. "They're ready for you now, uh, children?"

"Thank you," Avery answered flatly, too annoyed to correct him.

The attendant's eyes scanned each of them up and down, as though he were deciding if each of them were dressed appropriately enough to be seen by high society. His nervous eyes fell on Jack and narrowed with suspicion.

"Who are you?"

"Jack. I'm Moz's brother, I'm standing in for him 'til he gets here."

"Where is he? You can't just-"

"I sure as hell can! And he just saved all your butts, so I think he can be as fashionably late as he goddamn pleases."

Lily held a hand up to her mouth to cover her stifled laughter with only marginal success.

"Very well," the attendant said. "Follow me, His Majesty and the Royal Court will see you now. Do your best to behave yourselves, now will you?"

Avery bit her tongue both figuratively and literally. If she could just hang on a little longer, she would never have to deal with the aristocratic bullshit again. They followed the short, suited man into the hall.

It looked somehow even more grand than it did when Avery and Moz had seen it during the daylight hours. The crystal chandeliers above their heads were lit and threw dazzling warm light into the gilded coffers. An ensemble of musicians sat where they had not too long ago, playing a sweeping but high-brow piece that Avery didn't quite know herself. Even then, she found herself immensely jealous of the cellist in the black chiffon dress.

The attendant led them down a navy length of thick rug and toward the platform where a secondary throne had been established. When Avery saw King Harthmoor again, she reminded herself to play nice until they had the money in-hand. After that, she promised to treat herself to a verbal free-for-all.

"Wait here," the attendant ordered and hurried up to the Royal Guardsman posted at the King's right. He stood up on his toes to whisper something to the taller man adorned in a dark blue uniform trimmed finely with gold buttons and medals. The look on the guard's face never broke its fixed, stern frown. The guard then relayed whatever message he had just heard to the King on the other side of him.

King Harthmoor buried his face in his hand with visible annoyance and did not bother to keep his voice quieted. "Well we're not going to wait for him, just get on with it."

The Guardsman signaled with a lifted hand to the other officer posted on the other side of the Throne. This Guardsman lifted a knee high, bringing it back down to the marble floor with precise rigidity as he lifted a trumpet to his face. A blaring note arched over the dull hum of conversations from guests in colorful gowns and suits who had taken their seats at the tables in the back of the hall. The musicians fell silent and the air hung still as the first Guardsman marched towards the Reapers who had been left standing in an awestruck row.

He stood before them, throwing up a rigid salute. Avery gained some satisfaction in knowing that the Guardsman *really* didn't want to be doing that but had to anyway.

"You're supposed to kneel now," the attendant hissed from where he stood off to the side of the platform.

They looked at each other, Jack shrugging, and then they decided it was best to just go with it.

"We, the people of Brightloch, thank you for your valiant effort in the initiative to combat the surge of demonbeasts. For your actions, we bestow one thousand and three hundred gold pieces to Avery Porter, Lilian Clements, and, um, William Mosley's substitute, respectively."

Avery lifted her head up, looking towards Lily as they knelt. She exchanged grins with her best friend; she felt damned proud. Not for slaying the demon, that shit had been easy - she was taking their *money*.

The attendant held three velvet bags and handed a pouch to each of them. Avery's eyes widened with surprise at the weight of the gold in her hands. She didn't think she ever had so much money to her name and she remembered that she was going to have to surrender it immediately for their mission.

She watched Lily nod in thanks as the court dismissed them. Lily stood back up and took the bag Jack handed off to her in Moz's stead.

"Ave, gimme," she said and held out her other hand.

Avery pouted, handing over the heavy bag of gold. Lily took all three and placed them in the satchel she wore under her quiver. As she moved, Avery heard a faint clinking of metal far too delicate to be the coins.

"Lily, what've you got in there?"

"My dear Avery," she said with a sweeping gesture of her hand towards the circular tables dotting the edges of the hall "you'll notice that though this royal party is grand, not a single one of these dinner settings have knives."

Avery pinched the bridge of her nose.

"I'm not even gonna ask."

"You don't need to, Ave. Flying knives. *Gold* flying knives."

"That. Is. Kick-ASS," Jack interjected gleefully before turning to find Tristan in the crowd.

"We're gonna go now," Lily told Avery. "You be careful coming down, alright?"

"You got it, Coach."

Lily grinned before disappearing into the crowd to follow Jack. Avery turned in every direction and looked for a familiar face now that she had been left alone in the cloud of gilded gowns and tailored coats.

Avery almost didn't recognize Moz with his wild locks of hair smoothed down and away from his face. He grimaced, tugging at the sleeve hems of his navy coat that matched hers; unintentionally, she presumed. Avery saw the tattoos on his hand and wrist peeking out from under the stiff fabric and she grinned when he approached her.

"We sure don't belong here, do we?"

Moz shook his head. "Having my scabbard on still surely doesn't help. We stick out so terribly in a crowd."

"The gun in my pants doesn't feel too great, either," Avery said as she nodded in agreement. "And maybe we could have shown up in different suits."

"Well, *I'm* not going to change."

Avery grinned warmly at him, nudging him with a teasing fist before she turned her attention back to the crowd of ball goers around them. Having Hemlock still strapped across her back had warranted her some incredulous stares from the regal ball attendees. She knew she should have heeded Lily's warning of the feeling of being bizarre with a weapon on but Avery wasn't the one sneaking a knife from each dining setting to use as a telekinetic projectile.

Moz held out his hand and Avery raised a brow.

"Really? You're really going to do this?"

"If they're going to make me do this stupid shit to my hair, I'm pulling out all the stops."

Avery laughed, sliding her hand into his. Moz pulled her towards him, attempting to put his hand on her waist and they both snickered when they realized the giant scabbard would only allow him to hold his hand awkwardly on her side.

"Close enough."

She held her right hand on his shoulder, looking past him towards the other dancers to see if she was doing it right. The graceful movements around her didn't seem to match her fumbling steps and she wasn't sure if Moz was just as ungraceful or if it was only her who hadn't waltzed a day in her life.

"You don't have to worry about them." He said in a low voice towards her turned ear, "I think they're over the spectacle and won't be expecting much out of us as far as dance moves go."

She laughed but still studied the calculated footwork of the couples around her as she realized the clumsiness was just hers; Moz's careful steps were those of a long prac-ticed swordsman.

"What do you think it's like to be them?"

Avery looked up at him, puzzled by the unexpected question. A warm flush of shyness spread across her cheeks when he looked down at her, waiting for an answer.

"What do you mean?"

Moz's green gaze floated above her head and towards the people around them. "These people, what's it like to be them? Do you think they've lived here all their lives? Do you think they have tons of children? How do you think they stumbled on so much money?"

Avery shrugged. "Like Lily said, logging and mining probably. I don't see why-"

"But they're not Reapers."

Avery fell quiet, looking around her as they spun in dance. She caught a glimpse of a woman's laughing face, her skin glowing despite the lines around her eyes and corners of her smile. Her dark hair was piled atop her head in careful curls, streaks of silver glimmering unashamedly under the glow of the chandeliers. The woman had clearly lived long and lived happily, and she spun out of Avery's line of view in a joyous dance.

"I'd like to think we were chosen for a reason," Moz continued as she looked back up at his face. He was looking up and away from her, earthen eyes flickering as he tracked the dance movements of the mortals around them. "That this job is really as terrible as I think it is and that it requires a certain level of resilience. To withstand carrying everyone to death, to be almost gods of the undeniable end. Do you think most of these people could bear the burden that we do? They get to live out their lives so enviably ordinary while we were sacrificed, not because it is easy for us, but because our will is so ironclad. And if we weren't chosen for any reason at all and just drew a shit hand? Don't tell me."

"You know, you *are* one of them now," Avery reminded him.

Moz scowled. "Me? Never," he teased before looking back down at her with a boyish grin.

Avery grinned back at him, so comfortable in his warmth. She knew she should have felt overly aware and conscious of being in that ballroom with no dancing ability, wearing a suit when she was expected to wear a dress. But looking up at him was coming home after a long trip, it was a warm quilt and her favorite book on a rainy day. It was trust, but it was most importantly love.

She opened her mouth, ready to confess, but he spoke first.

"You know," Moz whispered, "she's watching you."

Avery began to turn around and Moz gripped her side tight to stop her.

"No, play it cool!"

"But I can't see her."

"You will when you dance with her. I'm gonna make you do it. I mean, obviously I'm a little biased towards a different lady, but she does look quite pretty."

"You're being kind of weird about this," Avery said frankly.

Moz looked down at her face and frowned. "Am I? I'm sorry, Ave. I'm not really sure what the right way to be is."

"No, no, it's not bad. Just takes getting used to is all, I suppose."

"Ain't that the truth," he said and laughed. "You should really see her."

Moz stopped dancing and let go of Avery's waist as he stepped back. She hesitated before nodding, uneasy with his acceptance still. As he walked backwards, he shooed her on with little sweeps of his hands.

"Go on!"

She watched him disappear into the crowd of aristocrats with a grin on her face and sighed before turning around. Avery searched the crowd to find the Princess but was unable to see past the frills of the ballgowns and tall gentlemen. She stood on her toes and still she could not spot Yumi.

The crowd suddenly parted and Yumi stepped through the people who looked on with adoring admiration; Avery stood frozen as she stared. Shintori's Princess stood tall and looked every inch regal and brave, the deep ashen blue of her skirts speckled with gold foil constellations like she wore the night sky itself. The glowing flickers of spirits danced about Yumi before melting into the living, vanishing from the periphery of Avery's vision. Then Yumi was looking down at her, brown topaz eyes glittering just above Avery's ordinary blue.

Without speaking a word, Yumi held up her right hand towards Avery's shoulder and Avery felt herself flush with embarrassment - she had forgotten what unscathed and unblistered hands had looked like. She slipped her left hand into Yumi's, ashamed of the way her callouses must have felt against Yumi's soft skin.

She smiled and placed her other hand onto Avery's shoulder, sweeping their steps into the fluid rhythm of the orchestra. Yumi's steps were fast, but she led with a grace that carried Avery with her so effortlessly that she had nearly forgotten that she knew nothing about ballroom dance. They held locked gazes and Avery was far too enchanted to break it, even though her animal instincts itched to turn her focus to the flickering spirits that flocked to their haunted dance. The gilded coffers beyond Yumi's head of careful curls looked like a foiled halo and Avery could have easily mistaken her for a saint.

"I spoke to Moz," Yumi broke the silence between them.

"About the Knight? What happened?"

"No, not about the Knight. About you."

"*Me*? What about me," Avery felt her ears flush hot at just the two of them having a private conversation about her.

"He mentioned something, I'm not sure I can remember. Poly-"

"*Fucking Moz.*"

A smile crept up in the corners of Yumi's lips. "Are you embarrassed?"

Avery glanced away, chuckling at the understatement of the century. When she turned back, Yumi was fully grinning and Avery was certain the flush that had crept to her cheeks was the color of overly ripe tomatoes.

"Yeah, really embarrassed. I don't even know you terribly well, but something about you feels so right," Avery confessed.

"Everyone had made you out to be this horrible monster, and at first, I believed them," Yumi admitted, and Avery flinched. "Then Owen came and showed me what he had seen. I was wrong, we were all wrong. You are brave and kind, that's hard to be sometimes."

"Yumi, you *are* brave. I mean, the way you handled the demon in the square? With the throwing knives? That was fucking incredible, I mean - sorry."

Yumi laughed, the sound a melodic tune. "I don't care, you're entitled to whatever words you please."

When Avery grinned, the Princess added "and thank you. I am very honored to know that you think that of me. I don't hear much of that from the people around me, not things that matter anyway. So to hear that someone thinks of me as being brave, especially from you."

Avery abruptly stopped dancing and her heart hammered. "Why especially me?"

Yumi's gaze was warm as she looked down at Avery, the world around them had melted into a gilded bokeh of light. The Princess tilted her head ever so slightly to the side, as though she suddenly felt bashful.

"I was enchanted by you, Avery. From the very moment you first spoke my name, I heard you. And again when Owen spoke your name and I have carried it with me ever since."

Her breath hitched in her throat, watching the Princess' lips as she spoke. Avery tilted her head up to meet Yumi's face, her movements timid until Yumi closed the distance. Avery's skin rushed with warmth as Yumi's skin brushed hers, the scent of her perfume washed Avery in a grove of neroli flowers.

Kissing Yumi was to kiss the stars, to kiss magic itself. Yumi's slender fingers slipped under Avery's ponytail and gently held her neck, sending hot waves down Avery's spine. Sparks of electricity fired off in every nerve ending and Avery felt she could combust right there on the dance floor. She admittedly would have been fine with that.

When they parted, Yumi looked down at her with a bright grin. Seeing that even the Princess's cheeks were flushed red, Avery began to laugh. Yumi laughed, too, for only a moment before she ducked fast to kiss Avery once more.

"Your laugh, I like it," Yumi said with her forehead against Avery's.

As her cheeks flushed hot, Avery quipped back, "You're quite-"

The doors of the hall burst open and the orchestra halted with a harsh screech of strings before the room fell silent. Avery's hands fell from Yumi's waist as she turned towards the commotion. She found the wall of uniformed bodies in the entryway, steel of their drawn swords glinting under the crystal chandeliers. Ball attendees scattered back from the intruders, sucking Yumi and Avery into a crowd with the sudden exodus. From between cramped shoulders, Avery saw the head of flaming hair before she heard the familiar voice.

"A Knight? In the ranks of the wealthy and significant? Color me impressed," Morgana teased with dripping vitriol as she stepped forward, the clicking of her heeled boots on the marble floor heard clearly in the tense silence.

"Hide," Avery instructed Yumi without turning her head to look behind her. "Keep the Knight silent. Don't let her catch you near Moz."

As Avery crept through the crowd, she fought the urge to look back to see if Yumi had listened. She reached over her shoulder for Hemlock from where she hid behind tall men and large ball gowns, circling her prey. With her left hand, she patted the gun under her coat to reassure herself; she may not have been an expert shooter, but she knew it would freeze many in their tracks. She pulled her sword carefully from its sheath, freezing when the metal scraped the hard leather.

"Berserker Witch!"

Morgana cried out and Avery's hiding place was compromised when guests scattered. More swords scraped as Morgana began to laugh, looking towards Avery.

"It would appear you can't live off gusto forever!"

"You settle with me first," Moz called out from behind Avery but she didn't dare turn to look even when she heard the familiar draw of Moz's sword.

Morgana looked past Avery, shaking her head in something resembling bastardized pity.

"I'm afraid that's irrelevant," she said. "She drew the blood of my child, therefore your witch is fair game."

"Never would I have imagined that the Berserker Witch was you, Avery," the softness of a familiar voice called out from somewhere within the formation of officers and she froze with Hemlock's blade pressing against her flesh. The Legion officers parted to create a pathway, letting the shorter figure step to the front and Avery's eyes widened in utter bewilderment.

"What are…. *you?*"

From behind her, porcelain crashed as table settings were kicked over in cacophonous fury. Avery flinched at the sound and found Kurosaki had launched himself onto the table, his rifle already drawn in the direction of the woman.

"I WANT THE BITCH'S HEAD ON A SILVER PLATTER," Kurosaki screamed in an awe-inspiring rage.

Riko Yamada turned a smug grin towards Kurosaki, pleased that she got such a rise out of the normally composed man. She twirled the blade in her left hand, spinning it nimbly like a child's toy as she spoke.

"How disappointing to see you here, Izaya. It almost overshadows my joy to see my favorite Baby."

"You've gotta be fucking kidding me," Avery heard Moz swear from a new location in the crowd. "There's no fucking way she's-"

His voice faded, Avery could only focus on the hideous monster before her. Riko turned her dark eyes to Avery, brushing the front strands of her dark bob away from her face as though they were having the most casual of conversations. Blood pounded in Avery's ears at the sight of her ex-girlfriend and almost muffled the words coming from her own mouth.

"I know what you did. What you continued to do."

Avery thought of the pockmarks inside of her elbow from the countless needles and what Kurosaki had told her about soul harvesting. Riko had used her when her body was uninhabited by her soul; Avery was forced into a plan to lure vulnerable people to their deaths via demons.

Riko's head tilted and the steel blade in her hand stopped spinning. She straightened up and sighed, sounding oddly pleased with herself. Avery recognized nothing about this person other than appearances, the same freckles and long fingers - only now the devil herself wore them. She couldn't imagine any scenario in which a human would agree to harvesting souls, kick-starting the demons that were no doubt swallowing Ardua by then. What had Riko been offered in return?

"I must admit," Riko said, pressing the tip of her blade against her own lip as though in careful thought. She began taking calculated steps to maneuver around Avery, though Riko never caught her backside unguarded. "I had whole-heartedly expected you to continue to play along with my soul farm. And to have you cut my rope as soon as you were a Reaper, just like that? Never in my wildest dreams!"

Riko's face then contorted into an expression of exaggerated grief. "*'How could you do this to me, Avery?'*"

Only after she repeated her own cries from months ago when Avery severed the relationship, her mouth twisted into a devilish grin and she unsheathed a second blade. Her right foot stepped backwards as she braced herself for a fight.

"I'll consider killing you an ample vengeance," Riko cooed.

Avery paused, the gravity of the situation weighing heavy on her. With shaking hands, she broke the flesh of her hand on Hemlock. Her hair floated upwards as the spirits emerged, more of them than Avery had ever seen at once before.

"Coward!" Riko snapped. "You accuse me of using souls and then have them fight your battles! Fight me on your fucking own!"

Avery screamed wildly as she threw Hemlock down upon Riko, stopping short of her grinning face when Riko caught the sword with both of her blades.

"Ex-lovers fighting to the death?" Riko cried out excitedly, shoving Avery away with surprising force. "This is the kind of shit I live for!"

Avery stepped backwards to reassess the fight, aware that too much of her focus was going towards holding back the spirits that itched to tear Riko apart. She ran forward, swinging Hemlock down across her body to strike Riko in the chest. Riko again countered quicker than Avery had anticipated, forcing her sword up with one hand blade while the other swiped towards Avery, forcing her to retreat again as she narrowly avoided being slashed.

"No, Avery! She's left-handed!" Kurosaki hollered from where he stood somewhere in the crowd and Avery grinned. She thanked the gods that Kurosaki was heavily invested in Riko's death.

Avery's focus was thrown off by Kurosaki's advice and in the small pause she left, Riko kicked her hard in the stomach. She stumbled backwards, Hemlock clattering to the floor as Avery fell. Panic rose and she scrambled to get up, her hands fumbling for her sword as Riko leaned over her with a devilish grin.

Riko suddenly jerked backwards as a narrow knife flew past her face from beyond Avery's vision. Avery watched Riko's grin change to a snarl of anger facing the direction in which the golden throwing dagger had come from.

"You stupid slu-"

Avery didn't waste time to see where the knife had come from before swinging her closed fist hard into the center of Riko's face. She felt the crunch under her fingers and Riko reeled backwards, holding the back of her hand to her spurting nose as she still held one of her blades. Moving quickly, Avery reached for Hemlock where it had fallen several feet away from her before stepping away from Riko; she knew she would need more fighting room.

Riko lowered her hand, blood dripping fast down her chin and onto the charcoal blazer of her uniform. The grin on her lips mismatched the fury alight in her eyes and she held up both her blades, waiting for Avery to strike again.

Avery ran fast, jabbing towards Riko's right side to exploit her weaker side. Riko swung her left blade across her body to deflect Hemlock's swing, slashing towards Avery's face and forced her to retreat. Avery swore to herself, careful not to let Riko hear as she wished she had spent more time refining her sword combat instead of relying on the spirits each time she came into a confrontation.

Riko must have heard, for she grinned. "What's the matter, Baby? Not doing too well without your ghosts?"

Avery snarled, lunging fast at Riko. The woman's blades crashed against Hemlock, blocking each swing Avery made with loud clatters. As Riko deflected a blow with her right hand, she jabbed at Avery with her left and caught Avery's right forearm. Avery winced, stepping back quickly as blood began oozing under her ripped coat sleeve.

Her arm radiated with pain as she stumbled, grabbing the nearest chair, and throwing it between herself and Riko. Avery backpedaled, giving herself as much distance as she could while Riko laughed.

"You're practically useless without them! Is this maggot really what you're all afraid of?"

Riko kicked the chair aside, driving at Avery with both knives. Avery stepped out of the reach of the weapons but jabbed Hemlock towards Riko's gut. The detective hesitated, sweeping to the side to avoid being pierced. The woman snarled and Avery knew she found an advantage; she didn't have to come nearly as close as Riko had to, even if Riko was admittedly faster.

Avery swung her sword again at Riko, their metal clashing and she felt the wave of impact roll up her arms.

"I'll show you exactly why your bitch of a Captain wants me dead so badly," Avery's voice was smooth, like she had been preparing to say the words since she had first left Ardua with Moz and Tristan. "Then you'll really understand the fear of the Berserker Witch."

— 🕊 —

Morgana watched the youngest of the Harthmoor family throw the dagger towards Detective Yamada and her manicured eyebrow arched in suspicion. Why did the Princess fight rather than flee? And for the Berserker Witch? *Could it be?*

"Hey Sparky, you can't just show up uninvited like that," William's taunt interrupted her trail of thought as he approached her, his blessed sword twirling at his side.

Morgana laughed. "Is that you under there, brother? You were the last person I'd expect to sell out just like that. And for what, a party? I'm very interested to know who you're here for."

She unsheathed her own sword, a close cousin to William's and crafted by the same ironsmith. The metal of her weapon was a stormy grey, wrapped with maroon leather around its grip.

"You can't kill me, brother. And I can't kill you either," Morgana spoke in a blunt voice "but I can prod at you. Poke you with holes until your Knight wants to play."

William smirked, sinister and childish, and he spun his sword upwards to wield it protectively in front of his torso. She knew it was a dare, but she would never be the first to transform. He had tried before to push her buttons to lure the Knight out, leaving her vulnerable to kill. If he managed to slay her Knight, she would go down with it.

Her focus flickered towards her periphery where the Guardsmen were surrounding Princess Yumi. The woman was shoving them away forcefully, a gilded dagger in her slender hand.

"Crush them between your teeth. The world bows and breaks to none but us. Go wherever you please, however you please."

The corners of Morgana's lips turned up in a slight smirk. Her Knight knew exactly what she was thinking: coax out the Knight of Spirit to confirm her suspicions. She watched as the Princess stopped thrashing, turning her head to find where the voice of Morgana's Knight had spoken from. That was all Morgana needed to know for sure.

In the glow of satisfaction with her own wit, Morgana almost missed William charging her with her sword aimed to pierce her. She shrank backwards with the metal, her skin squishing under the force as it plunged through her hip.

"Oof!"

The surprise of the blow hurt more than the wound, which was no more than a mild pounding as her flesh was already beginning to repair itself. Her Knight wouldn't let any of her wounds become grave as long as it still hummed within her.

"It's almost like I just found something you didn't want me to see," Morgana taunted.

She threw her head back towards the gilded ceiling of stars so that her voice would be carried over the clatter of crashing porcelain and swords.

"It's the Princess!"

William snarled, plunging his sword deeper through her until she ripped herself off the blade. Around them, her officers swarmed around the cluster of royal guardsmen. Gunshots rang out and a few of her men crumpled into heaps on the floor. Morgana swore; she had forgotten about the Reaper from Eyon.

Panic welled in Yumi's throat when the redheaded woman shouted, giving her away as the Knight. She heard the smoky voice coming from somewhere around her and couldn't keep herself from trying to find the source; she'd fallen for the trap.

Officers in charcoal jackets turned their attention towards Yumi, each of them swinging their swords in her direction. She swallowed hard as she reached towards the belt hidden under her dress sash. This time there was no choice but to kill.

"Sorry Owen," she apologized to the absent ghost boy, remembering their grave conversation about the necessity of violence.

Yumi drew two of her gilded daggers and the bodies sprang upon her. Their blades cut into the exposed flesh of her arm but the slashes were sealing just as quickly as they had been opened. If they weren't certain about the identity of the Knight of Spirit before, they undoubtedly were now.

Screams rang out around her, calling out her name. The armored bodies of the royal guards fell upon Yumi and the assailants, shielding her from the intruders. She looked on in terror; while she would not fall, they would. She shouldn't have been worth dying for and the act enraged her.

Yumi pushed as close as she could to the assailants and swung her daggers, not caring if she was temporarily cut. Her knives slashed a man across the throat and he sank to the floor in a pool of red. The spirits Avery rose with the blade of Hemlock flocked to her and Yumi surged with the tide of violence.

CHAPTER SEVEN

THE SUN

M oz seethed with anger and pushed his sword deeper into Morgana every time she tried to shrug herself off the hilt. Though the woman with a head of fiery hair was impaled, not a single drop of her blood tainted the pale marble floor beneath her. Morgana watched him with contempt, the eerie smile gone from her face.

"It pains me so," she said, her voice like hardened honey, "to see you shy away from something I know you want so very much. Imagine a world in which souls could never be parted by death. Do you remember the last time you saw your parents? Has it been so long since you became a lost boy that you have forgotten the face of your own mother?"

Moz ducked to the side when Morgana lazily swiped her own sword at him, his jerking movement ripping his sword sideways in her stomach. Already her skin knitted itself back together. The terrible Knight of Fire that lived within her would refuse to let her die.

"Do you remember the last time you saw *her*? Nora."

He froze. The chaos in the ballroom around them shrank to muffled silence.

William had been stalking the Leech for blocks. The humanoid mass of shadow darted seemingly without a destination, its white eyes focusing on a mortal for only moments before moving on. He watched on from the alleyway between two of many Centralia's taverns, waiting to see who the desperate soul was attracting the demon. Instead of reaching for the consecrated sword on his back, he waited patiently. If he could just tail it long enough, he might be able to see if he could help-

"Hey, mister! What are you doing creepin' 'round back here?"

"For fucks sake!"

William jumped, turning around. When his eyes met no face, he looked down.

She looked up at him with her fists balled up on her waist, the look in her glittering topaz eyes was accusing. The girl couldn't have been older than six, her height reaching only his belly even when he included the fluffy curls of her brown hair.

"Were you watching him?"

She pointed a finger in the direction past him and William turned. The Leech? He frowned; there was no way the mortal kid would have been able to see it. The black halo of a Reaper didn't surround her face upon first sight, and they were the only ones who could see the demons as far as he knew. Surely the kid meant someone else - like the gentleman who had been walking past.

"No," he answered, simply. "He's not terribly interesting."

The girl shrugged. "I don't know how much more interesting you can get than being made of dark clouds."

William turned again, looking down at the child with his eyebrows furrowed.

"Say, what's your name?"

The little girl grinned, proudly revealing that she was missing her two front teeth.

"I'm called Nora."

Something had been done to this child that made her able to see the demons, that he was sure of. But what?

"Nora, I'm William. Where are your parents?"

Her eyes lit up at the mention of his name. "That's my papa's name too! Mama's at home, she has a patient right now."

The two clues snapped together at once - the ship captain William Khan and his wife Isobel, the healer of Centralia. One of them must have done something to the little girl.

"Show me where you live, I have a wound I'd like checked out," he lied.

Nora hurried down the alley and into the street, energetic as a buzzing bee. William followed her through town until they came upon the navy painted house.

"Mama says you always have to knock first," Nora instructed, looking up at his face with a strained neck. "That way if someone is very ill, she can close him off first."

William rapped on the door and waited. From somewhere within the house, a shuffle of feet approached the door. Locks turned and the wood of the door creaked as it was pulled open, just wide enough for a face to poke through.

Isobel Khan was a beautiful woman, with long locks of dark hair and the same topaz eyes as her curious daughter. As Isobel examined William, he saw her jaw clench nervously.

"Nora, honey, please come inside and let Mama speak with our visitor."

Nora shook her head, refusing to budge. She wanted to be included in the grown-up discussion.

"What did you do to that child?" William cut fast to the purpose of his visit.

Isobel paused, looking stuck between his words and her child's refusal to leave them. She opened the door wider, as if she was about to jump through with a swinging fist.

"What are you insinuating?" Isobel was defensive, but frustratingly cool-headed.

"You may have fooled most of Centralia but I recognize witchcraft when I see it," he answered calmly "and I would like to know what it is you did to that child to give her the eyes that see demons. What was the price?"

Isobel's gentle demeanor snapped, and she threw the door open so hard that it hit the interior wall and bounced back, hitting her boot.

"Who do you think you are, to suggest that I would do anything to harm my flesh and blood? Just who in the goddess' name do you think you are?"

"I'm the boogieman."

Isobel pursed her lips, watching him as she formulated her next words very carefully. The witch understood his words perfectly while her daughter looked on in confusion. He was the lurking Death, unseen as he watched. The nightmare of all men.

"She is under Mona's protection now. I had no choice and no price was named. My little girl, the Goddess of Witches has taken her under Her wing."

"There is always a price," William spoke gravely.

The moon and sun exchanged places many times in the sky. The leaves of the forest shrank, died, and then bloomed again many times. Nora grew taller, her voice deepened, and in only a second she had become a teenager.

William heard her footsteps approach him across the creaking floor of the library.

"I've been thinking," she said, her voice the most familiar song to him even when it spoke hesitantly.

He lazily turned the page in the large tome spread out on the table before him and the sketch of the terrible serpentine beast stared back at him when he stopped. "And did you fair alright?"

Nora didn't respond to his poking joke.

"This whole time," she said and he heard the small wavers of nervousness in her voice "you hadn't changed in any way I can see. There are no wrinkles upon your face, no graying in your hair, and still you slay the demons quick as lightning. You are exactly the same as you were when I was a child. You're no witch."

He paused. There was no way she could have drawn up a theory pointing to him being what he was. Too many steps would have to be skipped. William felt his familiar stir in his pocket. Even Jack was too nervous to speak, uncharacteristic for his talkative nature.

"Then what do you make of me, Miss Khan?"

"You are Death."

William calmly closed the book and scraped his chair backwards across the floor slowly. He stood up, his height still towering over Nora and yet she did not shrink away. William knew exactly what was coming next.

"Did you kill her? Were you the one who took my mother from us?"

He watched the nervous flicker of her eyes as she stared him down, seeming ready to run if he so much as moved too suddenly. William was grateful that he didn't have to lie this time; he was not the one to take Isobel away only hours after birthing the youngest Khan.

"No, Nora," he spoke gently. "I did not Reap your mother."

A handful of years passed. Still, she changed and he did not. William followed the young woman through town day after day. He was the shadowy embodiment of Death that dared not touch her. Sweltering summer afternoons passed as they sat under shady trees, Jack squirmed in her gentle hands as she talked to the rat with light words. On that day they sat, and the dread sat heavy in William's stomach.

"Nora, I have to go away for some while. To Eyon."

She paused, still holding Jack in her hands as she looked up with a look of sour disgust on her mouth. "Why would you want to go to such an awful place?"

"Believe me, I don't want to. But there's someone I need to see."

"Who?"

He paused. William never outright lied to the girl; if she asked, he always told the truth.

"The Oracles of Neri."

"Sounds like your business is serious. I'll be waiting here for you to come back. And William?"

"Hm?"

"In case I haven't ever told you yet, you're my closest and dearest friend."

William looked on at her face, remembering that his did not shift and age as hers did. He had to take care of this and he had to do it quickly.

"And you are mine, Nora."

William came back from Eyon that autumn. The Oracles sent him away as answerless as he was when he first arrived on the hermit island. As he made his way back towards the one-room he called home, he searched for the witch.

Any moment, Nora would dart out from the alleyways like she did as a child. But she never did. The silence was heavy without her absent humming or the clattering rocks she kicked as they walked through town talking about nothing and everything.

"William," a man's voice called out from behind him.

He turned around as Jack disappeared under the collar of his shirt. William barely ever saw the owner of the library and was surprised that the elder knew him by name.

The old man stopped, leaning forward over his bad knees as he caught his breath.

"W...William, something terrible has happened."

William's heartbeat quickened in his chest as he already feared the worst.

"What has happened?"

The man fumbled with his hands, wringing his fingers over each other nervously as he picked his words.

"Nora Khan... she's been.... They took her in, they're executing all the witches who are still here, and well, we all knew-"

Dark growls swirled unheard in William as he closed his fist around the man's tunic collar.

"Where is she? Who did this?"

He shook his head sadly, struggling to move under William's pull. "My boy, this transpired days ago. Captain Khan, he was the one who told-"

"Her own father," William spat as he dropped the shorter man. "Is he overseas or is he here?"

"He's still here. I saw him just yesterday."

William said nothing about how he should have confronted the depraved man; he would save that for later. He tore apart the small town of Centralia looking for the captain. Tavern after tavern, shop after shop. William Khan was nowhere to be found.

He itched with anger, yelling out in unhindered frustration when he left another establishment empty handed.

"There! Down the road!" *Jack's small voice chirped in William's skull and his gaze followed the rat's small pink paw that pointed from his shoulder.*

William stalked towards the man in the red coat, not caring that he was with a group of other men. The captain's back was to him, but William recognized his wide stature and long hair pulled back with a leather band.

As he got closer, his hand was reaching behind his back for his blessed sword before he stopped. No, to kill him suddenly was too good for the monster.

The men around the captain saw William first, their eyes widening as if they knew what was about to happen.

"Cap'n!"

They didn't warn Captain Khan quickly enough; William's fist was already connecting with the man's cheek. A strike from behind was undoubtedly dishonorable; but so was lending a hand to the murder of your own child.

The blow knocked Captain Khan off his feet and he hit the dirt. Rubbing his cheek, the man was more surprised than he was injured and William stood over him, waiting for the captain to stand again.

"You know why I'm here," William growled. "You sick, fucking bastard. Get on your feet."

Captain Khan lifted himself up with his hands, reaching quickly for the sword on his hip.

"You... you think we don't know what you are? You hold the hands of demons as much as the witches do. Your kinds have killed by wife, ruined my daughter."

William smirked as the Thing within stirred.

"Is that so?" He kicked hard into the Captain's side just before the man could make it to his feet. William then stepped backwards, daring the man to step up.

"My sword will stay sheathed today," William taunted. "I wanna feel the crunch of your bones."

A sickening squish came from below and William looked down at the sword that had punctured him from behind. He looked over his shoulder at one of the captain's friends, holding the weapon that had impaled William.

"Run like the scared swine you are," William warned, "for I am far worse than Death."

William stepped off the sword, the wound in his sternum was already sealing fast. The men watched him with gaping mouths of horror.

"Gut them, my eldest son," *the living Thing within him dared.*

He didn't listen; he only wanted one.

William lunged at the captain's face with a swinging fist and blood splattered from the man's nose. The sailor kept his footing that time but stumbled out of William's reach as he drew his rapier.

William howled in laughter at the flimsy weapon. Captain Khan slashed at him, ripping William's tunic but still his wounds drew no blood.

"So did you miss your buddy's attempt or...."

Captain Khan looked at William's sealing gash and then at his own sword in horror. In the cracked window of time, William knocked the rapier out of his hand, sending it clattering to the ground. His fists swung, crashing into the captain's jaw. William felt the crunch of bone as his vision flecked red with anger. He kept hitting, his rage blinding him as blood and saliva splattered.

The captain fell to the ground and William pinned him down with a boot to the chest. Pushing down hard when Captain Khan struggled beneath him to get up.

"You didn't give her a chance to run, did you? So why would I?" William taunted darkly.

William grabbed the captain's ponytail, yanking hard to lift the man's head to face him.

"You have failed as a father and you have failed as a man. You were meant to show mercy and love to your child

and you killed her. You killed Nora. My Nora," William spat on the man before he pulled out his dagger, swiftly slicing the ponytail away from the man's head.

The captain's head dropped hard onto the dirt with the release of his hair as William continued. "I don't need to consort with the Keeper of the Crossroads to know that you're going straight to Od. You're demon grub now, you son of a bitch."

William lifted his boot, kicking the man hard in the face. Captain Khan was unrecognizable, squirming in pain.

William waited and the man blinked but did not move. He let a cruel amount of time pass with his foot buried in the sailor's chest. William wanted him to suffer.

But he also wanted to make sure there was no making it out of this one alive.

He leaned forward over his knee, keeping his foot planted while he spun his dagger in one hand.

"Are you in pain?"

The captain didn't answer him, his face broken and bleeding beyond recognition. Only a groan of air passed through his swollen lips.

"Good."

William drove the dagger through the man's heart and Captain Khan was silenced forever. He stood up, attempting to wipe the splattered blood from his face but only smeared it around as he looked down on the corpse.

"I'll be fucking damned if I ever share the same name as you again," he spat.

Mosley stood still, as though the man who fell to his violence would answer him. He wanted to feel satisfied - he had just killed the man who executed his only friend. Sure, he could punch and beat all those who participated to a bloody pulp, but nothing he could do would ever bring Nora back.

He turned and saw the librarian quivering from a safe distance. Mosley pulled out a cloth to start wiping the blood off his hands and then his face.

"What will the townsmen do to you, William? They saw-"

"That name will piss off right to Od. My name is Mosley. Moz-lee."

He nodded, accepting this without missing a beat. "Mr. Mosley, she's still out there. On the edge of the woods. Nobody has buried her."

Mosley dropped his dagger and cloth, frozen in his heartbreak. Even Jack and the Thing came to a total silence. He had never experienced that kind of quiet before.

He stood still for long minutes before he remembered how to move his feet again. Mosley scooped the dagger and cloth back up. The librarian stepped back and out of his path without another word. Moving at a crawl eastward, he floated solemn as a revenant through the town and passed the rotting shambles of a lonely house.

The line of trees came into view over Centralia's wheat-fields and he stopped. The grief was already overcoming him and tears welled down his face. He was unsure if he could will himself to move any closer.

Mosley knew he would have to. For her, he would suffer a thousand times over.

He walked to the edge of the forest, where he saw her on the rope dangling by her wrists. The image of her would be burned into his nightmares forevermore. He swung his sword at the scavenging birds drawn to the carrion, his tears turned to sobs as he shooed them away from her in a cawing cloud of feathers.

Mosley cut her down, trying to wipe the long dried blood from her skin and fixing her matted hair as best he could with his fingers. He gave her only a fraction of the death rites she deserved, but it was the best he could do in his grief and knowing so little of what the Priestesses did.

Nora Khan was buried with tender love from her closest and dearest friend. He collected rocks, building a stone mound to mark where she would sleep forever.

Death sat with a hardened heart, guarding her from anything that may come her way.

— 🦋 —

Avery and Riko's breaths became labored as the fight began to exhaust them. Pauses between strikes became longer, both bleeding and seething at the match that was too even for comfort. The exhales caught between Avery's teeth and became angry hisses falling in perfect time with her heaving shoulders.

Riko feigned a step towards Avery, throwing her knives up as though to strike. Avery fell for the maneuver, stepping aside to her left to dodge the oncoming hit. Riko swiped hard, her knife slashing across the shoulder of Avery's injured arm.

Avery's sword clattered to the ground as she howled in pain, a wave of energy swelled behind Riko as she pounced on Avery and knocked her onto her back. With a hard stomp, Riko planted a foot on Avery's chest and pinned her to the marble floor. The world spun around Avery as the air was forced from her lungs. As her vision was refocusing, Riko threw her arm against Avery's throat.

"You should have stayed home, Avery," Riko warned, tutting her tongue in pity.

Avery blindly fumbled for her sword but only slapped the empty marble floor with her desperate and sweating palms.

Riko laughed. "You should have stayed home. You shouldn't have quit your job. You should have stayed with me and let me care for you in the new world. You should have stayed my Baby."

Avery thrashed hard, trying to throw Riko off but with her foot planted she had just the right amount of leverage to keep Avery on the ground.

"You should have never followed them and you should have never come here. Now I'm gonna gut them all. I'm gonna gut them all and there will be nothing you can do because they will have already witnessed your death. Foolish and alone."

The words slowed Avery. Riko leaned closer, bringing her knife towards Avery's throat in such a fluid motion that Avery felt she was watching it happen to someone else. It was over.

Avery became aware of the cold metal in her belt. The hand that had fumbled for Hemlock swooped in the other direction to her waist and with a swift motion, she pulled out the handgun. She clicked off the safety and held it up. Her shot was clear. Riko's eyes widened.

"You bi-"

Avery's ears rang and the recoil sent burning pain shooting up her injured arm. Blood pooled around her in a fast tide and she lay frozen, the flash of the gunfire leaving her temporarily blinded. Salty tears stung her eyes and a coppery taste seeped between her lips from the warmth that had splattered across her face. She fumbled to push the mangled body off her and her tears broke into an agonized weep as she shoved the dead weight with wet hands.

Her vision wobbled and she saw the blurred shapes of party-goers fleeing; the danger must not have been fully re-alized until they saw a woman shot in the head.

Vengeance was hers - so why couldn't she stop crying? She turned and vaguely glimpsed the muddy shapes of Yumi and Kurosaki running towards her. Their voices were nonsensical warbles as Yumi's slender hands gripped Avery's shoulders hard. She flinched when more gunshots rang out, coming from the blonde shape that she thought might have been Kurosaki.

"We… we need to go," she blurted out and Avery was certain she was going to vomit.

A hand forced Hemlock's grip into hers.

"-help Moz," Kurosaki's voice became clear enough to discern words too late for her to fully understand what it was he had been saying.

Her vision grew sharp once more as the blinding effects of the gun flash continued to wane. The clashing that had been quieted under the ringing in her ears became clear and she saw the crashing of swords on the other end of the hall.

Moz and Morgana were both battered but too headstrong to admit their stalemate. She watched Morgana plunge her sword through Moz's shoulder. He stumbled backwards and her heart dropped to the bottom of her stomach, but he did not fall.

Avery hurried towards them, ducking around officers fighting royal guardsmen with her haunted sword in her left hand and the unforgiving gun in her right. As she drew closer to the fringe of their fight, Avery had a clear shot of Morgana. The air cracked and flashed when Avery fired several rounds, all but three projectiles missed their targets.

The bullets that lodged in Morgana's chest and stomach wouldn't kill her; Avery knew that already. Morgana was swept off her feet by the force and she hit the ground with a hard thud. Her wounds didn't bleed, just like Moz's after Kurosaki had shot him in the head. Morgana blinked with bleary eyes, unable to get back to her feet.

"If only it was that easy," Avery muttered.

Moz didn't waste any time to thank her for intervening. He grabbed her arm and she hissed as pain shot up to her shoulder.

"We need to leave Brightloch, now," he said as he urged her forward.

"C'mon, I got us covered," Kurosaki said, leading the charge towards the hall doors. With precise shots he picked off Legion officers who attempted to cut off their exit one by one. Watching his swift and methodical movements, Avery was again reminded of Alice's absence and she felt a sharp bite of sorrow. She sliced her palm on Hemlock and when the necromantic sword blinked to life again, she did nothing to restrain the magnetic pull it had on the spirits.

They scrambled into the hall, surrounding Yumi the same way that Avery had been protected from the demons in Od. Yumi clutched Mara to her chest and Avery held Yumi's free hand as they ran out into the chilly air. The early Novara nights were already biting in the foothills of the mountains. Aegis darted out from the shadows, catching up to them as they ran through the courtyard.

"Some warning that was, useless fucking cat!" Moz shouted angrily at Aegis.

"*I did warn you. They had a witch with them. Guess we know what she does. Did you catch anything I was saying to any of you?*"

Aegis weaved around Avery's strides, looping between her and Yumi as he waited for Avery's response.

"*You look worse than usual, girl. What happened to you in there?*"

"I killed Riko."

The sentence felt numb in Avery's mouth and Aegis hesitated with his usual snarky reply.

"*That couldn't have been easy. I'm sorry I couldn't help you. If I wasn't stuck as a-*"

"Don't apologize," Avery cut him off as they approached the iron gates of the castle grounds. She didn't want to hear it. Nothing her familiar said could have changed what injustice had been done to her and what she had to do as a consequence.

The Guardsmen that had been posted at the entry were gone, presumably called in to the bloodshed of the dance hall. Moz ran ahead and threw his whole body weight into turning the crank to open the gates. With a cacophonous screeching of grinding metal, the gates slowly pried open.

Not bothering to open the gate all the way, they impatiently slid through the parted bars and sprinted down the cobblestone road toward town.

"Avery, I know it must be hard," Kurosaki shouted from where he ran ahead of her "but you gotta keep it together! Look at all these Leeches!"

He pointed toward a flurry of black orbs bobbing near the front door of a half-timber home, bouncing against the door as they tried to force their way inside. Were they trying to get inside to someone feeling terrible despair? Avery felt the terror erupting through her body, in the beading of her sweaty palms and in her eyes scanning for fledgling demons getting ready to charge her. She knew the fear would lure them in just as much as grief but putting a conscious effort into tamping it down made the fright bubble and bloom.

Moz led them through town, weaving his way through the gaps between shops and taverns as though he had already memorized the route toward the docks from any given point in town. Avery held the gun limp at her side, feeling her own pulse all the way down to the tips of her fingers held around the murder weapon.

From the corner of her vision, Avery saw a flicker of shadows dart on the street. Kurosaki must have seen it as well, for he gently nudged her forward with his shoulder.

"We can't waste time fighting them," he said calmly, "so we just have to give them a wide berth."

She thought of walking back to the castle with him from the graveyard and holding his hand. In the darkness around them, she felt the small and warm glow of gratefulness for Kurosaki.

They stumbled down the steep staircase leading to the docks and Avery feared that she would stumble under the insufficient light from the lanterns on the street above. Humanoid shapes came into view, seeming at first to be Leeches in the fog until Avery caught sight of the flaming ball glowing in the hand of one of them. Cassie.

The faces of their friends came into view as their feet hit the creaking boards of the pier. They were standing in front of several rowboats illuminated by hanging lanterns and Avery was unable to voice her confusion. They were *rowing* to Eyon?

Lily was the first of their friends to catch sight of them and she ran to Avery, clutching her bloodied face between her hands. Jack stood just beyond her friend, looking at Avery with wide eyes of concern.

"What happened to you? Are you okay?" Lily turned Avery's head gently, looking at each side of her face before examining her pupils.

Avery couldn't choke up an answer but was thankful that she didn't burst into tears again.

"The detective is dead," Kurosaki answered for her.

Lily's eyes turned back to Avery's with a look of heavy pity that wounded her.

"We only have a small sliver of time to leave port," Moz changed the subject and Avery was grateful for him too. "Were all of the preparations made?"

He stepped past Shank and Tristan, climbing into the first rowboat and took both oars.

"All that's left to do is row out to th' ship and pull up anchor," Tristan answered as he climbed into a different rowboat, the vessel jostling under his weight. "Get in, kids."

As Rowan and Cassie climbed into Tristan's rowboat, Theirrin stayed on the dock with a watchful frown as she was overseeing everyone else getting into boats. Kurosaki turned towards the exorcist.

"Where's the familiars?"

"Already ferried Ina out. Grim an' Oonlok swam to the tow raft."

Shank helped Maria into the third rowboat before they took both the oars. Lily looked from the boat back to Avery.

"I'll be fine. Go with her," Avery said.

Lily climbed into the boat after Maria before she turned, looking back at Avery with a frown that clearly meant she wasn't sure about leaving her.

Avery climbed into Moz's rowboat, locking her knees in reaction to the swaying of the small vessel on the water. She looked up and held out her uncut hand toward Yumi.

"C'mon, I got you," she assured Yumi with forced bravery and a flat affect.

Yumi hesitated before grabbing Avery's hand, quickly stepping into the boat to keep the rocking as small as she could.

"Well, I'm not going to be the fourth wheel!" Jack teased before climbing into the last rowboat. "Twin and Theirrin!"

Kurosaki groaned as he climbed into the boat after Jack and Theirrin hesitated before being the last to board a rowboat.

Moz reached out a long leg, using his foot to shove off the dock and push the dinghy forward. With the momentum he began to row the oars in deep sweeps and ferried them into the thick marine fog.

The damp air collected on Avery's skin, dripped down her face and carried blood in the droplets. Horrified, Avery tried again to wipe her face of Riko's blood. In the dim light of the lantern hanging on the bow behind her, she looked down at the sleeve of her soiled coat.

"I'm sorry," she apologized in a whisper to Yumi even though Avery's back was to her.

Yumi's fingers curled tenderly around Avery's good shoulder. "Clothes are replaceable, the person inside them is not. I'm glad you're okay."

The thick fog swallowed the lights of the port behind them and muffled the voices of their friends in the boats around them. Jack's laughter came from somewhere out of sight before they fell into silence broken only by the whooshing of water as Moz pulled the oars.

"Why did that woman attack you, Avery?"

"Yumi, I wouldn't," Moz warned.

Avery shook her head, unsure of what she was even to say.

"Unspeakable things, really... I don't want to... I can't deal with this right now."

They rowed the rest of the way without speaking. Yumi gently held Avery's shoulder the whole time, moving only to give occasional rubs of comfort on her sore back before her hand settled again.

Dim lanterns came into view high above their heads and muffled voices leaked through the fog in front of them. They sounded deep and unfamiliar to Avery and she looked to Moz.

"Who's up there?"

"Tristan paid off an entire crew to help us get there. We can't even consider competing against the Legion's fleet unless we had some serious experience."

Moz stopped rowing and the boat bobbed toward the shadow of the three-masted ship that came into view. Avery heard a faint splash and she looked up to the humanoid shadows upon the deck.

"Starboard!"

A man shouted from the deck and Moz swore under his breath, pushing the oars furiously through the water so they could circle the stern to the other side of the anchored ship. Their small vessel nudged against the side of the ship with a jolt and Moz put the oars back into the rig, standing up with fluid ease and grabbing hold of a rope ladder that had been thrown over by the crew.

"Grab hold and climb," Moz said to Avery "I'll hold it steady, you'll be okay."

Avery hesitated before standing up, unsure of her balance as the small boat rocked under her shifting movement. She reached out towards the rope ladder and took it in her hand. The fibers of the rope felt sharp in her already-cut hand and Avery winced before planting her foot on the nearest rung. Moz held the ladder as taut as he could and Avery began to climb.

Halfway to the top, a gust of wind picked up and Avery's muscles locked in fright as the rope swayed in the gale.

"You're almost there, Ave!" Tristan called out from somewhere beneath her, but Avery did not dare turn to look.

When the wind subsided, she scrambled up the ladder as fast as she could until her wet boot slipped on a rung and her body dipped. With her left foot still sturdy on a rung, her hands burned against the strain of the scratching rope and Avery thrashed as she tried to hoist her other foot back to safety. Her fright subsided when she found the purchase of a lower rung of rope beneath her foot and she climbed the remainder of the ladder with stronger caution.

Another burst of fear radiated in her belly when her arms were grabbed by two sets of burly hands. Fingers closed around the wound in her shoulder and she wailed in pain. The hands hoisted her off the ladder and over the rail of the ship. Avery crumpled into a heap on the deck, despite the sailors trying to set her down firmly on her feet, and she looked at the blood seeping even farther down her sleeve.

"What happened to you, Miss?"

"You look like you fought the devil herself!"

Avery didn't answer either of the men and her breath quickened when she realized she was completely encompassed by much bigger bodies than hers. She was in no condition to wield Hemlock and win.

A pair of feet hit the deck behind her and slender arms wrapped around her waist to help lift her upright.

"For god's sake, give her some space," Yumi said, letting go only after Avery had regained her footing.

The rest of their group climbed the ladder and boarded the ship as a sailor climbed down a separate ladder, descending to attach the rowboats to another tow line.

Moz gently put his hands on Avery's shoulders, ducking down so he could speak in a low voice to her.

"You know I don't like telling you what to do and I know you don't like me telling you what to do, but I really think rest is a good idea," he said softly. "We can cover your work getting the ship to Eyon. We really need you to take care of yourself."

Avery blinked at him.

"C'mon, I'll show you where to go," he said as he gently took hold of her hand and turned to lead her towards the door that presumably led to the decks below.

Avery quickly pulled her hand back and out of Moz's grip. He turned around, looking puzzled by her retreat.

"I can't." She shook her head. "Not yet, I have to be certain it's safe."

Moz looked at her, the gaze of his eyes flickering as he examined her face. He paused before he spoke, certainly looking for ways to convince Avery to suck it up and rest.

Instead he said "Okay. I think a lot of us could use some reassurement. Wait here a minute."

He disappeared below deck and left Avery alone until she found Aegis slinking around her boots, his tail swishing.

"What do you suppose he's doing?"

His black tail curled and then unfurled as though it were a feline version of a shrug. *"How should I know? Bone Brain is lucky if he forms any idea at all."*

The door opened again and Moz emerged, holding a cloth bundle in his hands. Whatever was inside the cloth sack clanked with each determined step Moz took towards the center of the deck.

"Gather round," he called out as he carefully set the bundle down, letting the edges of the cloth fall to reveal what had been gathered inside.

On the center of the cloth, Moz placed a metal dish with an incense cone directly in the center. He reached into his coat pocket to extract his matchbook. With a snap, he lit a match to ignite the incense. A swirl of smoke rose from the cone, immediately reaching Avery's nostrils with a strong scent of musty earth.

In his left hand, Moz rang a copper bell thrice.

"Children of the earth have come to honor the gods," he bellowed out, his voice echoing off the thick walls of fog that surrounded their ship.

Avery watched Yumi where she was sitting on the side of the altar cloth opposite from Moz. Her eyes were wide with enchantment and she dipped down in a bow with her forehead nearly pressed to the deck when Moz rang the ceremonial bell.

Moz led a ritual of prayer on the deck, making each rehearsed movement with strong intent. He called out to the sky and Yumi's softer voice lay just under his; she knew the words by heart. The glow of dead sailors gathered around Yumi as she followed Moz with a truly happy grin on her face. Avery wanted to feel their religious joy, but she was just so tired.

Avery sank to the deck, toppling when her legs folded underneath her. Beside her, Rowan ducked and looked at her with dark doe eyes. When he spoke, her ears heard a numb nothing.

The detective is dead.

Suddenly Moz was standing over her as the crowd dispersed. She watched the shadowy shape of him duck down and felt him slip his arm under the crook of her knees. His other arm braced her back as he picked her up and the words he spoke were unintelligible during Avery's state of shock.

The world around her became dim as she was carried into the below decks. Moz turned corner after corner, confusing her sense of direction until he stopped to kick open a door with his foot.

Avery was gently lowered into a canvas hammock; Moz handled her with great care as he draped a wool blanket over her. He was speaking and still she heard the warm mumble of his voice as he crouched low to her, brushing his thumb across her cheek.

Her bones settled into the canvas. She had never felt this tired before. Her eyes fluttered, and then she sank.

CHAPTER EIGHT

JUDGMENT

Moz emerged from the lower decks and stopped in the doorway. Yumi had been leaning ever so slightly over the starboard rails but she turned to watch him when he approached. Her jaw muscles flexed once as she swallowed hard. Moz stood beside her, looking out into the choppy ocean but said nothing.

"What's going to happen to us when they kill the Knights? Are we going to die, too?"

Moz couldn't answer. It was a question he had been actively avoiding in his entire search for Yumi. He feared the thought that he was to die as a consequence of killing his Knight of the sea, but he hadn't given his pipe dream of growing old and frail much thought either.

He looked over at Yumi as she waited for his answer, the wind whipping her long hair as she leaned in closer to urge him to speak. Moz saw not the love of his love, but his sister in shared doom. Whatever happened to him was to befall her as well. He wasn't sure what overcame him to do so, but he gently put a hand on her shoulder.

"I wish I could say."

Yumi didn't shrug him off. She lifted her fingers to touch his and he knew then that she understood him in a way no one else ever could. They stood for a long moment in silence looking out into the nothingness the sea fog. Moz's wet skin and dripping hair felt suitable for his dampened mood.

"We should take it as a lesson," he finally murmured, "to stop living in fear. Especially to stop taking what we have now for granted. To preach it is easy, but to actually do so? That's a different beast entirely."

Yumi said nothing as she searched the emptiness of the marine layer to find whatever had captured his attention. She gently lifted his hand from her shoulder, easing it back down. After a long moment, she spoke again.

"Best we get our affairs in order."

What kind of affairs? When Moz turned towards her, she had vanished.

Avery came back to wakefulness much later than she would have liked. Her stomach turned in the dark cabin when she tried to sit upright and the canvas hammock beneath her swayed. The dense scent of salt and damp that hung below-deck certainly did not help the queasy feeling.

"How are you feeling?"

Avery flinched. She hadn't seen Yumi sitting on a crate beside the support beam at the foot end of her hammock. Avery held her hand to her sternum and steadied her racing heart before she was able to answer.

"I feel like I was hit by a train, Yumes," Avery answered. Instead of acknowledging the raised brow response to the nickname, she continued, "and then hit by a car. And then beat with the Fuck You stick."

Yumi nodded in one slow, singular gesture. Like the therapist in Ardua that Avery had seen only one time and then never returned to. "Sounds serious. Do you think it will help to go stand in the sunshine, can you walk? We've saved you some bread and fruit."

"Yeah, that sounds good, I think."

Avery stood up, having a much easier time with the sway of the hammock now that she was expecting it. Yumi offered her hand when she wasn't sure if Avery was going to be able to walk without falling again. She wasn't, but Avery took it anyway.

"I'm so glad you're okay," Yumi murmured before she kissed Avery's forehead. Avery didn't remember much of what had happened after she climbed the rope ladder onto the ship, but she didn't want to be reminded either.

She followed the Princess through the narrow walkways and halls below deck, feeling awfully grateful that she was with someone who knew where they were going when they turned corner after corner. Yumi led her up creaking steps and into the blinding light of the sun.

Avery held her free arm to shade her eyes when they stepped onto the main deck. When she had finished blinking herself into adjustment, she saw the sailors buzzing about them. Tristan and Shank were helping to pull a line. Moz, Maria, and Lily were huddled around a map laid out on the topside of a barrel and speaking in low voices as they formulated a plan. The teenaged Reapers looked awfully busy doing nothing, milling about until the next adult would tell them what they could be doing instead.

Yumi's fingers slipped from hers and then Avery felt a loaf of bread stuffed into her palm.

"Eat," Yumi commanded. When Avery lowered her arm from her eyes, Yumi forced a metal canteen into that hand as well. "And drink. You'll need it."

Avery hurried to unscrew the cap off the canteen first and she pounded back the water, immediately relieved when her dried throat felt cool again. *Holy shit, when was the last time I drank water?*

"We've got a tail," she heard one of the sailors say to Moz, collapsing the brass spyglass into his hand before offering it up to Moz. He frowned but didn't take it. Moz's narrowed eyes were fixed on the masts of the ship far behind them, a black smudge on the empty midday horizon that Avery struggled to locate as quickly as he had. The sails billowed wide while their own hung limp in the doldrum.

"Peter," Moz cursed the name, turning on his heel as he peeled off his jacket. He stormed towards the stern of the ship and a heavy air of anger swirled around him as he passed Avery.

Avery quickly followed. "Moz! What are we going to do?"

"Peter is using the winds to carry them. But they've forgotten, this is *my* fucking domain."

He stopped at the stern rail, kicking off his taped boots and the thick socks stiff with dried sweat. Moz looked up and past where Avery stood with a scrunched nose.

"Kurosaki, mind the nest."

Avery watched Moz climb the rail, gripping a rope to hold him steady for only a second before he dove into the water. She hurried to the rail's edge, leaning forward to figure out what on earth he had been planning. The water churned and bubbled, but Moz was nowhere to be seen.

"Where the fuck did he go?"

A long moment after she called out, a dark shadow moved just under the surface, spanning far longer than the ship itself. Avery quickly moved away from the rail just as the Knight emerged in an explosion of bones and water. A hard splash of cold seawater seared the deck, drenching Avery and everyone else who had been observing a little too closely.

The sapphire beast began to circle the ship, high above where Kurosaki sat perched in the crow's nest. Droplets of the ocean rained down from the beast and Kurosaki laughed in glee, swinging his legs off the edge of the perch as he looked straight up. His hand was held over his eyes to block the sun and Kurosaki swung himself upright to survey the tailing ship as the Knight of Water circled their own vessel.

Avery watched the Legion ship expectantly as well and she was surprised when she didn't see a rival burst into scales and wings.

"Are they not going to challenge him?" She wondered aloud.

"It's too dangerous," Shank said, and she jumped in surprise at their voice behind her. "They're probably wondering what on earth he's even doing. There's nowhere to spread out supporting troops below - both for them, and for us. Sitting ducks like that, it's not worth the risk. They're calculating what he can really do out here. Will it be a splash of rain, or will the sea swallow their entire ship? Big fuckin' risk, that math."

Excitement pitched in Avery's throat and she gasped. She turned fast towards the Knight circling the air between the two ships, its movement was lazy but cocky. It knew exactly what their advantage was.

She beat on the wooden rail with a flat palm, screaming as loud as she could, "MOZ! YOU CAN FINISH THIS! RIGHT HERE!"

Still the sapphire Knight circled as it assessed their watery battleground with reptilian eyes. Behind the Legion's sails, Peter's winds were carrying in a wall of fog that emerged as quickly as the Knight of Water did.

The water between the vessels began to churn, the gentle caps rolling faster as they turned white with foam. Avery slapped her hand wildly on the rail.

"MOZ! MOZ! SINK THE SHIP!"

Choppy water began to rise to waves, their curls and crashes beating upon the Legion vessel. Avery watched as the ship rose with the swelling water and bobbed back down with great swaying before the next wave beat against the bow. Her heart was racing as she watched the ship struggle - *will she capsize?*

The progress the ship had been making with Peter's winds at her back was beginning to subside, all while the ship Avery stood upon was sailing in near perfect waters. Distance between the two ships began to grow wider as they were gliding faster while the Legion was hindered by thundering walls of water.

Avery stopped her wild fanfare long enough to look down into the water below the stern and notice that the water swirled and churned differently along the curve of their ship. The current was carrying them!

Soon they were sailing through calm waters under a sunny sky, the storm that the Knight created for the Legion was only a thumbprint on the horizon. The beast flew in a glide down into the water of the starboard side. Kurosaki finished his descent from the crow's nest, hitting the deck with his heavy boots.

"Toss him a rope!"

The Knight had disappeared into the water in a storm of bubbles and foam, but a drenched Moz surfaced with a heaving gasp for air. One of the crew members tossed a mooring rope over the rail and men huddled along it to begin hoisting Moz up.

Moz climbed up over the rail and collapsed onto the deck, gasping for air and drenched to the bone. Avery pushed her way through the men, holding him by the arm to help him sit upright.

"Moz! What became of the ship?"

As he tried wringing out his soaked shirt, he took labored breaths. Water dripped off the tip of his nose as he looked up at her.

"Slowed…down," he said between the heaves meant to force salty water out of his lungs. "Even though… this is my element… I can still…. only do… so much."

A sharp pang of guilt hit Avery and she frowned. She hoped he hadn't heard her while she was screaming; she didn't realize she was pinning all stakes on Moz. That certainly wasn't fair of her.

"Moz, you did amazing," she praised him and pushed some of the wet hair away from his face so she could plant a proud kiss on his forehead. "Stay put, I'm going to find something to dry you off with."

$$-\text{✼}-$$

From the thick blanket of fog settled around the hermit island of Eyon, the tops of skyscrapers crept up from the horizon like hands held to the heavens in solemn prayer.

"What strange towers," Yumi muttered beside Avery as they watched from the portside rail of the ship, heads leaning over to get a clear view. Or as clear of a view they could possibly get in the milky air.

"Gather round!" Moz shouted from the center of the ship, holding a parchment roll in his hand.

As the Reapers formed a circle around him, he squatted down onto the balls of his feet and unrolled the parchment onto the deck to reveal a map. Drawn out in blurry black ink was a jagged circle, a moon-shaped bay cut out in its northern shores. Moz pointed a tattooed finger, 'E', towards the middle of the crescent shore.

"We land here," he said. "Inland about half a mile is where the city becomes dense. This spot right here to the east is the Temple of Neri. Before this is a gate and a wooded area, blocking off civilians from the temple and sacrifice pit. We need to get this open in the shortest time possible from the moment our boots hit sand."

"How do we get it open? If they won't even let civilians in, I doubt we'll be able to walk in," Maria said.

"We bring Lily there and we force it open."

"No pressure or anything," Lily snorted and Avery felt her unease. She put a hand on her sister's shoulder before reassuring her:

"What we can't open with mind, we'll break down with force."

Moz nodded in agreement without looking up from the map.

"I reckon we've got 'bout an hour before we can get the skiffs on the shore," Tristan said from where he hovered over Moz, his big fists held on his hips as he looked with squinted eyes from the map towards the towering shadows of Eyon.

Shank was the first to break from Moz's huddle and snap into action. "Look alive then, yeah?" They held up a hand with thick rows of woven bracelets to wave everyone to follow their lead. "Load up. Only what we need and nothing more."

Soon again they were rocking about in small dinghies on a sloshing and foaming sea. The crew carried them to the shoreline with deep strokes of the oars. When the hull of the rowboats hit the pebbly surface of the beach, everyone but the crew hurried out with the crunch of small stones under their boots.

"Follow that footpath up," one of the sailors instructed them. "It's just a quick hike through some brush before you hit the first street downtown."

The Reapers thanked the sailors before they trudged their way uphill. Small beach stones became bigger and sharper under Avery's feet the farther they got from the erosive power of the crashing waves. Tall sea grasses and brush rose all around them as she followed Shank in front of her, winding left and right to keep to the flow of the path. Before she could register the change in terrain, she was standing on smooth concrete. Flat pavement felt alien underneath her after so many days outside of the steel and concrete hotbox that sat within the Ardua walls.

Avery looked up in wonder and she tried to find the tops of the skyscrapers from where she stood so small on the pavement. Countless balconies wrapped around them and stretched in open bridges that crisscrossed high above the streets. She watched people travel the high veins of the city and the black clouds that buzzed around their heads. Avery gawked in amazement; she had never seen so many Reapers in one place.

"Follow me close and don't wander off," Kurosaki called out from the head of their group as he took the lead.

They followed Kurosaki through streets much wider than what she had become accustomed to in Brightloch. Their two-by-two lines were quiet as they each focused on the sights and sounds of the city to separate commonplace from potential threat. Nobody spoke and it seemed that Avery wasn't the only one slightly frightened by the strangeness of the island.

"Izaya!"

Kurosaki froze at the head of the group. He looked at the group of young men approaching them from the side street nearest them. Black clouds swarmed around their faces; more Reapers.

"Izaya. Where is Alice?"

Oh no. The fog faded and it was the young man at their forefront who looked at Kurosaki expectantly. His wavy hair was dyed a deep maroon that was shorn short along the sides of his head and opaque, black sunglasses sat over his eyes in round discs that didn't quite look right on such a square face.

Kurosaki turned his head, spitting tobacco-stained fluid onto the pavement. He looked down at the ground in front of him and then up at the maroon-haired man. The smile on his face was exasperated, tired of answering to the same grief in every encounter Kurosaki had.

"She's dead, Todd," he said flatly. "And where were you? Holed up a-"

Kurosaki was cut off by a blow to the mouth. He rocked backwards with a bleeding lip before lunging hands-first at Todd. The other men began to swarm around the fighting Reapers, and Moz dove in, swinging fists and yanking Todd by the collar of his black leather jacket to pry him away from Kurosaki. Todd turned and threw a punch hard into Moz's shoulder to free himself from the grip.

"*You* again? Will I ever be fucking rid of you," Todd snapped at Moz when he had been pushed farther away from Kurosaki.

Avery jumped into the scuffle, kicking one of the young men hard in the hip and sending him crashing into the ground. She planted a boot on his ribcage, her handgun aimed into his forehead.

"Damnit, Avery! Don't be fucking foolish!"

Avery looked up when Kurosaki scolded her, only to find four more guns pointed at her. Todd, unarmed, only laughed.

"You gave this idiot her gun? Izaya, I knew you were a goddamn bastard, but this is just fuckin' unbelievable."

Kurosaki was breathing hard, spraying beads of blood with every exhale. He held a hard gaze at Todd. Avery didn't know a single thing about any of these Reapers, but she detected the heaviness of the silence.

"Todd, we need some bikes." Kurosaki's voice had softened. She had never heard the jagged edges of his voice so soothing and low.

The man pulled the sunglasses off his eyes, folding them patiently and hooking them on the collar of the white shirt that peeked out from under his zipped coat. He looked back up at Kurosaki with chestnut brown eyes.

Avery was confused by the turn this exchange had taken and she turned to Kurosaki. For the first time ever, she read nervousness on his face. She took her foot off the man on the ground beneath her, letting him go.

"Where are we going?"

As Todd spoke behind her, Avery watched Kurosaki's face light up in a grin that she had only seen once or twice before. Moz was wiping the splattered blood off the side of his own cheek when he answered in place of Kurosaki.

"The consecrated grounds. The Beldam's Legion is not far behind us."

Todd looked from Moz back to Kurosaki before nodding his head.

"We deal with this now. And then you'll take us to Alice later. Did you bury her?"

Kurosaki nodded and Todd exhaled sharply, running a flat palm down his face before shaking his head. Avery caught a glimpse of glassiness in his eyes as he looked away.

"Damnit, 'Zaya. That's my sister…"

Nobody spoke until Todd wiped his eyes and looked back at them. "C'mon, follow me to the garage."

Todd waved his hand for everyone to follow and Avery hurried to walk beside Moz.

Under her breath she hissed, "please tell me you are able to explain what just happened."

"Alice's older brother, two years difference. One of the only two instances I know of both siblings becoming Reapers. Gang leader. He and Kurosaki have a *thing.*" The last word held an audible bite of displeasure.

"But I thought he and Alice were?"

Moz shook his head with barely detectable movement. "One-sided. Kurosaki has loved him for years. He asked both of them to come with him. Only she came. Todd and Kurosaki are twisted and complicated, with Kurosaki distracting himself with other people along the way, but it's a thing nonetheless."

"What other people?"

"Well, me, for one."

"*Oh*," Avery answered softly and wasn't sure what else could have been said. So she followed in silence until they reached a squat building with a rippled metal door.

Todd knelt, grabbed a handle on the bottom of the garage door and yanked it open with a hard shove. The boy with the blonde hair that Avery had jammed her gun into helped Todd lift the door high enough to pass through, turning on the fluorescent lights inside. The lights buzzed, flickering before stabilizing and casting an assortment of motorcycles in a cold glow.

Todd looked back at Kurosaki with a half-smirk, "will these cut it for ya?"

Kurosaki had a wild grin on his face as he threw his arms up and went inside the garage to inspect the vehicles. "This is more than I could have hoped for!"

Kurosaki turned around, looking back to his group. "How many of you know how to ride? I'm already counting Moz and Tristan."

Avery reminded herself that this wasn't the time to laugh about the time Moz had struggled to drive an automatic transmission in Ardua.

"Me and Lily do," she instead volunteered. Lily's brother only had a dirt bike for a single summer before having a son and selling the bike, but it was enough to have it figured out when Byron let Avery and Lily zip around the streets with every method of protection available apart from fifteen layers of tightly wound bubble wrap.

Jack threw up his hand and waved it wildly in the air. "Ooh, because Moz knows, I know too!"

Kurosaki nodded. "Great. Pair off with someone who doesn't."

Within seconds, the group had formed pairs: Tristan with Shank, Moz with Theirrin, Jack with Rowan, Lily with Maria, Kurosaki with Cassie, and Avery with Yumi.

"Right," Todd said and pointed towards a shelf in the back of the garage. "Nobody's going anywhere without a helmet. I won't be responsible for cleaning up any road spatter. Casper, go jump on the radio and rally up any Reaper you can. These guys are gonna need help and we take care of our own."

The blonde boy ran to the back of the garage and disappeared through a door with a newspaper covered window.

"What do you think the best way to the grounds would be from here?" Kurosaki asked.

"North end of main strip. Left at 36th, right at 44th," Todd answered without missing a beat. "We'll round up Grims and anyone else we can think of and meet you there. Don't want to draw too much attention to you and risk getting picked off by heat. Stagger your bikes."

"Consider it done," Kurosaki turned his attention from Todd to Avery and the others. "Gear up and get out, we need all the time we can get."

After they had all found fitting helmets, Avery's eyes scanned the rows of motorcycles to find the one that suited her short frame best. Her attention locked onto a beautiful dual sport in a candied cherry red. A little different from the dirt bike she zipped around the streets on when Byron would let her and Lily try, but it would fit both of them and it looked far too attractive for her to pass up.

Avery found Yumi wandering the rows, looking a little lost as she searched the bikes. When she had the princess's attention, she waved her over. She didn't need to see Yumi's face behind the tinted face shield to notice her body freeze in terror.

"Oh gods."

When the bikes were roaring on the pavement it took quite a bit of convincing to coax Yumi into getting on the seat behind Avery. She finally did and locked her arms under Avery's ribs in a near-choking grip. Hopefully, it would be a quick ride because she was unsure of how long she could bear the tightness.

Yumi yelped when their bike jolted a few times as Avery was getting back into the rhythm, but soon they caught up to the rest of their friends with ease. Kurosaki and Cassie led the group, following the directions that Todd had recited. Though her careful focus was on the road ahead, Avery caught glimpses of people on the sidewalks stopping to watch the thundering procession of engines and she was again very aware of how little she knew of what she was doing. Bases of skyscrapers passed in a blur as they thundered by, their structures swallowed up by the fog that had devoured the sun.

They came to a gate that struck Avery as eerily similar to the one that stood at the base of Credence Lot where Alice was buried. But something seemed wrong when Kurosaki sped up faster to the sidewalk before it, turned off the engine and kicked down the stand. He didn't bother to take off his helmet before he rushed up to the wrought iron gate.

"Fuck!" He screamed in frustration.

Avery took off her helmet as Yumi scrambled to get off the bike and onto pavement as fast as she could. Walking to meet Kurosaki, she immediately understood the need for profanity.

They stared at the broken gate left in a mess of twisted metal and powdered explosive residue. The padlock still on one of the doors was left untouched. Bikes rumbled behind them as Todd's first wave of reinforcements arrived.

Panic welled in Avery's mouth and she felt a sick acidity bubble in her throat, but she willed herself not to vomit. Her heartbeat raced and she looked back at Moz behind her, desperately wishing he had the perfect solution. Instead, she found him with both his hands atop his head as he looked at the scene. Even he was dumbfounded and said nothing, his mouth agape in shock as he tried to calculate why.

"There's a couple of options here," it wasn't Moz who spoke, but the familiar voice woven of velveteen and whiskey. Avery turned back around to face the broken gate, where Balthazar stood and rubbed the patch of beard on his chin.

"Either Morgana had recruits planted on the island already," he continued, "or someone else we had not yet factored in yet wants their cut of the immortality pie."

Avery's eyes widened; both options were awful. One meant Morgana had been a step ahead the entire time and could have more tricks up her sleeve; the other meant they had been fighting with their backs turned to an enemy the entire time.

Balthazar turned around and the Demon of the Crossroads smiled devilishly. "Ah, but I have a plan. We lay a trap and cut this monster off at the head."

Morgana watched the handoff from her hiding spot. The Demon of the Crossroads held the familiar, thick tome in his gilded hands before Avery Porter took it from him, placing it gingerly in her knapsack: Mona's spellbook. The Berserker Witch then followed Balthazar into the darkened temple of Neri's Oracles. She furrowed her brow. *What were they doing?*

She raised herself slightly from her crouched position, moving light on her toes through the dense ferns. With a hurrying pace she approached the side of the Temple of Neri opposite the one her opponents had just entered. She had to retrieve the spellbook and kill the witch if she was going to prevent the exorcism of the Knights. It was Avery's skin or her own in the eyes of the Beldam.

The rear portico of the temple was darkened by columns, holding up a pediment adorned with low relief sculptures of holy bodies. Morgana glanced up but didn't pause as she passed beneath the images with determination bubbling in her belly. She knew it had to end here. For her daughter.

Morgana stepped into the darkness of the temple and froze, waiting for her eyes to adjust to the red cast of light that allowed her to see the faint outlines of black scrying mirrors. She looked up at the dim tubes of red neon that seemed terribly out of place for a temple. Her mouth twisted into a scowl.

"Fucking Eyon," she mouthed to only herself. She hated the hermit island and everything on it.

When Morgana was confident in her regained vision, she began slowly weaving through the narrow walkways made by the tall mirrors. Reflections of her red hair danced around her from every angle and she was even more luminescent under the bizarre light. Her handgun was raised in front of her and the muzzle butted into glass on more than one occasion when she mistook a black mirror for a pathway.

A hushed whisper floated from somewhere within the labyrinth of mirrors and Morgana stopped, listening for it again. In the corner of her vision, a shadow darted across the mirror at her right shoulder and Morgana spun around.

"One, two, three
Think you'll best me?
One, two, three
But it's better if you flee."

The witch's voice floated around her with the haunting tune of a siren. How appropriate that she had managed to lure in the Knight of the Sea - Morgana's oldest and dumbest brother. She scoured the reflections for her enemy and found only darkness and the reflection of a desperate mother. If she had been willing to kill her own husband to solidify Sera's place in the world free from death, why would anyone else dare to stand in her way?

> *"One, two, three*
> *Devils whistle through your teeth*
> *One, two, three*
> *And she plants the hangman's tree."*

Movement flashed fast and her heart lurched. The face of the witch stared at Morgana from every direction but none of them gave away which one belonged to the real Avery Porter. The younger woman's square chin was tucked down, her eyes looking sinister under thick eyebrows; her face was still freckled with the blood of Riko Yamada.

Morgana spun in each direction, dizzying quickly under the neon that cast the house of mirrors in blood red. It was then that she noticed the handgun in the Berserker Witch's hand, held limp at her side as though Morgana was not even a threat to her. She felt rage building up around her bones, bolstering her strength. There was only one beast in the hall of mirrors and it certainly wasn't the Berserker Witch.

"You're the biggest fucking hypocrite I've met," Morgana shouted, her voice bouncing off the mirrors closest to her to swallow her in an echo chamber of her own fury. "You fight, and you kill, and you try your damnedest to keep the dead from walking the earth. And look how you use Paion's sword! Do you even know what you are?"

Freezing air swirled around her and Avery disappeared from the mirrors.

"*I'm the boogieman*," the witch hissed next to her ear before Morgana's eardrums split with the crack of a gunshot and a sharp rain of shattered glass.

— ❦ —

The wrong Morgana. Avery had shot at the wrong Morgana.

She sprinted out of the temple, holding a hand to her bleeding cheek. Luckily, she was able to pluck out the bits of shattered mirror that had cut both the Legion captain and herself. But Avery wasn't foolish; she had fled after her location was given away by the gunfire. Balthazar's plan to trick and injure Morgana to buy more time would have worked if it were easier to pick out the real one from the crowd of reflections. *What a stupid fucking plan.*

Avery looked over her shoulder to make sure she wasn't followed as she ran back to the meetup point. No one else had emerged from the small temple as far as she could tell. She looked ahead and kept sprinting with the weight of Mona's grimoire in her rucksack slapping hard against her back. Though irritating to run with, it was comforting to have back in her possession. She wasn't sure how she would use it if she needed to, but she knew Tristan or one of the others would know. A dark shape slunk next to her and ran at a darting pace.

"Did you get her?"

Avery scowled, frustrated even more by Aegis' question.

"No, I missed! Did he really think this would fucking work?"

Her breathing labored and heaved as she ran hard back toward the dirt trail where she had left the rest of the Reapers. The isolated Temple of Neri didn't feel far from the path to the sacrificial site, but the thought of being chased made the distance stretch further in Avery's mind than it truly was.

What felt like hours later, she saw the subtle flashing of Shank's reflective beacon from the thick underbrush. Avery ducked and slid onto her side, skidding across the damp grass and into the bushes that enveloped Shank and Kurosaki in camouflage.

"What happened?" Shank whispered as they put the contraption of mirrors and a lightbulb back into their rucksack.

"I almost... had her," Avery explained between gasped breaths. "I don't know why Balthazar... thought shooting in a hall of mirrors was a... great idea."

She gulped in a big breath of air and steadied herself until she could speak normally again. "It gave away my location immediately when I shot a mirror. I was damn sure I had her, too. She didn't chase me, so I think she's counting on us meeting her at the pit."

"Don't worry about it," Kurosaki reassured her. "That would have been a difficult hit for anyone. Let's go meet up with the others."

Kurosaki stood up first, offering his hand to help Avery upright. The trio moved in silence, scanning the brush around them for any signs of danger as they made their way to close the rest of the distance to the trail. With every step they took towards the sacrificial pit, the dread in Avery's feet grew heavier and heavier.

This was it. They could all die. Some of them probably would die and Avery could barely even remember who had told Moz and Tristan that this is what they must do. Guilt mixed into the flurry of anger and fear when she remembered that it was the High Priestess of Centralia and that the Knight of Earth had already killed her. *Who else would have to die?*

Avery was nearing another panic attack when she saw Ina's form of midnight fur emerge from the brush. Hushed voices floated from behind the wolf familiar as the rest of their small faction of Reapers followed.

Moz locked eyes with her first and instantly his expression changed to a concerned frown when he recognized that something was wrong. He closed the distance between them quickly in long strides.

"Fuck, are you okay?" Moz gently turned her cheek with fingers under her chin as he examined the last ribbons of blood. With his other hand he brushed remaining shards of glass from her navy coat that she had missed.

"Moz, I need to tell you something," Avery said breathlessly.

Like the last time she confessed to him, he watched her with waiting eyes to let her know that he was focused on her every word. This felt right. Whatever happened to them now, she was terrified and she needed him to know.

Should there have been a lead-up? Should she talk about all the ways her feelings had changed since she had first pointed a chef's knife at him in her apartment kitchen? So many things had happened and certainly she needed some kind of preface to how they had gotten there or a full disclosure that she had once hated him. But then the words found a life of their own and wrestled free:

"Moz, I love you."

His face lit up like the warmest sunrise over the ocean. He dropped his consecrated sword onto the ground in an unusual carelessness for the prized object. Strong arms wrapped around her waist in a rushing embrace and the ground disappeared from under her feet. Moz held her up to him and the happiness that radiated from him was infectious. His face was buried into the side of her neck with how she was lifted above his head and Avery wrapped her arms around his neck - equally out of joy and not wanting to be dropped.

Moz pulled his head away from her neck to look up at her. A glassy film had developed over his eyes like he might have cried but the tears never came.

"I love you too, Avery," he echoed and an immense wave of relief washed over her. She finally had said it. He didn't take it back, either. "You ran to me that day and I have loved you ever since."

Her feet found the ground again as he set her down and as Moz held her face in both of his hands, he kissed her with warmth. Avery's heart swelled and bloomed even after he parted from her lips and pressed his forehead to hers.

"When this is over, we're going to go on a date, okay?" He said. "Anywhere you want to go at all. You want to see a movie in Ardua? You got it. You want steaks in Bright-loch? Done deal. We're going to be fine."

Avery nodded and suddenly she was the one who had tears rolling down her cheeks. "Yeah, I'd like that," her voice was soft and broken. She wanted nothing more than to believe him.

Moz smiled and closed his eyes, still cradling her face in his sure hands. The smile spread to her own mouth and Avery closed her eyes as well, blocking out any part of the world that wasn't Moz holding his forehead to hers.

Then the hollering began.

"FINALLY!" Jack shouted, clapping his hands over his head.

Moz let go of her face when Avery turned to see their friends. Jack was still clapping quite a bit too enthusiastically and Maria was clutching Lily's arm with a face usually reserved for gushing over a small puppy. Her gaze then trailed to Yumi's beautiful face, watching with the corners of her soft mouth turned up in a smile and her arms folded in regal satisfaction. When their eyes met, Yumi's smile lifted more and she gave a knowing nod in Avery's direction. When this battle was over, their time too would come.

She just had to make sure they got there in one piece.

CHAPTER NINE

FOR ALICE

A very looked out on the field. The shadowy forms of the stone circle loomed at a distance but made her dread heavier in the bottom of her stomach. They had arrived at the sacrificial pit. Avery knew that her chances of dying in a gruesome battle suddenly sky-rocketed and that though she was lucky enough to have survived the arrow wound, she doubted Onja would grace her with victory again.

As the band of Reapers slowly approached the pit, the archers pivoted their aim all around them. None of them truly believed that they were the only ones to have arrived at the sacred grounds as they scoured the undergrowth of the forest for any trace of the rest of the Legion. Something was wrong.

Avery nervously twisted Hemlock in her grip as she carefully stepped up the sarsen stairs. Inching slowly, she leaned forward to look over the edge of the sacrificial pit. Crumbles of stone broke away from the edge and dropped into the chasm, tumbling into infinity. The overcast sky shone no light down into the pit where impenetrable darkness lived. She crept backwards to safety, careful not to disturb any more stone and lose her footing. When she turned, she found Moz had been peering into the pit as well. He let out a long, low whistle.

"Shit, make sure your shoelaces are tied."

He turned back to the rest of the group, headed by Yumi and Tristan as the range shooters continued to scan their surroundings.

"Yumi and Kurosaki will be the ones to draw the blood and follow the ritual," Moz instructed. "I don't want her in any position where the Knight could break out. Kurosaki, you're our only choice for Saved blood because I can't do it. I'll be a little wrapped up with the other Knights. Tristan, you conduct the ritual for them and provide additional cover. Avery, have you already handed off the book?"

Tristan patted the book in his rucksack dutifully.

"Good. When the exorcism ritual gets going, we need to push them all towards the cliffside and cut off any pathways to-"

"Time's up!"

Shank cut Moz off and Avery's head whipped up to look to the trees. A mass of charcoal uniforms and men in plainclothes emerged under buzzing clouds of black. Coyote familiars snarled at their feet and birds of prey shrieked from the treetops as they flew towards the pit with full fury.

"TRISTAN, GO!"

At Moz's urgent shout, Tristan grabbed an arm from both Yumi and Kurosaki and dragged them to the pit.

"Don't let anything happen to her!" Avery cried out.

Moz clapped a hand on her shoulder. "She's going to be fine when you've got her back."

Avery nodded. She patted the bulky outline of the gun on her hip to reassure herself it was still there.

She slashed Hemlock across her left palm, crimson beads of her blood glittering down until it pooled on the hilt. The sword's golden eye blinked to life as the spirits rose from underground underneath her. Avery's blood went cold when she saw the sheer number of spirits who had been lingering around the sacrificial pit.

"You're going to be unstoppable here," Moz murmured. "I believe in you."

Avery nodded and for a moment she worried that he may have misplaced his belief. She watched as he stepped towards the approaching Legion, swinging his blessed sword around in his hand like a toy.

"Come any closer and all who wear the Legion colors will die!" He called out with a puffed chest, arrogant and proud.

None of their horses nor their men hesitated. Instead of raising his sword, he sheathed it. He turned around with one more look at Avery before he said, "don't forget our panic switch: if the ritual cannot be completed, one of the Knights must die. Even if it's me."

Moz exploded into sapphire sinews and bone while dread came over Avery in a heavy wash. The Knight of Water flapped its wings hard, and the Legion fighters hesitated when the beast stood tall on its rear legs, defensive in front of Avery and the others. Avery didn't want to think about whether any of her friends had it in them to kill Moz or Yumi if the ritual failed. She knew she didn't.

"Alright, you ready Cassie?"

Lily called out to the younger girl as she soaked her gold knives in alcohol.

"You got it, Coach!"

Lily carelessly tossed the bottle aside before gathering all the knives into one hand. She threw them upwards into the sky, holding her hands upright as they froze midair. One by one, the gold knives caught fire.

"Let's light 'em up!"

Lily turned her focus towards the Legion soldiers and the flaming projectiles cut through the air like deadly comets. The knives whizzed past Avery's shoulders and beyond the Knight before the onslaught punctured Legions shoulders and ribs. What missed the riders hit the horses, forcing the officers to dismount to stop the fire from spreading.

Behind Avery, Tristan began to recite the ritual.

"I beseech Ara, the Mother of All - hear our cry!
I beseech Yve, the Womb of thy World - hear our cry!
I beseech Mona, the Hands of Her Heart - hear our cry!"

Tristan's voice was shaken and breaking; the sheer power of the ritual the exorcist was performing clearly overwhelmed him. Avery didn't know what true prayer was but she found herself asking whoever was listening to grant his words power. The leaves in the trees swirled, heard only for just a moment just beneath the rumbling rolls of thunder. *Malo?*

Rain began to drizzle as the Knight of Water took off and circled over their heads, daring the Legion to strike first. Daring Peter and Morgana to play his game. For Sera to pay for what she had done to the Priestess.

"Protect your Children from this scorching of your fruits!" Tristan carried on as the wind picked up and whipped his ale-blonde hair.

Avery turned to Kurosaki and Yumi on the opposite side of the pit from him, holding their hands clasped together in tight desperation. She saw the pale glaze of fear on both the Knight and the Saved Reaper.

"Seal away forever the demigods of destruction, the demons birthed from the womb of the Beldam, Mistress of Od! Seal away forever the titans of war, forced by the hand of Paion, King of Unrest!"

"I can't, I can't," Yumi stammered as her nose began dripping fast with blood. "I tried and I can feel it -"

"Yumi, Yumi you have to," Kurosaki tried to soothe Yumi as she stepped backwards away from the pit, wriggling her fingers free from his grip of silver rings.

Avery heard the first heavy footsteps of a Legion officer approaching her. She turned her attention back forward and hit his sword with her own and a gratifying metallic clang rattled through the electrified air.

"Yumi, you have to keep going!" She shouted as loudly as she could manage over the clashes of swords.

The ground beneath Avery's feet rumbled and she staggered, spreading her stance to keep herself upright as best she could. The Legion officer before her shrank away out of Avery's swinging range so that he could frantically look about, trying to find out what was happening to the earth beneath him. He stumbled, hitting the ground and the sword he held clattered out of his hands when he lost full balance. With a sudden advantage and a sweep of her arms, Avery brought Hemlock down upon his neck and she wobbled at the knees with the earthquake.

The dirt began to stir in patches across the field, bubbling and churning underneath her dark revenants. Small tree roots emerged from the dark soil and began to stir and stretch to the heavens. *No* - Avery's eyes widened with terror when she realized they were not roots, but bones.

Fingers sprouted from the ground, reaching blindly for the mist of Avery's revenants. Skeletal bodies heaved themselves to the surface by the dozens, gripping the revenants and pulling them inside what little form they had left to their bodies.

Inside their splintered rib cages, the darkened clouds of spirit stirred like a spitting swarm of hornets before the bodies swept into quick motion fully upright. The bones and the revenants were becoming one. Avery knew of only one cataclysmic event that could have raised not just the spirits of the dead but what remained of their bodies as well.

She turned towards the sacrificial pit where she saw Yumi's bloodied face from the nostrils down. Her eyes were a ghostly white, illuminating her delicate features in a haunting halo.

"Avery, you are the oil to my flame. Take them and go," Yumi spoke, the only sound on the battlefield as she watched Avery with glowing eyes. *"The levee has finally broken, and you must cut down the Legion in waves, for you have finally reached your peak of justified violence."*

Yumi's bones violently snapped and she shrunk inward, white smoke clouding fast around her as she exploded into scales. The serpentine monster roared an atomic shrill cry and the force of the explosion crumbled the columns around the sacrificial pit, forcing Tristan and Kurosaki to retreat. Avery watched in frozen terror as the opalescent Knight of Spirit launched into the sky.

"We failed," she murmured.

All those blistering hot days trekking on foot. All the monstrous horrors they had witnessed along the way. All the death, all the murder - all for nothing. The Knight was here and there was no putting it back inside the beautiful body it called its host.

Her heart raced, remembering Moz's Panic Switch Plan. One of the Knights had to die for the Beldam's force to be broken - and she had to make sure it wouldn't be Moz or Yumi.

"Alright, three out of five odds isn't bad," Avery finished the thought to herself out loud. She held up Hemlock, ready to strike the Legion officer on horseback running full speed at her.

"Batter up, boys!"

Her revenants, now encased in skeletons from the earth beneath her feet, swarmed the horse. Their bony hands closed around the ankles of the officer and yanked him hard to the ground. He struggled to right himself and the skeleton-cased-revenants shrunk away as Avery leapt upon him, Hemlock plunging into his torso.

Hemlock's golden eye widened and the blood it received made the air around Avery thrum with energy as the dead sought out their next victim.

Look how you use Paion's sword.

Morgana's accusations from the neon labyrinth inside the Temple of Neri surfaced in her racing mind and Avery gave them pause. She watched the skeletons - people she and Yumi had reanimated together and now had acting under her will.

She couldn't move her feet. Her arms were frozen at her side, even as she watched the Legion forces choke tighter and tighter around their small faction of Reapers.

How am I different from the Beldam?

How was she a good person if she even had to ask herself that? How was she supposed to stop evil if she embodied it? How could she-

"My own fledglings so dare turn against me?"

The air went still and Avery's blood froze in her veins. She recognized the voice as old as Death, the very one that each Reaper had heard in the square at Brightloch. Avery turned her head to look at the figure standing before the Legion across from her.

They stood only just taller than Avery herself - before accounting for the twisting black horns that looped atop knotted black hair. Their skin was the grey of a crumbling slate headstone, eyelids sewn shut with coarse black thread and serpentine nostrils flared where a nose may have been. They were adorned with black robes and the matted fur pelts of wolves and bears. In the grip of long, black tipped fingers was a staff of wood, topped with a yellowing human skull.

Avery's skull vibrated and nausea overcame her as the figure spoke again.

"I birthed you from my own womb of nightshade, and you dare defy me?"

Their mouth was overcrowded with fangs stained black. Avery's stomach sank when she realized who had graced them in the rotting flesh.

Beldam turned towards her terrible Knight of Water circling in the sky above her horned head.

"Many chances I granted you, my eldest Son. But now you must see suffering and recompense for your defiance. You will die an eternity over."

Beldam planted her staff in the blackened earth that withered beneath the skin of her bare feet, lifting her clawed hand in the direction of the sapphire Knight. As she flexed her bulbous knuckles, the beast suddenly hurtled towards the earth and slammed with a hard impact that shook the ground beneath Avery. The Knight shrieked and writhed on the ground under Beldam's psychic grip.

"NO!" Avery cried out, breaking into a sprint towards Beldam to break whatever control she had on Moz. The Goddess of Death turned her stitched eyes to Avery and she saw the draped limb turn in her direction.

A flashing wall of movement cut Avery off with an impenetrable boundary of fluttering and chirping. She took a step backwards and saw that she had been blocked off by a dense stream of sparrows, forming a living wall between her and Beldam. Avery turned towards the forest where the swarm of birds had shot from, where the strange and beautiful figures emerged.

The towering woman wore a dress of red feathers that matched the tall crown sitting atop her thick locks of black hair. Feathers of garnet stemmed from her skin, glimmering like jewels cast in bronze. Her hand was held open, large and strong as it directed the moving wall of birds to come between Avery and the goddess of death.

Avery's confusion was replaced with shock when she saw that the woman was flanked by Balthazar and another woman - this one wore a crown of flowers in her thick halo of curls and was very pregnant under her lilac gown.

"Azura, hold fast for Onja to strike," the woman with the flowers commanded, and the feathered woman nodded.

Azura? Onja? Avery felt herself go woozy. Those were *goddesses.*

The Goddess of Birds nodded and the wall of sparrows grew denser, refusing to let Avery through. Beside her, the pregnant Goddess regarded Avery with a tiny shrug.

"Sorry my Daughter, but you're not getting to this one."

That must have been Mona.

"Avery!"

She looked over her shoulder enough to see Shank behind her, their frantic gaze shifted from the officer falling at their feet to the crumpled heap of sapphire where the Knight of Water had crashed.

"You gotta go!" they shouted, "I got your back!"

They held their ready bow, powerful and elegant as they scanned the battlefield beyond Avery. Between heaving breaths, Avery smiled at them and turned to run. Behind her, she heard Shank call to the sky:

"*I call upon my Father, Malo of the Wood!*"

As Avery sprinted towards the Knight of Water, her eyes widened at their words before the sound disappeared under the rumbling of the earth; "you *what*, now?!"

Beneath her feet, the soil split and rose in chunks as the tree roots deep under the surface writhed. Both Avery and her skeletons were lifted in the air, she dropped Hemlock and fumbled quickly to get it back in her palms before it could disappear into the dirt. With her tightened grip she turned to look over her shoulder.

Malo had returned. The tree roots swirled behind Shank to give the god His form, towering high over the heads of the Reapers and the other gods. His head, a ten-point stag skull, materialized from the thick vines forming His body. Malo held His hands of branches above Shank's head, as though the god were to use them as His marionette and chills ran down Avery's spine.

"Avery, I said *go!*" Shank shouted again. Their voice held an eerie tone lying just beneath the surface.

Avery nodded, knowing she should not make them repeat themself a third time. She began to run to the sapphire Knight across the field from her, where its big belly heaved to try and recoup from the choking grip of Beldam's influence.

The sky above her illuminated with cracks of lightning that cast the shadows of two serpents in the sky clashing, disappearing before their shrill roars reached them on the ground. As she ran, determined to reach the Knight of

Water, she evaded Legion swords in dodges and desperate dives. She didn't have time to get into a scuffle, Moz needed her *now*.

She didn't see the coyote familiar coming from her left before it knocked her feet out from under her. Saliva sprayed as the animal gnashed its teeth into her leg, breaking through both her pants and her skin with sharp pain. Avery shrieked as she fought to kick the demon off with her other leg.

The small beast wriggled out of her short kicking range, ducking and lunging again. She was pinned down by her leg where the coyote lay claim to her, and she rolled her torso as far away from its mouth as she could. With her right arm, she swung Hemlock as hard as she could but could not land her strike. She screamed again with the coyote pressed down on her gushing wound with a paw.

"I'm not… fucking around!" She yelled, not to the demon but to herself.

Avery set Hemlock down on the ground beside her, using her right hand to reach across her torso. Risking losing a finger or two when the coyote lunged at her, she reached where her handgun was holstered into her belt.

The demon growled and began to retreat, but Avery was faster. She fired a shot into the familiar's chest, the force knocking it away from her. The demon wailed, slumping, but did not become still. Seeing not a Legion-aligned demon but a wounded animal, Avery pushed it away with her boot as she stood up to get away. Her stomach felt sick with what she had done.

She didn't have time to grieve what she had done to the coyote, a Legion officer was shortly behind their wounded familiar. The woman wielded a black-edged battle axe and she screamed wildly as she lunged towards Avery.

Without time to reach for Hemlock, Avery fired two rounds into the woman. The third pull of her trigger yielded only empty clicks. It wouldn't have been needed anyway; the woman lay still on the ground. Terror choked Avery as she looked from the struggling animal to its dead Reaper.

She wanted to cry. She wanted it to be over.

Avery rose to her feet and scrambled for the grip of Hemlock. Weight on her injured leg caused the limb to throb and she felt the hot blood dripping down into her sock. She turned to run towards the Knight of Water, with her steps slowed as she favored her right leg. The pain finally let the tears break.

"You have to keep going," she said to herself, trying to forgive her sniffles between the words.

Her bone armored revenants guarded her back as she limped towards the Knight. She felt warm blasts of air as she approached the beast head-on and its titanic exhales enveloped her with relief.

Up close she saw the reptilian eyes blink first with an inner lid and then again with the two outer. Its eyes were the brightest gold, watching Avery with a slivered pupil of black that could have easily been as tall as her. Her braid blew back as the beast huffed again with flaring nostrils.

"Moz," she said softly, knowing that somewhere in there he could hear her. "We can do this. We have to do this. Yumi is up there alone and she needs our help."

A deep vibration rumbled from somewhere in the Knight's belly. Avery reached out a flat palm cautiously, slowly moving towards the Knight's snout. With gentle movement, she laid it flat on the sapphire scales. She smiled, sweat beading on her face and rolling down her cheeks with her tears.

"I believe in you, too," Avery said.

The Knight of Water stirred and she pulled her hand back. With rumbling earth beneath it, the demon-beast turned to expose more of its flank where Avery could scale the exposed ribcage. It was inviting her.

Avery grinned as she gazed into the Knight's eye. "Good boy," she joked.

The beast huffed and she knew somewhere inside it Moz was laughing. Avery found comfort in just recalling the melody.

She hurried as much as she could on an injured leg and sheathed Hemlock on her back. As she found footing on scales and bone, Avery winced as she struggled to put weight on her bitten leg. It took much longer than it had previous times but finally she climbed onto the back of the Knight and perched herself at the base of its neck between two spiked bones.

"The ritual failed," Avery said to the Knight. "Yumi is up there. We have to kill a Knight. Doesn't matter if it's Morgana, Sera, or Peter."

The Knight huffed under her after she added, "but I bet you can guess who my preference would be… It's not going to be either of you, it never was. I'll protect you always."

The giant demon rose on its taloned feet, the spiked tail swishing to knock the officers and familiars who approached out of their way. Avery gripped a bone in a tight lock and held fast as the Knight launched into the skies.

Wind whipped Avery's braid around her and the sky around her rumbled with thunder, matching the stirring belly of the beast she perched atop.

"Oh, *fuck*."

Avery knew that it wasn't just Yumi in the skies, but had initially suspected only one of the other Knights were dueling with her. She watched not just the pearl Knight of Spirit, but the emerald one clashing with it. The sleek, black Knight of Air. And the ruby Knight of Fire that sent chills down Avery's neck. If there was one thing she could have been wrong about, this was easily the worst one. Yumi had taken to the skies alone and fought hard one-on-three just to keep herself airborne.

Sera, the Knight of Earth, chased Yumi down and was closing in fast. Morgana surveyed from above and watched from where Peter's shadowy beast was circling around Yumi's trajectory to cut her off.

Thoughts raced through Avery's head as she calculated the best move to end the battle as swiftly as possible. As she worked, she watched the black Knight of Air change course and barrel towards Avery and the Knight of Water.

"Get me as close as you can to Morgana!" Avery yelled as loud as she could over the wind and the flapping of titanic wings.

The Knight of Water ducked to evade the lunge of the Knight of Air and Avery felt the sensation of falling as the air rushed around her. The Knight recovered fast and soared for the Knight of Fire. Avery readied herself as the beast aimed not for the other, but for the air above it.

He won't let you fall. You have to believe.

Avery bolstered her trust in Moz as hard as she could when the Knight of Water passed over that of Fire and she dropped into the empty air between them. Her vision turned blurry with fright, the sensation of falling overcoming her. Avery landed hard on the spine of the ruby Knight and she scrambled to latch her footing and grip. Her foot found bone and she wrapped her arms around the middle of a spiked vertebrae.

Avery let herself relish the few seconds of relief before she had to move quickly. She slid downward, using her body to wedge herself between two of the spikes with her feet and a free hand gripping a rib bone tightly. With her other arm, she reached backwards and quickly pulled out her sword.

The ruby Knight beneath her suddenly jerked violently, thrashing about as it tried to throw Avery off its back. In her instant reaction to keep herself from falling, she gripped hard on the horns of the beast's spine with both hands. With her grip no longer tight on her sword, Hemlock slipped down the curve of the Knight's ribcage and plummeted.

Avery watched as her sword disappeared into the ocean below and the splash Hemlock made just before it was gone forever. Her eyes widened; *screwed*, she was absolutely screwed.

She cursed herself up and down for not accepting Kurosaki's offered ammo. All that Avery had left was an empty handgun and a dagger.

"The dagger," she whispered to herself below the whipping howls of the wind.

The Knight of Fire swerved left and right, making any attempt it could to throw Avery off its back. Avery gripped a horn with two hands, using it as a handgrip to haul herself up the spine and towards the demon's head. Rain pelted her hard in the face and the roars of the sparring Knights nearby broke through the thick clouds.

Avery hoisted herself farther up the spine of the beast.

"Almost there, Avery. You can fucking do this," she said to herself.

Her footing slipped on the exposed bone and her heart lurched as she gripped the horn tighter. Avery lodged her foot at the joint of two vertebrae and she paused just behind the largest horn atop the Knight's head. Carefully, she held the spike of bone and shimmied around it until she was above the Knight's face. Nothing protected her now from the violent wind and she lowered herself carefully with both hands holding the large horn. With one hand, she quickly grabbed the dagger Moz had given her what felt like years ago.

Avery knew she had only seconds as she sat atop the Knight's skull. Her mind flashed only with images of Moz and Yumi, of Lily and Maria, of her little brother. She would never see any of them again and she was struck with a choking loneliness.

With the dagger gripped in her hand, Avery Porter was prepared to die.

She swung her arm down and let out a primal scream, driving her blade into the right eye of the Knight. Blood spurted and the demon wailed in pain, the lift of its jaw felt under Avery's legs. But she pulled the dagger out with a sickening squish and stabbed again, faster and faster as she grew desperate for mortal damage. Her strikes hit the hard flat of bone and the spurts of blood became a mess of gore.

The Knight's wings stopped flapping and they hovered in empty air for a fraction of a second before the air shifted and they were both plummeting down. Avery gripped the

Knight's horns with her bloodied hands and closed her eyes, knowing the smack of her body on the water would snap her spine and kill her. An instant and merciful death.

The hard blow of the sea's surface against the Knight's belly sent her flying off its back and she soared limply through the air before she struck the cold ocean with a loud slap. Avery didn't have time to suck in air before her head slipped under the surface and her throat stung with the absence of oxygen. She pulled her arms, struggling to crawl back to the surface.

If her waterlogged boots felt full of concrete, then her arms could have only been lifeboat paddles that had already been blown to useless splinters. The impact of her spine on the water hadn't killed her, so why couldn't she make it to the surface?

Ahead of her was the titanic body of the fiery Knight, unmoving and pouring glittering bubbles as it slowly sank down into darkness where she hoped that the terror would be forever forgotten. Avery would never see the peace in Shintori that followed the collapse of the Knights of Od because she knew she would soon be buried in the sediment of the ocean floor with it.

Warmth bloomed in her ribs and she knew she must have been bleeding out. Her vision began to darken as she realized her arm was twitching violently. Avery's back cracked with pain and she stopped her struggle to swim. Spasms in every muscle prevented her from pulling her arms upward and she thrashed just beneath the surface. Water filled her mouth as her numbed jaw slackened. Pressure clamped around her middle and the world frosted over white.

Yumi had always wondered how it felt to fly. She didn't think there would be so much exposed bone and the gnashing teeth of monsters involved. Even less that they would be hers.

The demon that had taken up residence in her body had finally overpowered her and she was thrown into the dark recesses of its true form, watching through its eyes instead of her own.

Bring me back!

She had no use for her voice where she was and she threw her thoughts forward as hard as she could, but the projectiles meant nothing to the Knight. Yumi watched the beast of Spirit lurch for its emerald sibling with a gaping mouth, missing the ulna bone of its wing by only a narrow margin.

Why are you fighting them? Is this not what you all want?

Yumi was answered not with words, but with a feeling: tomb-cold rage. The minute the Knights of Earth and Air chose to go after that of Spirit, they became its enemies. She felt it was a tentative motive, but Yumi gladly accepted it.

The Knight of Air lurched in their direction, a shrill roar piercing the sky as it unhinged its great jaw. Her Knight dodged in a calculated drop, banking in the opposite direction towards where Earth had tried to pin them. Spirit shot upwards into the belly of the green beast, horn hooking into an exposed rib bone.

Sera's Knight screamed out, trying to wriggle free from Yumi and Spirit. The Knight of Spirit began to pull with the intent of dragging the other beast back towards the ground where it could be outnumbered and vulnerable. Yumi felt the hard jolt from the other side of the dark veil when the monstrous Knight of Air rammed hard into Spirit's side, knocking Sera free from their tangled bones.

From a break in the clouds, Yumi saw the shape of the Knight of Fire plummet into the ocean. She expected it to emerge from its dive, but it disappeared into churning foam and never resurfaced.

Yumi felt the hesitation enveloping her in the space she occupied in the Knight's stead, in the circling of the two other beasts as their teeth pulled away from Spirit. *What does it mean if a Knight is dead?* She was met with silence. No words, no wash of vague emotion; only the hollow darkness around her that swallowed the thought she projected into the void.

Just as quickly as they had wrought violence upon Yumi and Spirit, the other two Knights fled back toward the ritual grounds. Her anger flared, hot licks of heat filling the void between her demon's vessel and where she lay dormant inside as they lurched to follow the beasts.

Spirit snapped its jaws, desperate to close its fangs around the emerald tail in front of them but the distance was too great. Yumi felt the tether between her and the Knight of Od beginning to weaken and panic washed over her in frigid waves. She couldn't let them get away, not after everything they had done.

Keep going - we can destroy them if we can just catch them!

The Knight of Earth suddenly nosedived, breaking formation with its brother when its leathery patagium wings stopped flapping. Yumi was certain that it, too, would plummet into the ocean to follow the Knight of Fire into the depths but the trajectory of its fall put the beast just over the jagged cliffside when bones began to snap inward. It was a slow implosion to watch the emerald dragon break down into the woman of flaming hair - wings retracted, bones and horns crumbled into dust and then there she was, hurtling back to the earth where she had been born. The broken Knight crashed into the ground below like a terrible fallen star before she took off running.

Yumi didn't have time to see where she would flee to when the oil-slick Knight of Air led her on a one-on-one chase. She feared that he was luring her into the maze of fog and skyscrapers before it suddenly banked to the left just over the threshold of the leveled ritual grounds and the forest beyond.

Where are you going? Why turn around?

She looked down at the clash below, letting Spirit control the chase without her commentary. Through the eyes of the Knight she followed the trajectory of Peter's careful path of descension, gravitating around the small fulcrum of two archers on the ground no matter how many times they looped around the field.

Lily!

Yumi had heard the call of his Knight just before he had chased her into the sky, seeking to draw Lily to him the way Moz had with Avery. *My witch* - they called out the same way, just as she had heard in the grand hall when William Mosley and the Berserker Witch were bound before her. But where Avery obliged, Lily resisted. What good would it have been to call out to the witch it claimed when the death bells had tolled now for the Knights? *Avoiding a march to the grave alone*, she decided.

I'll kill you before you lay a hand on her, Yumi could have screamed with the way the words burned in her bones and yet she doubted he would register it even as a whisper. Just as she started to worry that she wasn't strong enough to win on her own, every good deed Yumi had ever done returned tenfold. Every prayer she ever whispered in the dark of her chamber was answered, every song of praise she ever sang for the gods echoed back at her in the thundering air around her: Peter's bones began to crumble.

CHAPTER TEN

SWORDS

Moz felt the full force of the sea when the Knight made impact with the waves. The Thing that lived inside him for so long was finally sputtering into darkness and though he felt it had wanted to wreak as much damage as it could on its march into death, it chose to dive after its Witch instead.

They found the sinking body of the Knight of Fire first in the cloud of blood that fogged the frigid depths. Bones of the wings and rib cage were beginning to snap off as the beast advanced in decay, being the first of the demon creations to die.

There they found her.

Their Witch was sinking lower and lower with a faint stream of bubbles trailing from her perfect and smart mouth that had lashed him many times with quick wit and that he still wanted to kiss anyway.

They cut through the water in a serpentine flash. Moz wasn't sure how they were going to get her to safety, but the Knight already knew. They bobbed their head down, pushing Avery against the flat of their unholy face and swam. Propelling her with quick care just beneath the surface, they almost made it to the cliffside before Moz began to feel the demon peel from him.

No, no, no! After all these years, can't you hang on just a little bit longer?

He felt the pain of shrinking back inward, his bones rearranging, and he wanted to scream. Moz threaded his arm around Avery's waist and pulled her up the rest of the way to the surface. When he broke the water, he finally screamed. She made no sound as her muscles jerked.

Kicking and paddling as best as he could with both of them, he was almost grateful with each lashing of a wave that carried them just a little closer to the base of the stairs carved into the cliff side.

Finally, he felt the ledge appear under his feet from the sea god altar at the bottom of the cliff. It sloped upward into the rock and Moz dragged their bodies up as high as he could to get them out of the salty foam of waves.

Setting Avery onto her back, he saw the spasms of movement in her limbs and head. He took her wrist between his fingers and felt the slowed flutter of her pulse.

"Avery?"

When she did not respond, panic welled and Moz fumbled to begin compressing her chest in rapid succession. Her body jerked and on the third try, seawater began to erupt from her mouth. He called out her name again and still she was silent.

"Okay love, we need to get you help," he said, mostly to stay collected and to keep himself from believing he was now alone on that cliffside.

He lifted her carefully onto his back and looked at the steep incline of stairs that wound across the broad face of the cliff above them. Moz inhaled deeply. He'd have to be careful but quick, there was no safety rail to keep them from plunging into the depths if he made a wrong step.

"We got this. You and me, okay?"

Silence.

He took the first step of many. It felt lonely on that cliffside and so he continued to talk. Anything to keep his fear at bay.

"Avery Porter, I love you for standing between me and that beer fridge and not knocking my teeth out when I was rude to you. I would have deserved it a thousand times over."

Another step. Silence.

"I love you for telling me I don't know how to drive. You're right. I still don't and at this point, please don't teach me."

Two more steps. Silence.

"I love you for swatting Tristan with a giant branch when you found out he drugged you to sleep. I think he deserved that one and even though at the time I only found it funny, I'm glad you always stand up for yourself."

The longer the silence carried on from behind him, the more panicked his steps became.

"I love you for… running to me. Protecting me when no one else wanted to."

That silence broke him and Moz began to cry, trying so much faster to get them both back to the ritual grounds but the crash of the waves was a frightening distance below them now and there was only a narrow purchase his feet had on the stairs before it became open sea air that would send them both tumbling to their deaths.

"I love you for that glow of your heartbeat when we were in Od and though we had to hide it, I'd swallow the sun just to feel a fraction of its warmth."

"I love you for coming back for me. They wore your face so many times in that prison to force my hand, but I knew with no doubts when it was really you who came to save me. I would recognize the shape of your soul in complete darkness. In the loneliest corners of Od."

"I love you for the first time I held you and you stayed there. You took my goddess bell and I prayed every night since then that it could keep you safe and that I would hold you again."

His voice was beginning to waver.

"I'll love you when I hold you again."

"I'll love you when you eat my pancakes during breakfast even though you said you weren't hungry."

He took more steps now between affirmations, both out of concentration on moving efficiently and trying to think about the future with such clarity that it had to come true.

"I'll love you when we play our music together for hours and have only stopped because we wanted to dance. I don't know how to dance Avery, and I really need you to live so that you can teach me how to dance. And drive. I was lying earlier."

"I'll love you if you agree to be my wife even after all these times I defended you from being accused that you already were... I need you in my life, Avery Porter. And I won't let you go. Not like this. I won't let you die a hero when you should get to live the rest of your life... I'm selfish and so afraid now and I can't do any of this without you."

It felt like he had been climbing up the cliffside for hours when he finally found the stable ground of the plateau beneath his feet. He was gasping for breath between sobs and looked around frantically for the nearest help.

Lily and Maria were nocking arrows into their bows as quickly as they could, their backs to him.

"Guys... guys, we need help!" He cried out, hoping they would hear him. Lily was the first to turn towards Moz and her eyes widened in horror when she watched him lower Avery off his back and onto the ground.

She lowered her bow, instructing Maria "Cover us."

To Moz she asked, "What happened to her?"

Lily fell to her knees at Avery's side and set down her bow carelessly at her side. She peeled off Avery's chest plate and Moz froze when he saw it.

On a red cord, the silver bell with bent prongs from having the clapper pulled out. His gift to her from what felt like so long ago with how burned into his memory that moment was; from then on, he had tried to be better.

"She took out Morgana from right on top of her. I didn't see how she did it, but she doesn't have her sword anymore."

"We saw the red Knight fall out of the sky," Lily said grimly as she began to attempt chest compressions herself. "I didn't realize Avery was there too."

There was no more seawater for Lily to push out and she too felt the slow beat of Avery's pulse between her fingers. She then held a hand beneath Avery's nostrils, feeling her breath.

"I don't understand," Lily said with a frown. "Her breathing is steady; her pulse is slow but it's there. Why is she unresponsive?"

"I don't know, but she was seizing like mad when I pulled her out of the water."

Her eyes widened as the information pieced together perfectly in her mind. Lily turned around to look at Maria behind her.

"Maria! Avery needs out now, she's down for the count!"

Moz's panic flared as he watched Lily. "Waitwaitwaitwait, what does that mean? Down for the count?"

Lily didn't answer but grabbed her bow and stood up to make her way to Maria. She looked over her shoulder at Moz before she said, "We're going to cover you, but you need to make your way back to the Temple with her. The Legion is trying to take as many of us down with them as they can."

Moz nodded. He scooped Avery back up, struggling to hoist her onto his back again.

"Follow me," Lily said. "I've got you."

He followed Lily and Maria as they hustled away from the cliffside, back towards the sacrificial pit and where the gates to safety waited for them beyond the trees. The women moved quickly as they launched arrows into Legion members, then nocking the next arrow to do it again. It reminded Moz a lot of the way Kurosaki and Alice moved together and he felt the immense sadness in his stomach deepen.

The ground beneath their feet jolted and almost knocked Moz onto his back. Lily and Maria both stumbled but found their steady hold much quicker than he had, as though they had already known it was coming.

"What the fuck was that?"

"North by northeast," Maria said simply, instructing him where to look to find his answer.

Moz turned his gaze to look ahead and off to his right. There he found a tall mass of tree limbs towering over the much smaller bodies of the Legion officers, the size easily rivaled that of the other Knights that were nowhere to be seen. It was molded into a humanoid shape, swinging a large arm to sweep bodies with a crushing impact. At the head of the giant was not a head at all, but the shape of a much smaller body that easily could have been missed against the darkness of the trees twisting around it. Their eyes glowed white, pulsing with power. Moz squinted his eyes before dropping his jaw when he recognized the body.

"The fuck is Shank doing? How is Shank… What?"

"Keep moving!" Maria snapped.

Moz hurried in obedience, grateful that he had found help at all. The ground shook again as the beast of trees caged around Shank took another step and hurled a uniformed body into the ground with a sickening crunch of bones. Moz scanned the biker Reapers for Todd and wondered if Shank would take requests.

"Is this how you guys felt seeing my Knight?"

"More or less," Maria answered. "You're a lot uglier, though."

He frowned but was relieved that Maria wasn't feeling too worried to avoid giving him shit. They drew nearer to the sacrificial pit when the dirt next to them exploded into clumps and flying grass. Something had fallen out of the sky and narrowly missed them. As they passed the crashed projectile, Moz caught a glimpse of Yumi on her back with a streaming nosebleed, struggling to get up from where she had hit the earth.

"Wait, stop," he called out to the witches ahead of him and hurried to Yumi. Still holding onto Avery, he leaned over the Princess and held out his arm as steady as he could to help her up.

"Do you… feel that?" Yumi choked, struggling to sit upright. "They're gone."

Moz nodded. "Avery did it. We have to go now. Can you get up?"

Yumi gingerly propped herself up on her arms, hissing at the painful movement. She grimaced as she held in a cry but instead of wailing, she just nodded. "Yeah, yeah, I can do it."

When she was upright she grabbed hold of Moz's outstretched hand and pulled herself up the rest of the way. She held him there with her fingers gripped around his wrist and his around hers.

"You did good," he said and Yumi nodded her head once, accepting his sincere praise quietly.

They hurried to where Lily and Maria had been covering them, with Yumi stumbling at first on her feet before she steadied herself to keep up with the quick pace.

"I didn't realize Shank was a dedicant of Malo," Yumi said after the ground shook again. The gears turning in Moz's head stopped once she mentioned the forest god - that made sense now.

Maria suddenly stopped and Moz nearly tripped over her small frame with how closely he had been following her. She held out her wiry arms and bow, motioning for everyone else to stop.

"New plan," she said gravely. "Stay out of *their* way."

"What are you talking about? We need to get- oh, *fuck*."

Moz found his protest changed quickly when he saw the wretched form of the Beldam standing with her back to the gate. Her staff was planted firmly in the rotting earth beneath her feet and she stood a short distance across from another woman.

The woman in glistening silver plates of armor stood heads taller than the Beldam. Her figure was strong, solid, and still so graceful. Her ginger hair was pulled back into an elaborate knot on the back of her head and streaked through with plaits. At her side she held a shining broadsword with ease and grace as if it weighed a mere nothing.

"Onja," Yumi murmured, instantly recognizing the Goddess of Victory.

"Shit's about to go down," Lily grabbed Maria's arm to pull her off towards the treeline to the west. "Hurry, this way!"

Before Moz turned to follow, he caught a glimpse of the tall figures standing behind the Beldam. He recognized Aegis easily in his humanoid form from his time seeing it in Od; the tall blonde woman he had never seen before must have been Mara, watching with a stare as serious as her Reaper. Aegis watched him with eyes completely glazed in black. Silently and with careful gestures to not draw the attention of his Mistress, he pointed low at his side towards the treeline with a long claw. They then reshaped into a thumbs up; it was safe to go. Moz wanted to nod in thanks but didn't want to risk giving him away either, so he hurried to follow the women to safety.

They crashed through the trees in thundering and desperate strides. Lily stopped to fire into a Legion officer who had broken off from the pack to follow them and he crumpled to the ground in a gurgling heap of grey, an arrow protruding from the throat. She quickly caught up to Moz and Yumi, following Maria's lead.

"How much further ahead is the Temple," she asked.

"Not terribly far," Moz answered.

Dodging and weaving through the scattered trees, they came to a much smaller clearing than the one on which the sacrificial pit sat. A jagged pathway of worn sarsen stone cut through the overgrown grass. Long-dried fountains lined the path and the nude goddess sculptures atop them sat in an eerie silence. At the far end of the path a temple of crumbling marble loomed waiting for them like the transept in a basilica of trees. It was a modest and simple structure on the outside, but Avery had warned them of the hall of scrying mirrors and neon that lay within. Moz had never been inside and up until that point he had hoped to keep it that way; but he would do anything necessary to get Avery to help.

They stopped in the center of the clearing and scouted the columned portico of the temple for any movement inside.

"Hello?" Yumi called out. "Is anyone here?"

Moz looked around. No one. The silence was heavy without any crash of metal from the battle cutting through the thick embrace of trees on all sides.

"*William.*"

He heard the familiar voice behind him and turned to find Balthazar's looming shadow. The Demon of the

Crossroads looked at him with a stern gaze; he was not here to offer congratulations.

"You and the Princess must leave immediately," he said. "The Oracles of Neri want you both in the ground."

"But a Knight is dead, I thought it was over?" Yumi was the one who spoke from behind Moz.

The demon shook his head. His dark eyes were bagged as though he had been stewing in worry for far too long. "That wasn't good enough for the Oracles. They did not want the vessels to remain either. They entrapped Mona and I in a thinly veiled threat: kill you both or risk our child."

Moz's mouth suddenly felt dry. "You… kill us? Balthazar, I thought you were our ally."

"I am and that's the only reason you're still standing. We don't have much time. Leave my daughters here and you both run, they'll be back any moment."

He shook his head. "You know I can't do that."

"Just as you know that when it comes to it, my child will win every time. You have one minute, William, and you better hope you never see me again. Don't make me kill you."

Moz swore violently and he stumbled to follow his friends when they broke into a run again. They might be safe if they made it all the way into the city again. Maybe. But *damn*, he was so tired of running. He'd much rather avoid Eyon altogether than have to flee from some hooded freaks, too.

"Avery, when we get home we are sleeping for four days straight," he whispered to her on his back. Again, no reply.

Even Yumi and her proper mouth were swearing up a storm as the group tumbled through the trees. "I'm going to gut those charlatan bastards… Yeah, the minute those sons of bitches set foot on the mainland… Not even real fucking scrying, you fucking cunts. I'll fucking lop off your heads."

Colorful.

Moz felt Avery begin to slip several times and as he tightened his grip around her legs at his side. He began to worry that she would be left with terrible bruises on her thighs. If that was the worst of their injuries, he did not mind apologizing at all.

"Guys, I see the gate!" Maria shouted excitedly, pointing ahead at a gap in the trees.

Moz could barely make out the blurs of iron in the shadows cast by the woods. He struggled to run faster, feeling his body was on the verge of quitting and he knew time was slipping fast through his fingers. His lungs burned, his muscles ached, and he couldn't ever remember feeling this tired before. There was an eerie stillness within his skull and he could feel the thrum of his heartbeat much too clearly. It was the feeling of absence.

He'd spent lifetimes wishing to rid himself of The Thing and now that it was gone, he wasn't even sure how he felt. Helpless seemed like a good place to start.

Lily was the first to run through the gate that divided the city from the wilds. When her feet hit the pavement where the motorcycles stood waiting, she buckled forward with her hands on her knees and heaved for air. Moz, Yumi, and Maria were shortly behind.

"Yumi… Moz… find Avery help and keep away from the forest... You can't let any of the Oracles catch you.… Me and Maria need to go back to help."

Maria's face had a stern fix to it but she nodded in agreement.

"Are you sure you will be safe?" Yumi asked. "I am not afraid of Balthazar nor the Oracles. My murder would rain chaos down from the Crown if they dared to try."

Lily straightened up, her hands on her sides to open her ribcage for easier breathing. "Yes, I'm sure. Moz will need cover since Avery is slowing him down."

Yumi and Moz exchanged glances and the Princess nodded. "Of course, I have his back."

"We'll come find you when we have everyone back," Maria said, adjusting her bow and quiver on her back. "Be safe."

Moz nodded. "You too."

Both parties turned their backs to each other as they headed in opposite directions - Maria and Lily back to the woods, Moz and Yumi deeper into the petrichor of the concrete jungle. Moz readjusted his grip around Avery's legs and followed the former Knight of Spirit.

Yumi's attention swung on a swivel, studying the faces of people who passed them on the slick asphalt. It struck Moz as strange that they hadn't sought shelter yet - surely the commotion from the sacrificial grounds could be heard? He waited, listening. Nothing but a low rumble from the direction they came in; the thick canopy of the woods swallowed the sound. He looked up and the drizzle of icy rain leftover from the Knight of Water hit his burning cheeks. If it was over now, why had the rain continued?

"Where should we go now?" Yumi asked with her back still to Moz as she led the way to nowhere in particular.

He watched her and the tight grip of her fingers around the gilded throwing knife.

"We're not going to make it all the way back to Todd's garage on foot like this," he answered. "Kurosaki's place isn't too far from here; we can regroup there. I'll give you directions if you lead the way, take a right at this next corner."

They wound through the city grid in jagged lines and stopped only when Moz had to recall where they were in relation to Union Street. He looked both ways on the corner as cars and motorcycles zipped past; *was it left or right?* The dumpling house with the neon red lights looked familiar to him and that was probably a good omen.

"Left feels correct, let's go left," he finally decided. Yumi had folded her arms, trying to wait patiently as he mentally walked through the directions and she raised a skeptical eyebrow.

"It just feels correct? Moz, we need to get her help and we don't-"

"Crossing!" He cut her off when the pedestrian light changed to a blinking green and he walked ahead of her.

They passed shops and apartment lobbies. Nothing was striking him as a threat or out of the ordinary and despite the weight of Avery on his back, he felt a little lighter knowing that they were all going to be safe soon. Then they passed an alleyway.

Moz might have missed the figure if he hadn't still been assessing their surroundings to make sure they were even going the right way. Yumi had missed them entirely and kept walking a few paces ahead of him even after he had stopped to stare at the person draped in a red robe. Their hood was drawn, but there was no mistaking the hue of sky-blue paint scraped across the bridge of their nose.

"Yumi," he called out without taking his eyes off the Oracle.

She rushed to him, immediately picking up on the danger in his tone. Yumi looped her arms under Avery's and eased her off his back, freeing up his scabbard and sword.

Moz and the nameless Oracle strode towards each other, stopping just shy in the middle of the alley to be out of sight of the city. Neither of them drew their weapons. He wasn't sure what kind of encounter this would be, it was a bizarre sight to see just a single member of the Oracles of Neri.

"The lone sheep has strayed far from the flock, hasn't he?" Moz taunted.

The Oracle's chin tilted up, but the features of their face were still obscured by hooded shadow.

"You have done the world a great service and we are grateful," the Oracle spoke, his voice carrying a strong undertow of implication. "You must also understand why then, we must never allow for the Beldam's monsters to roam again. We give you the opportunity, William Mosley, to come to your end willingly so that no more innocents must suffer."

"When were you bestowed the authority to decide who is innocent? Am I guilty? Is the Princess guilty? None of us chose any of this. Please just let us take Avery to safety."

"I cannot let that happen, William. Though he did not speak of it explicitly, Balthazar has alluded to the bond the Knight of Water shares with the witch. It has latched onto her and we must not leave any tethers to this world. There is no reason to spare her life, Saved or not."

Moz drew his sword, shifting his stance to hold it down at his side. "At least now I know I don't have to pretend to ask you nicely."

He watched the Oracle reach into one of his bell sleeves and pull out a long gold needle with a loop on the end. The other end was poisoned by the looks of the oily black sheen that coated the sharp tip. The Oracle threaded his pointer finger through the circle of gold, gripping it firmly in his hand tattooed with spirals.

Moz rushed the Oracle, his sword cutting through the air like snaps of lightning. The Oracle was faster and lighter on his feet, evading Moz's strikes with ease. It seemed impossible with such a small weapon; he was completely sidestepping the attacks Moz dealt. He was growing increasingly frustrated until he began to read the patterns. *Step, step, dive, step, dive.*

When Moz learned the steps of the deadly dance, he stopped it abruptly. He swung his sword low when the Oracle expected it to go high. The weapon cut a deep gash in the Oracle's thigh, forcing him to buckle. Metal clattered on pavement as the poisoned needle fell and the holy man scrambled to find it again. When he looked up, Moz was standing over him.

Moz crunched the needle under his boot, careful to not let the poisoned end so much as touch the sole.

"You will be my messenger," Moz spoke to the Oracle, just above a whisper. "And the words you will say are: *they live.*"

He laid both his hands on the Oracle's cheeks, pushing back the red hood. Moz saw his pale face and ash blonde hair shorn close to the scalp and the ice of his eyes frozen in terror. The man's hard jaw was trembling, unsure of what was coming next. Moz wasn't sure himself. All he knew was that he felt the tide rolling out fast, leaving him standing alone on the sand as his feet sank in the place once occupied by The Thing.

"*They live. And they continue. And they are free.* But you will say them not with your words. No. For threatening me. For threatening Yumi. For threatening Avery. You will say them with your corpse."

The Oracle cried out, "Please, William, no! I-"

The tide came crashing back.

The nameless Oracle of Neri began to choke as Moz held his face. Sea water bubbled over his lips, dribbling down his chin and splattering on the scarlet robe. Between coughs, his lips shifted to blue and the panic in his eyes bulged. He sank lower and lower to the asphalt, fighting the landlocked drowning as hard as he could and Moz only waited patiently, holding his head. The Oracle fumbled weakly, trying to get a grip around Moz's hands to pry himself free, but it was no use. Where Moz once heard the fury of the Knight, something else to pin the blame on, he now only heard the thundering of his own tsunami.

Movement stilled as the Oracle stopped fighting him and he crumpled at Moz's feet. He looked down at the puddle of sea water and though he knew he should have felt confused as to how he was able to drown the man without the Knight, Moz did not want to waste time running through the cycle of emotions. Avery needed safety.

He sheathed his sword. "And when you tell them, don't forget to say my name is Moz. None of this William shit."

Moz carefully took Avery back from Yumi and hoisted her onto his back. They didn't dare speak a word the rest of the walk to Kurosaki's apartment, a middle floor in a high-rise building. He was grateful for Yumi's ability to kick the door hard enough to force the lock plate out of the door frame; he couldn't remember where Kurosaki kept the spare key and there was no doormat or potted plant to be an obvious hiding place.

They walked into the darkened apartment that was stale with prolonged absence. Moz felt a visceral jolt when he remembered that the last time he had been at Kurosaki's apartment, he had kissed him goodbye. Despite the changes since then, it was nice that the home still felt familiar. Like it was half his. Grey light from the rainstorm outside leaked in from a crack in the heavy blackout curtains hung in front of a sliding glass door. He half expected the Princess to turn her nose up in disgust as they passed a darkened galley kitchen into the living room, but Yumi was solemn and silent.

She helped Moz ease Avery down onto the cognac leather couch that was far too old and far too squished. Yumi took the scarlet patchwork quilt that was draped over the back and laid it tenderly over Avery, tucking the edges carefully under her. The Princess smoothed her hand over Avery's cheeks to push back the wet waves plastered to her face, lingering just a moment to watch the shallow breaths of the woman they both loved. She then looked up at Moz with a serious stare.

"That's going to come back to haunt us, isn't it?"

Moz couldn't answer her; he knew she didn't mean the broken door at all.

— ❦ —

When Maria and Lily found their way back to the battle-field it had been littered with corpses adorned both in char-coal uniforms and street clothes. Maria wanted to begin flipping bodies out of the mud to make sure none of them had belonged to someone she loved.

Shank could easily be accounted for as they struck down Legion officers with the borrowed power of Malo's tree limbs. Why did the forest god need them anyway? She had no time to consider the answer as she followed Lily head-first into the fray.

Fireballs flared on the south end of the field and Maria easily tracked down Cassie and the other Reaper children. They stood with their backs together to take on Legion Reapers twice their age. In front of them was Kurosaki, firing crack after crack of gunfire into anyone who came too close. Maria knew him well enough to recognize the act of protecting the children was not only for them, but for Alice.

When she watched him, she realized the bodies charging the children had too many limbs. They were too tall and the sounds coming from them sounded more animal than human. And then she caught sight of a set of wings and a tail. Panicked, Maria turned to Lily and the woman seemed to have gone into high alert with the way she quickly scanned the field.

"Oh fuck, over there!"

She followed the direction of Lily's pointed finger towards the horrible figure of the Beldam. Between her and the Goddess Onja was a deep chasm glowing a sickly green. Bodies of swarming darkness crawled their way out of the earth, screeching and flailing in all directions. Those who chose to hurtle toward the Goddess of Victory were pierced with her broadsword and discarded like rubbish.

Maria turned back towards Kurosaki, in hopes of projecting her voice over the clash to be heard, "Your place! Take the kids and go, now!"

Thankfully, he heard and understood. Maria knew it was going to be difficult without the gunman, but she would be undone if they lost another child. She helped provide cover for Kurosaki and the Reaper teens, nocking and launching arrows as fast as she could into demon bodies. Lily and Maria swept to retrieve their blessed arrows as they inserted themselves between Kurosaki and the gaping wound in the earth. She yanked one of her feathered arrows out of a blackened body that might have been a dog - if a dog were a seven-foot tall bipedal and oozed black when she yanked out the weapon with a sickening squish. Nocking another arrow into her bow, Maria whirled in the direction of the godly figures flanking each side of the terrible split in the earth.

Shank's winding limbs of trees struck down stray demons as they rammed their way through the horde, forging ahead towards the Beldam and where she set her demons upon Onja with each flick of her bony hands. The body of trees hoisted up a giant arachnid demon in both hands, tore the body in two and tossed it aside like a ruined paper doll.

Maria had never felt so small. Her blessed arrows were finding their targets and sending demons to the ground, but she still was nothing compared to the destruction the gods left in their wake. The way Shank used their own body as such a weapon left her frightened. *How did the gods decide who to loan their power to? What were the conditions?*

She dropped her bow.

Lily called her name beside her, but she heard only a muffled sound as she watched the large demon with a vague feline shape charging her head on. Wet curls around her face floated upward and her eyes inked over when her vision filled with the internal miasma and skin that held the demon together. She held up her hands in the air to reach out and touch it even though she still had the safe distance to run away. Weaving through the darkness of the demon's insides, she found the silver thread holding it all together.

Maria crunched her fingers into fists, pulled back with all her strength and the demon crumpled into a stilled heap. *To save, never to resurrect.*

Her vision cleared of the demon's internal darkness but she knew that her eyes had not lightened. She wasn't done yet.

"*I've waited for you,*" a honey-sweet voice of a woman behind her said. "*You have been haunted for too long,*

Daughter. Your greatest sin was only the lengths to which you would go to save those who you love. Do you forgive yourself?"

"No. If I have doomed myself by trying to save, I may as well plunge all the way and kill," her own voice was ragged and the words felt wrong in her mouth.

Maria reached into the next demon and yanked the thread until there were no bones to hold the terrible creature upright. She joined Malo's marionette in the war path to the Beldam, yanking and ripping, tearing and forging on. Lily's warm presence followed, her arrows guided by the gift Balthazar and Mona had forced on her. She was Maria's beacon to return home before she sank too deep into the miasma.

Maria wasn't thinking when she reached into the next demon. Her fingers sank into the vision but she felt stunted, like there was a barrier of frigid water and she was nothing more than an oil slick gliding across the surface. She stumbled out with clear eyes and the sobering fear hit her when she saw that no other demons stood between her line of sight and the Beldam.

"Sending your bitches after your own kind is an act of treason, Mona. I will not hesitate to slaughter my own Creations and you will not be warned again."

Maria looked past the Beldam and across the chasm, where she found the Goddess of Victory watching her back with narrowed eyes. She caught just the faintest nod of her head and the shift of her grip on her broadsword slick with inky demon blood. Maria knew the signal. If Avery could do it, so could she.

She reached her hands up again and slipped into the dark space of witchcraft easily. Her vision swam with darkness that she could not penetrate. Maria was met with overwhelming terror each time her fingers brushed the barrier that gave with the coldness of the grave, but did not break. Her fingers swam in the empty air in front of her, looking for a way in when she felt the darkness shove her hard.

Her feet dragged through the mud as she was pushed back, and Maria's fingers clenched as she tried to hold on to whatever she was seeing inside the Goddess of Od. The Beldam howled and the animalistic sound terrified Maria far more than any threats the goddess had woven with words. She felt a choking grip around her throat and her instincts urged her to drop the magic to save herself. Maria resisted and shoved her hands forward as hard as she could.

"You wretched Reaper. For your actions, you will suffer a-"

Maria felt the strong pull from behind her as an unseen force worked to pry her out of the vision. Branches around her cracked and snapped.

"Maria, leave," Onja boomed.

She obeyed, pulling her hands out of the darkness and her vision cleared. Beldam was pinned down with a twisting mass of Shank and Malo's tree arm. In her ribs, Onja's broadsword pierced her all the way through.

"Take your friends and go," Onja commanded her again.

Maria looked to Lily, where she saw Tristan and Jack had joined her. Tristan nodded, already ushering Lily and Jack back to the treeline. The exorcist looked around at the other Reapers that Todd and the Grims had rallied.

"Everyone out!" His voice was a sharp cut through the air and Maria's feet carried her fast before she had time to hesitate.

"For your crimes Beldam, I punish you," Onja's thunderous voice carried behind her in a strong tide of sound. *"You will be a prisoner of your own kingdom, guarded forever by those who once were your captives. You are banished from the Realm of the Heavens, as is your co-conspirator, Paion. May you suffer greatly at the hands of consequence."*

Maria's thoughts raced with the pounding of her feet and soon she heard Shank running behind her more clearly than the rest of Onja's sentencing. They were heaving air, struggling to reacclimate to their own wiry body again. She wanted to comfort them, to praise them for becoming such a force to be reckoned with - but she could only think of that name.

Where had Paion been? The God of War never surfaced once. Never to reclaim his stolen sword from Avery, not to command the Knights that were just as much his as they were Beldam's. *How ironic that the god of war is a fucking coward.*

Lily fell into step with her as they ran. She fumbled for Maria's free hand, weaving her fingers slick with sweat and rainwater clumsily through her own. Maria squeezed her hand tight, their footsteps thundered together through the safety of the trees.

"Holy shit," Lily gasped between breaths. "We fucking did it! *You* did it!"

At Lily's praise, Maria was thrust into hyperawareness: she was running, she was breathing, she was with her friends who ran and heaved for air right alongside her. She had been able to step through the veil of witchcraft in their darkest hour and they were all still alive. Not only did she manage to not kill anyone in her last-ditch effort, she felt like a hero. Or what she imagined heroes were supposed to feel; she decided it was probably close enough.

Maria suddenly stopped and their interlocked fingers yanked Lily back. Lily looked back at her with panic, like something had gone wrong but Maria was looping her bow onto her shoulder. She eagerly reached for the taller woman's face and pulled her into a kiss that Maria hadn't even been aware she was waiting for until she felt the electrical thrum of life in every tendon of her body.

When Lily kissed her back, she tasted like the mulled wine of victory. She was the first two interlocking pieces of a puzzle, the real starting point and not the moments before when the image could twist and warp into something it wasn't meant to be. Maria started here, in love, not in death.

Lily eased out of the kiss first and she held Maria's waist with her free hand. The amazement painted on her striking umber face was tender and she smiled, her secret dimples forming at the corners of her quick-witted mouth.

"You are just my kind of extraordinary," Lily declared.

CHAPTER ELEVEN

THE WORLD

Avery opened her eyes and she knew she had died. Her surroundings were bleached white and she laid on her back with cold marble beneath her hands. She wasn't sure at first if she would be able to move, not with the bite on her left shin.

The more she thought about the injury, the more she realized that her leg was no longer throbbing. Avery sat up easily, to her surprise, and looked down at her legs. There was a tear in her pants about the size of a coyote's mouth, but the leg beneath it was perfectly unmarred. Not a single hair on her shin was out of place.

Avery's eyebrows furrowed and she looked up at the hall around her.

He looked so out of place with the white colonnade to either side of her and the vast hall of white marble that stretched beyond him.

"You could probably guess that this isn't how this would normally go," Balthazar said, folding his ringed hands neatly in front of his waist. "My wife said that I would be the one most comfortable for you to see."

"Balthazar, did I die?"

Avery spoke the words and knew she should have been afraid; but she wasn't. Even the absence of fear on the matter should have made her squirm. It didn't matter to her that the Demon of the Crossroads, the one who arguably made Avery the witch she was, stood across from her in the strangest of places. The sunlight pouring in from the clerestory windows and the sweetness in the air was so soothing that she didn't think she would have minded if she really were dead.

"You should have," he said with sharp frankness, "given how hard you crashed into the Stillmaw. But you did something, just beforehand, that saved you."

Avery was rising to her feet gingerly, "what did I do?"

"*Saved you,*" he repeated. When Avery looked up at his face, she saw a warm beam that could have been pride. "You were Saved. You were never lonely, my fierce daughter. Even when you were alone, you found company in the moon and in the trees. But it seems that when your moment of reckoning arrived, you knew the awful truth of it all. We are all born into this world alone and at the core of it all, we will all die alone. It is the most terrible loneliness and you felt it all. So suddenly, so awfully. And that Saved you."

Loneliness.

She thought of those final moments in the sky above Eyon. When she was driving her dagger into the skull of the Knight she knew her chances of survival were slim if at all. It wasn't her own life she had thought of, but the lives of the people she would never see again. Lily's. Moz's. Yumi's. Tristan's. Soren's.

That day she was pulled from her monotonous life in Ardua, she didn't think she would have so many people to miss. Now that she had found them, the thought of never hugging them again made her feel lonelier than she had been before them.

Tears rolled down her cheeks and the loneliness gripped her again by the spine and squeezed. She stumbled away from Balthazar and even though she was grateful for his familiar face, she feared what his presence would bring next.

Sympathetic to her overwhelming feelings, Balthazar reassured her, "you will get to return home, that I promise you."

"I know… I just," she sniffled, wiping the tears off her face with the sleeve of her coat. He waited for her to continue, but she had trailed off.

"Being Saved is a powerful thing, and while you may take a rest knowing your burden is done - not that you did much to begin with - your journey is not yet over."

"What do I do?"

"That is not for me to say. It's time for you to go home."

"But wait, what am I supposed to do? What do you mean it's not over? Aren't you coming, too?"

From the open clerestory windows above their heads, a crow soared into the hall and perched on Balthazar's broad shoulder. The bird regarded her with a curious cock of the head, its iridescence matching the green brocade of Balthazar's coat and stovepipe hat.

"We will meet once more, Avery Porter. Our business will not be complete until that final day you come with me. You will greet me as an old friend and you will go without a fight. And I will bring you to your well-deserved rest, my strangest daughter."

A smile spread across his face and he lifted his gilded fingers to tilt the brim of his hat down towards her. And just like that, the demon was gone.

Avery blinked and when she opened her eyes again, she was violently coughing up water. Her surroundings had changed and the peaceful hall around her became a darkened room. Beneath her was the soft cushion of a bed, now wet. She fought to wriggle out of her cocoon of blankets, and she freed herself just enough to turn onto her side so that she could examine her surroundings.

It was a sparsely furnished bedroom, with the bed she laid in jammed into the corner opposite the door. A wooden bookshelf was overflowing with books that spilled onto the floor and motorcycle helmets with scraped paint were arranged in a row on the top. A black coat hung from a hanger on the back of the closed bedroom door, along with silver wallet chains of varying thickness.

Avery felt relief when she saw Shank's familiar locks of hair, though their back was turned to her where they laid on a sleeping mat spread across the floor. She struggled to move again; every muscle was sore.

When she could finally reach over the edge of the mattress, she poked Shank's shoulder gingerly. They didn't stir, so she tried again.

Finally, they let out a tired groan and rolled onto their back. Shank rubbed their face with their hand and blinked hard.

"What are… oh good, you're awake," they grumbled.

"Shank, what happened," she whispered.

"Why are you whispering?" they said in their normal tone with sleepiness mixed into its warm depth.

"Oh, what happened?" she repeated herself, louder.

"What happened is we thought for sure you were dead," they said. "Except Lily, who pointed out you were convulsing just like Moz did when he was Saved. So, congrats on that. While that was happening, Malo and Onja led a siege on the Beldam. We didn't know what was happening up there until we saw Morgana fall out of the sky. Peter and Sera fled."

"Did we win?" she murmured.

"*Win* is subjective. Peter and Sera are still alive, some demons escaped Od. And since you can't kill a goddess, the Beldam was imprisoned in Od. Another gate for Balthazar. Paion was nowhere to be found, but safe to say the God of War has been banished, too."

They sat up, rubbing the patch of hair on their square chin. "You able to get up?"

Avery looked down at her leg. The wound on her leg was still absent and though she was healed, she felt weary. She rolled onto her side, propping herself up on her arm to try to get to her feet.

Shank got up, extended their hand down to her and helped her upright.

"Thanks," she murmured.

"Don't mention it," they said. "You can lean on me. I'll help you to the others."

When she was taken gingerly into the other room, she found that there was a whole crowd of people mending from the battle.

The first person she saw was Tristan, who spotted her easily from across the room.

"Ave!"

Lily was the one who got up and hurried around the maze of Reapers, throwing her arms around Avery in a tight hug.

"Are you okay?"

Avery nodded. "Just very, very sore."

"Oop, sorry!" Lily released her embrace but kept her hands on Avery's shoulders in a comforting grasp.

The rest of her friends were shortly behind Lily. Moz pushed past her hurriedly and cupped Avery's whole face in his hands. He held her cheeks as he kissed her hard, like she was gossamer in a rainstorm about to disappear and this was the last chance he would ever get. Moz pulled away just enough to hold his forehead to hers and for Avery to see the glassy tears building.

"You scared the absolute *shit* out of me. You absolutely cannot keep doing this!"

Avery choked up a small laugh, "I don't think I'm going to have to."

Moz pulled her into a tight embrace, cradling the back of her head with his hand to hold her against his chest. She let herself stay there with the flutter of his racing heart against her cheek. The comfort of the embrace mirrored the warmth of voices around them, safe and ordinary.

Long minutes passed and his hold on her never faltered. When Avery lifted her head to look at his face, Moz relaxed his arms just enough for her to move freely.

"Have you seen her?"

Moz nodded. "Kurosaki's bathroom is down the hall and to the left. She's been cleaning herself up, but I think she might really be struggling mentally with all of this. She's barely spoken."

Avery stepped out of his arms, the flesh of his forearm brushing against her like he wanted as much as he could possibly get from the touch of her before she walked away.

"I'm going to go check on her," she told him and he nodded.

"Let me know if there's anything I can do."

Avery nodded a thank you before she turned into the hall lit by a dim, orange overhead lamp. She followed the damp smell of old carpet until she reached the only door on the left side. Though it was closed, Avery was sure she could force the flimsy wood barrier open if it turned out to be locked. She held an ear to the door, listening, and heard the faint running water from a faucet.

"Yumi?"

When she received no answer, she tried turning the round knob of peeling silver. To her surprise, it did not resist her, and Avery carefully pushed open the bathroom door.

The inside of the bathroom was lit with cold fluorescents that starkly contrasted the orange glow in the hall. Avery stepped onto the white linoleum in the narrow space in front of the toilet.

Yumi did not look back when Avery closed the door behind her, but stared at her own reflection in the chipped mirror above the running sink. Her face was streaked red, her almond eyes puffy from tears. Avery gingerly stepped towards the sink, turned the faucet off and looked up at Yumi.

The Princess didn't react, only stared at her own reflection.

"Yumi," Avery murmured softly. "Everything's okay now, you're safe. It's over."

Avery watched Yumi's lip tremble, and her shoulders shake as she tried to hold in a sob. She looked down at Avery as more tears began to stream and Avery carefully pushed silken hair away from her face.

"I feel nothing," her normally composed voice was cracked and broken. "There is nothing where it was, but I don't feel like this is over. Not with the way Moz killed someone."

Avery's hand stilled and she frowned. "What do you mean he killed someone?"

"He drowned an Oracle from the inside out. How could he do that if the Knights are truly gone?"

Avery thought of the softness she had seen in him in their moments before falling asleep in the castle, of their winding fingers laced together in a place as frightening as Od. The cruelest edges of him that she had seen in her earliest memories of him were not gone; only buried. She considered this for a moment before saying, "It was such a big part of both of you. And strong, too. Maybe it's just a lingering piece of it that will go away with time."

Avery reached for Yumi's hand, holding it tenderly in both of hers. "But I know it's going to be okay. You both did it and I'm so proud of you."

The Princess smiled, faint but hopeful. "We would be gone without you."

Avery let go of Yumi's hand to wind her arms around her waist, easing her into an embrace. Yumi, the headstrong Princess of Brightloch, allowed herself to be held by the Berserker Witch she had once feared and nestled her face on Avery's shoulder. Avery smelled the sweet perfume of neroli lingering on her skin and tasted the salt of dried sweat when she kissed Yumi's forehead, exposed by her messed bangs.

"It's okay, I've got you," Avery whispered.

They stood together in a lovers embrace for long minutes. Avery's lungs drew in air when Yumi's released it and their chests moved together in a dance that made her grateful that they were both still very alive. She wondered if to some extent they had always moved in sync with each other: the necromancer and the Princess of Spirits.

Avery kissed her cheek, letting her body sway on the balls of her feet as she gently rocked Yumi. "I've always got you."

She heard Yumi draw in a deep breath next to her ear and she lifted her head to look at Avery. The topaz of her eyes flickered as she scanned Avery's face and she smiled, the fog of sadness lifting.

Yumi bent her head down and kissed her with a gentle touch, winding her fingers through Avery's as she did. She felt the crackle and fizz of magic on her lips, feeling safer than the first time they had dared. Avery didn't remember the last time she had prayed, but when they parted she prayed she could keep Yumi forever.

"Sorry to interrupt, but I fear I haven't got much longer."

The voice was as familiar to Avery as her own, but she had only ever heard it outside of her own head once before. She let go of Yumi and stared into the golden slivers buried in inky black sclera that looked down at her from an unsettling height.

"Aegis... why do you still look like a demon? I thought... Jack changed, why didn't you?"

"I'll see myself out," Yumi murmured with a red face and pushed past Aegis out of the small bathroom.

He folded his arms, the long claws of his fingers stretching halfway up his forearms underneath a black trench coat. It was strange seeing him under the buzzing fluorescent lights and not the sickly green glow of Od. The terracotta warmth of his skin and the short mess of wet, black hair all looked so normal that Avery was sure she could have mistaken him for anyone had his back been turned. But Aegis wasn't just anyone and she knew that under his calculating stare of black and gold.

"Avery, you've always known that you deserve so much better than what Reaperdom could give you," Aegis said, his voice lowered. "You wanted a life free from the ledger and free from the Beldam. You can't have that if I'm still around."

"Aegis, but you wouldn't even be a demon anymore. It wouldn't be like that."

"I know," Aegis admitted, "but you're operating under the assumption that I'm not a selfish person. I'm not done being me. I wish I could for you, girl, but I can't."

Avery didn't know what to say. Aegis wouldn't change for her; she knew she should have expected it, but she didn't think it would make her so sad.

"I'm going to go to another Reaper," he calmly said, "and will help them in whatever way I can, with everything you taught me. I'm going to help them hopefully make the right choices and when their work is done, I'll help them be Saved too. The cycle will repeat a few more times and I know you'll see me again, Avery."

Tears dribbled down Avery's cheeks. She knew she had not even been a Reaper for unbearably long; her months were only a mere blink compared to the lifetimes Moz had lived Reaping. Would Aegis be saying otherwise if she had taken longer?

The demon towering over her raised a clawed hand, smearing away the salty droplets from her face with the back of his hands.

"You're tough shit, Avery Porter," Aegis said. "You've worked so hard, and now I'm going to tell you how to get what it was you wanted this whole time. How you get to the Pool of Pasts Remembered. Are you ready to find out who you were in your last life?"

"How much farther do you think it is?"

Avery paused, waiting for Moz to keep walking ahead of her when he had stopped to survey the forested mountainside around them. The soupy fog that embraced the mountain to Brightloch's north receded the higher they climbed. Beams of sunlight began to break through the mist and speckle the crisp leaves, gilded in the warm shades of Novara. The last of the birdsongs were faint, not yet daunted by the season of snow that would soon ice them out to warmer climates.

"Well, Aegis said that when you pass Azura's temple at the base, it's about an hour hike. So we should probably be coming up on it soon," Avery encouraged him. "On the bright side, at least we'll know what to expect next time we make this trip."

Yumi stopped behind her. "What trip?"

Avery turned around to face Yumi, whose face was painted with furrowed confusion. Her sleek, black hair had frizzed from the mist in the ponytail she had tied. The princess looked every bit an adventurer with her skirts of tulle and gold traded for a long-sleeved black shirt and the grey cowl that Moz had kindly loaned to her.

"Yumi, I promise you that the very minute you are Saved, we're coming back here for you to know."

Yumi shook her head. "That's very kind of you, Avery. But I don't think I want to know."

"Why not?"

"I don't think I could live with the knowledge if I had been someone awful. It seems there is an incredibly good chance of that happening if the gods decided I needed another go at life as a Knight."

She gave pause to Yumi's words. Should she even be trying to find out who she had been? There was a gaping hole in her life where she was an absent Avery Porter before she had become a Reaper and she hated nothing more than even just the idea that her parents had been right. That she was a vessel and nothing more. She refused to be satisfied with that hollow space and would happily fill it with anything she could devour. It was an all-encompassing hunger for knowledge and the price she could end up paying was not enough to dissuade her from sating herself.

Yumi and Moz had both lived in far graver circumstances than she could ever understand. She recognized that and so she did nothing to persuade Yumi to sink her teeth into the carrion of a dead life.

"I understand, Yumes," Avery spoke softly. "Thank you for coming with me anyway. I'm really happy you're here."

The Princess smiled that half smile that showed more in her eyes than in her mouth and made Avery's heart skip and leap. The Reaper and her two Saved companions climbed higher up the mountain, into the golden maples and evergreen pines. As they hiked, they talked in loud conversations both to alert any lurking animals of their presence and because it felt to Avery that matters seemed relatively normal. They traded secret ingredients for the perfect dumplings, complained about books in ways that they couldn't seem to come to a consensus on, yearned for things they could have done while the weather was still warm and inviting.

"I'm just saying," Moz continued talking from the head of their group, "I think it would be a good idea when it's hot again to just take a small boat out and see the coast. It sounds like it- holy shit, there it is!"

Avery looked up from where she had been watching her footing on the narrow dirt trail. Amongst the leaves she caught sight of a glimmer of gold, far too reflective to be a cluster of dying leaves.

Higher up the trail a structure of weathered gold and sarsen stood hidden amongst the dense trees and thick underbrush. It didn't appear to be an enclosed space, but rather a gathering of stone columns and glittering arch haunches. Avery hurried faster up the steep trail; she didn't want to wait any longer now that her long awaited skeleton key was in sight.

Avery stepped through both sides of the open-air arcade built around the glittering pool. The sun shone down, warming Avery if she stood still long enough to bask in the light that nourished the ferns unfurling in thick combs around the water.

She turned and looked back at Yumi and Moz behind her.

"Moz, I think you deserve to go first. You waited this whole time," she said.

Moz looked down at his feet, pausing before he looked back up at her with a look of almost sheepishness. "Avery, I've been thinking and I'm with Yumi on this one. The Beldam thought I deserved to be one of her Knights. I think we've both suffered enough."

Avery was bewildered and this time she couldn't hold it back. "Then we came all this way for me to do this by myself?"

Moz nodded. "This is what you wanted and we want you to have this."

She then looked to Yumi for her words on the matter, but she simply nodded gingerly in agreement.

"We love you, Avery. You deserve this."

Avery paused.

"Thank you both," she whispered gently as she began peeling her boots and socks off. She turned towards the pool, dropped her rucksack, and unclasped her green cloak to let it fall to the stone ground. "If there is anything I can ever do for either of you, ever, I'll do it all."

She dipped her foot into the water, standing on the first step of smooth stone leading further into the water. To her surprise, the water was warm despite the cool air around them. Avery closed her eyes and relished the moment, feeling the sunbeams on her freckled and scarred face.

When she opened them, she looked down at the glittering surface of the water. She opened her mouth, took in a deep gulp of air, and plunged beneath the surface. Light filtered from the surface and danced across a thick cloud of glittering bubbles. Instead of floating to the surface to pop, the jewels of air hung suspended in the water around Avery in a bubbling embrace. The sunlight shifted, changed colors, and began to take shape.

The light became a projection of a person and it took her a moment for her eyes to focus on the figure the sunlight had created. She was young and radiant, with a thick waterfall of dark curls flowing down her shoulders. Her brown eyes held a warm intensity that made Avery want to fall into the young woman's gravity, not pull herself out of it.

The projection rearranged and the image grew darker, spreading across all the bubbles around her. Avery realized she was in the watery imitation of a library she had never seen before. Tall stacks of books swallowed up the light coming from a window beyond what the vision could show her and she was in front of a desk. Seated at the desk was a different figure flanked by tall towers of old tomes that threatened to topple over. It was a man, head down and nose all but buried in a thick book. Avery could only make out the fact that he had dark hair shorn close to the scalp and that the tunic he wore was a sage green. She heard footsteps on creaking wood from someone she couldn't yet see. Avery waited for the second figure to appear until she realized that she drew nearer to the man at the desk and that the footsteps were coming from whoever this memory belonged to.

"I've been thinking," a woman's voice spoke, and Avery felt the sensation of speaking within her skull, as though she had been the one the words came from. There was a warble that came from hearing it underwater, but she could make out enough of the tone and annunciation to understand what had been said.

The man flipped another page in the book he was engrossed in. *"And did you fair alright?"*

This second voice was familiar, but with the warp of the water Avery couldn't be sure she was fully recognizing it.

"This whole time you hadn't changed in any way I can see," the young woman's voice sounded nervous, shaking and unsteady, and Avery found it strange. It didn't seem to match the energy radiating from the woman she had been shown, if this was even the same person. *"There are no wrinkles upon your face, no graying in your hair, and still you slay the demons quick as lightning. You are exactly the same as you were when I was a child. You're no witch."*

The man paused his reading but did not look up from the book. Avery felt the confrontation happening before her eyes was a long time coming.

"Then what do you make of me, Miss Khan?"

"You are Death."

The man calmly closed the book and finally looked up. If Avery hadn't been underwater, she would have gasped at the surprise of seeing Moz's face. It was strange seeing him without the scar through the eyebrow or wavy tendrils on the top of his head, but she'd recognize that handsome look of pointed skepticism anywhere. The chair scraped across the wood floor as he pushed it back, standing up. Whoever this woman was, she didn't have much height on Avery, for Moz still towered above them.

"Did you kill her? Were you the one who took my mother from us?"

Avery watched as Moz studied her from the perspective of the memory and she was hanging on to every word. She prayed her lungs would allow her to stay under long enough to continue listening to the conversation unfolding.

"No, Nora," Moz's voice was gentle. *"I did not Reap your mother."*

Avery was yanked quickly out of that memory and images flashed fast across the screen of bubbles at a rapid-fire pace. She watched as a child named Nora met an adult Moz. Mona laying her gentle hands on Nora's forehead and speaking witchcraft into her. Nora running through the tall grass, chasing her older brothers. Nora giggling. Nora kissing the cheeks of village boys. Nora holding the white speckled rat in her hands, Nora waving at a three-masted ship leaving port, Nora concocting remedies and healing the sick.

Radiant Nora. Vibrant Nora. *Nora, Nora, Nora.*

The images went dark and Avery found herself again watching through Nora's eyes. Nora was writhing, screaming under a night sky, looking down at a rope around her hands and desperately trying to grip enough of it in her fingers to work her way out of it.

"Help me!"

Fear consumed Avery when she realized what was happening. She could not bear to witness Nora's murder through her own eyes, it was too much. Avery thrashed her arms, struggling to swim to the surface as her lungs began to burn. Memories of not one, but two brushes with death came back to Avery - one in the forest and one in the sea.

Avery finally surfaced, choking out water.

"I'm… I'm Nora," she cried.

Every moment she ever felt sadness for the murdered witch came back to herself. She was the one who lost her family, she was the one who was left for dead; and here she was again. Is this what Balthazar had meant about knowing her, when they spoke in his graveyard for the first time? Somehow, she knew that he was the exact reason why she was birthed again into the world; this was all mapped out before she was ever put into her body as Avery Porter.

She heard splashes and couldn't see through her tears as a pair of arms wrapped around her shoulders and pulled her into a hug. *Moz.* There was a jerk of movement from where his head might have been and a splash of water as Yumi followed him into the pool as well. Yumi's smaller arms encompassed her from behind, her small chin rested on her wet shoulder, and she spoke with such sweetness that made Avery fall even more in love:

"No, you're Avery. You'll always be."

EPILOGUE

FIVE YEARS LATER

I'll bet you all the candy in the world that you can't make a sillier face than me," she challenged the reflection of the toddler in the bakery window.

Right on cue, the little boy fished his hands out from the sling that held him safely to Avery's hip. He hooked a little finger in each corner of his mouth and pulled to warp his cherub cheeks, looking from his own reflection up to his mother to see what she would say.

"Hmm, that's going to be a hard one to beat," Avery said very seriously and he giggled. The sweetest sound she still had ever heard.

With her left arm still supporting him from underneath, she lifted her right hand to squish her own cheeks that she had puffed up with air. She watched her own reflection to show her son she was taking this very, very seriously and forced the air out, knowing the sound would make him howl in laughter. When he did, she grinned at both of their reflections - hers with long braids streaming from either side of her head and a band of gold on each of her ring fingers, and his with a head of soft, dark hair and the faint appearance of his first freckles coming through.

"So, who do you think won?"

He wasn't fully verbal yet at his young age, but still he pointed at his own chest with a sheepish smile.

"I've lost *again*? I think you've been practicing behind my back," Avery playfully accused, feigning defeat with a bowed head and he giggled again.

She turned around from the bakery window, supporting her child with both arms again. Banners of silver and green were strung overhead and hanging from lamp posts as the crowd milled about for the Lume equinox festival. The warming weather meant Avery could only use the canvas sling in shifts before sweat began to bead down her back even when the linen of her green tunic was lightweight.

From the less crowded sidewalk Avery saw a break in the current of moving people and spotted the top of Moz's head. He was nodding his head diligently, engrossed in whatever Yumi was explaining as she walked next to him. Avery was grateful every day for their close friendship but prayed her wife wasn't trying to talk shop on his day off.

"Look, there's Dad and Mimi. You have to tell him you won all the candy in the world, okay?"

Her son nodded enthusiastically, ready to stake his righteous claim on the world's supply of sweets. Avery walked with him to meet Yumi and Moz. When they approached, Moz looked down at his son's devious little smile and then at his wife.

"Why does it look like you've both gotten up to something?"

"Griffin has earned the rights to all the candy in the world. Since you are the keeper of the candy, he is reporting to you to claim his reward," Avery informed him.

Moz looked down at the paper bowl of candied orange slices in his hand and then back to the child.

"Well, you're in luck, bud, because I have in my hands *all of the candy in the world*," Moz played along, knowing that the boy wouldn't have noticed the vendor on the corner behind them selling bowl after bowl of candy just like it. He turned to Yumi at his side.

"Yumes, do you mind holding this?"

"Not at all," she said, taking the paper bowl of fruit out of his hand. Moz reached into the sling at Avery's side, lifting Griffin up and out.

"Alright, fasten your seatbelts, Daddy doesn't know how to drive," Avery teased and Moz shot her a dismayed look as he lifted the child out of the sling and onto his shoulders. Griffin obeyed, locking his little arms and legs around Moz's neck. His father pretended to choke but held on to Griffin's legs to keep him securely in place. Griffin giggled wildly, patting his palm against Moz's stubbled cheek to rouse him from the choking.

Moz turned around carefully to face Yumi and Griffin looked down on her with a big grin and fit of laughter. Yumi smiled sweetly at the boy that was not of her blood but of her small family all the same. She and Griffin truly adored each other. Avery watched them as she peeled off the sling; every moment was to be cherished while he was still little.

"Griffin, what do we say to Mimi?" Moz prompted the boy, who was watching the bowl of candied orange in her hands with wide eyes.

Griffin said something in jumbled toddler-speak that might have been a "please" if Avery had been listening much closer and there was no noise of crowd around them.

"Why yes you may, sweet boy," Yumi answered and lifted a slice of orange for Griffin to take. He babbled again something somewhat resembling a "thank you" before eagerly shoving the orange into his little mouth.

Moz started to walk with his son on his shoulders, Griffin nibbling on the orange with one hand as the other gripped tightly onto his father's head. Yumi followed, trying to pace Griffin's desire to eat slice after slice by handing them over as slowly as she could. Avery stayed in place, watching her husband and her wife and her child as they walked away from her. Moments like this one brought immense joy but a small pain flecked around the far edges.

From ahead of her, Moz turned around to see why she had stopped. Griffin's wondrous face nested on top of his father's head and again she was astonished at how much the two looked alike already.

"You coming, Ave?" Moz called out. "I think the balloons we spotted came from over here, we can grab one for Jude too before we meet with Shank and Angela."

"I'll catch up, just give me a second," she called back. Moz nodded and they continued ahead.

Avery stood in the center of the Brightloch town square that had haunted her. Not with the ghosts of people, but specters of what could have been. Years and years had passed, showing on her aging face, and even now she was thinking of Katherine and Harrison Porter. Of their faces when they had seen her in the same square, like they had just been woken from a bad dream.

She'd turned it over in her mind many times to try to understand how her hidden emotion could have been loneliness when she had been left behind by the people who were supposed to have loved her always. Avery had been bolstered so strongly by Lily and the Clements family, and then again by the Reapers. The mere notion that there would be anything on this earth to leave Griffin behind for was unfathomable, it just couldn't be done. Her pain was not one to be passed down, not when the love from the family she had found was surrounding her son as well.

It had taken her until she was standing at the altar with Yumi Harthmoor - that beautiful bride of golden sun - to realize that sometimes families aren't just born, they are made.

And theirs would be crafted of boundless love.

ACKNOWLEDGMENTS

This book never would have been possible had it not been for the fantastic mental healthcare team at Swedish in Edmonds, Washington. Having another trans person help me navigate the things that befell me between the publishing of HEMLOCK and KNIGHT was life-changing and while I will not name you, I think if this gets back to you that you will know exactly who you are.

Thank you, Heather, for the love and space to be bonkers about this book and letting me drag you into the circus. I'm glad all the jokes make sense now and I love you endlessly for making them as well.

Thank you, Kalina and Emily, for making me excited about this story again. Both of you truly gave it a new life and I might not have crossed the finish line at all had it not been for your enthusiasm.

Thank you, to the Congregation. Having the space to rave and commiserate with people who understood the muck and grime of being an author did wonders for this story. I cannot wait to get my hands on every single one of your books.

Thank you, to Johnny Hollow for all the music that was the soundtrack to my late nights with my face planted on the keyboard so I could just sit in the atmospheres you created.

And thank you, dear reader, for all the time and love you gave this story. I'll see you again soon.

Love and Swords,

ELLE SAMHAIN

ABOUT THE AUTHOR

Elle Samhain is from the Seattle area and began writing *The Shintori Chronicles* while earning their Bachelor of Fine Arts at Washington State University. They are active in the pagan and queer communities, which have impacted both their writing and visual arts.

If they're not writing or making resin collages, they're probably binge-watching *The X-Files* or talking to cats in sing-song.

COMING SOON

GRIFFIN THOUGHT THE MONSTERS ONLY LIVED IN HIS HEAD.

He was fine with that. In fact, it's far more preferable than his father sitting him down to talk about the regular visits from the things that go bump in the night and hearing him say "yes son, I see them too."

The delicate fabric weaving Griffin's sense of normalcy begins to unravel when his best friend, Jude, is called upon to do the work of a fractured relic: The Reapers.

When a string of grisly murders plagues the capitol city of Brightloch, a tragedy that has haunted Griffin may have been anything but accidental. With a suspect list that includes an ancient demon and a band of Oracles gone rogue - Griffin and Jude find themselves way in over their heads.

Who died and put the kids in charge?

COMING SOON

9 798989 104703